THE
TURQUOISE
TATTOO

A DEVON MacDONALD MYSTERY

NANCY BAKER JACOBS

POCKET BOOKS

New York   London   Toronto   Sydney   Tokyo   Singapore

POCKET BOOKS, a division of Simon & Schuster Inc. 1230 Avenue of the Americas, New York, NY 10020

Published by arrangement with G. P. Putnam's Sons

ISBN: 0-671-75535-8

First Pocket Books printing April 1992

10 9 8 7 6 5 4 3 2 1

Cover art and design by Todd Radom

Printed in the U.S.A.

For my father

Noble and common blood are of the same color.

ANCIENT PROVERB

Part
1

1

The day I first met Ben Levy, my six-year-old Honda had been acting temperamental and I'd had to wait more than half an hour in a downpour for the Auto Club. By the time I reached the office, I was wet, chilled and grumpy, not in the best shape to meet a new client. But the man in the reception room obviously had been waiting for some time. A tall, slim type with a narrow, angular face, he sat scrunched onto one of the low Naugahyde sofas my partner Sam Sherman bought before I joined the business. An interior decorator Sam is not. I nodded at Paula, who was devouring the latest issue of *Cosmopolitan* at the reception desk, and barged past her, dripping, into my tiny office. My raincoat left puddles on the worn wooden floor.

By the time I had my coat off and my face wiped dry, Paula had entered and closed the door. The cloud of perfume that came with her gave me a sinus headache, but it was right for the clinging, low-cut red knit dress she was wearing. I made a mental note to talk to her again about proper office attire. Really, Sam should do it—he hired her and she might be more inclined to listen to him—but I suspected he rather enjoyed gazing at Paula's abundant cleavage. She fit into his Mickey Spillane fantasies. My point of view was somewhat different; the way I saw it, in that getup, our receptionist was setting equal rights back twenty years.

She half-whispered in her breathless, little-girl fashion, "Devon, he refused to talk to Sam, insisted on seeing *you.*" Paula's tone implied disbelief, and well it might. Most of our clients prefer to deal with the male half of Sherman and MacDonald, Private Investigators. I usually have to turn on the hard sell to get them to so much as greet me, although Sam is nearly twice my age and has had two heart attacks in the past eighteen months.

"Who is he?"

"A doctor. Dr. Benjamin Levy." There was a certain reverence in her tone as she handed me his business card. I read that Dr. Benjamin Levy was a dermatologist in practice in the Lowry Medical Arts Building, a couple of miles away in downtown St. Paul. "You s'pose he's single?" she asked. Ever since her twenty-ninth birthday, Paula Carboni has had one major interest. It's not her job.

"Give me two minutes." I pulled the roll of paper towels I keep for days like this from my desk drawer and blotted my hair, then wiped up the worst of the puddles on the floor. I gave myself a short, silent pep talk on positive thinking and salesmanship, then arranged what I hoped would pass for a congenial, intelligent look on my face.

Seated in my compact quarters, Dr. Levy still looked uncomfortable. Everything about the doctor was long and lean. He was about six-foot-three and dark-haired. His face was an elongated oval with a dusting of freckles over a slightly hawkish nose, and his eyes were an unusual pale blue. His suit was an expensive charcoal-brown wool blend, slightly rumpled from the day's humidity, and I could see an inch or so of wrist protruding from the jacket's sleeves. As he spoke, his bony fingers nervously bent and unbent a paper clip he'd found on my desk. "Ted Towers thought you might be able to help me."

My congenial expression faded. Dr. Theodore Towers was a name from the past, part of a piece of history I'd tried my best to erase from my mind. Dr. Towers is a decent man and a good doctor, but he's connected with the worst period of my life and I've decided to get on with it. A strong gust of wind drove the rain against my office window, rattling the panes of glass. I shivered. "I don't know about you," I said, "but I'm freezing. How about some coffee?" As we waited for Paula to bring our cups, I said, "I'm surprised Dr. Towers knows I'm in this business." The last time I'd spoken with Ted, I was still teaching third grade at Linwood Elementary.

"Ted likes to keep up with people, and you impressed him. He says you're very bright, ethical, tenacious. Lord knows that's what I need. He thought you might understand what I'm going through . . . be willing to help."

When Paula had brought our coffee and I'd had a long sip of mine, I asked Dr. Levy to explain how he thought I could help him.

He leaned forward and stared directly into my eyes; his gaze was sad and somehow magnetic. "My son, David, is eight years old," he said, "and he's dying."

"I'm sorry." I looked away, realizing now why Ted Towers had sent Benjamin Levy to me. "Dr. Towers told you about Danny," I said. My voice was brittle. Ted Towers had been my only child's pediatrician and he'd done everything humanly possibly to save Danny's young life. It just wasn't enough.

"Yes."

I swallowed. "How can I help you?"

"David has leukemia. The doctors have tried every-

thing, or nearly. Nothing . . . nothing is working."
Levy's eyes filled and he sucked in air audibly. "Sorry. I
don't find it easy to talk about this."

"I know how you feel, Dr. Levy, but I don't understand what you want from me." That old lost, helpless
feeling I'd had when Danny was in the hospital began to
creep over me. I had trouble breathing.

"There's one thing they have left to try," Levy said. "A
bone marrow transplant. If the doctors can transplant
some healthy bone marrow—the right bone marrow—
into David, there's a chance his body will begin produc-
ing healthy blood cells." I could see naked hope on
Levy's face. I knew what he was feeling. When your kid is
dying, you grasp at any straw you can find. You believe in
miracles. You have no choice. "The bone marrow has to
come from someone who is a close genetic match," he
explained. "Both Gloria—David's mother—and I have
been tested and we're . . . neither of us . . . we don't
match close enough."

I would have given my life if it could have saved
Danny. "I'm sorry," I repeated. It was inadequate. All
words were inadequate.

"Gloria and I don't have any other children. It took us
five years to have David. A brother or sister with genes
from the same two parents would be the best match, of
course, but . . . This is where you come in." Dr. Levy
leaned his long head toward me expectantly. I nodded.
"There . . . there could possibly be half-siblings. We
need you to find out, and find them, before it's too late
for David."

"There's a former marriage?"

"No. Not exactly."

"An illegitimate child, then?"

He played with the coffee cup, turning it around and
around in his hands. "No, not really. Truth is, I . . . I
don't even know if there are any children. That's why I
came to you—" He hesitated.

I was confused. Was Levy asking me to search out his

past lovers in case one of them had produced a child she'd neglected to tell him about? Maybe it was his wife. Had Gloria Levy given up a child for adoption in her youth? Yet he'd said half-*siblings,* more than one. "We can play Twenty Questions if you want to, Dr. Levy, but things'll go a lot faster if you just tell me straight out what you want me to do for you."

He sipped his coffee, by now lukewarm. "I'm sorry. I thought it was going to be easier than this. To tell you."

"If you're worried about shocking me, I promise you that won't be easy."

He forced a smile. "When I was a medical student at the University, I used to earn money by donating at a sperm bank."

"You mean for artificial insemination?"

He nodded. "Lots of medical students did it. We were what were called the sperm donors of choice—young, healthy men, college graduates with good minds. Twice a month or so . . ." He colored slightly. "We used to joke about it. Go to the sperm bank, make a deposit, withdraw thirty bucks and you've got a week's grocery money. It didn't take much time and the work wasn't exactly strenuous." I nodded encouragement. Despite his medical background, Levy clearly was embarrassed giving a woman such intimate information. "In recent years," he told me, "I've begun to think more about the ramifications and the ethics of that sort of thing, but at the time . . . Well, I did it, my friends did it. We told ourselves we were helping some desperate infertile couple and making a few bucks, so what's the harm?"

"You want me to find out if these . . . uh, donations of yours resulted in any children?"

Dr. Levy nodded.

I shook my head. It was impossible. "That kind of record just isn't available, Dr. Levy. In any case, artificial insemination is still a closely guarded secret. Chances are, if you did father any children, they know nothing about it."

"I know. I know. I've thought of all that. But we have to *try*. David's dying. Unless we find a brother or sister to help him, my son is going to die and there's not a goddamned thing I can do about it." He pressed his palm against his forehead. The flesh beneath it went white. "I'm a goddamned *doctor* and I can't even save my own son." Grief and dejection weighed down his shoulders. I know how heavy they can be.

"Dr. Levy, even if I could find these children, assuming there are any, I couldn't disrupt, maybe ruin, their lives. You have to realize what this could mean to them."

"I'm willing to pay," he said. "I'm not a poor man."

"I never take a case just for the money—"

"I didn't mean you. I meant that, if there are children and one of them can help David, I could offer something in return. College tuition. Anything. Anything I've got."

He pulled out his wallet and I held up my hand to protest. I didn't want a retainer for this impossible case. I didn't want the case. But cash was not what Levy offered.

"This is David," he said, handing me a snapshot.

I saw a young boy, thin-faced like his father. But the child's body was shockingly gaunt and he'd lost most of his hair. What little remained rested in wispy dark patches on his head. His body was so emaciated that it seemed too small for an eight-year-old's. Yet his near-baldness made him seem oddly older than his years. Despite his condition, the boy had managed an engaging smile for the camera. I set the photo down and looked away, feeling as though I were stepping into quicksand, knowing full well that I could sink, yet unable to stop myself.

"Ms. MacDonald, I've already been to two other investigators. One turned me down flat and the other . . . well, I could see he was going to find a way to hold me up, bleed me for the money and do nothing for David. I knew he couldn't be trusted. So, when Ted suggested you, I felt you were the answer to a prayer. Lord knows we need one. Just *try*, that's all I'm asking. Just try."

"There's really nothing I can do, Dr. Levy."

"Please."

"You'd just be wasting your money."

"Let me be the judge of that. Don't make me beg, Ms. MacDonald . . . Devon. My son's dying. I know you understand what that's like."

I bit my lip to keep it from quivering. "I'll do this much, Dr. Levy," I said. "I'll look into it. I'll see what I can find out. There's no guarantee I can locate any children, even if they do exist. If I do, I'll plead your case with the parents. But I will *not* turn them over to you without their consent. If you'll accept those ground rules, I'll do what I can."

Levy leaned over my desk and grabbed my hand. "I knew you'd help," he said, gripping me almost painfully. "I knew it."

By then, I was already into the quicksand up to my knees, and sinking fast.

—— 2 ——

"Don't eat that!" I said, entering Sam's office.

Looking fleetingly guilty, my partner set down the remains of his chocolate doughnut. "Jesus H. Christ. It's not enough Rose is on my back at home, I gotta have you in the office." Doughnut crumbs dotted the May billing statements he had spread on his desk blotter.

"You know you're not supposed to eat that crap, Sam. Thirty pounds off, that's what your doctors told you. This junk is full of sugar, fat, chemicals, everything you shouldn't even *look* at. And don't bitch about Rose and me. We're just trying to keep you from having another heart attack and you know it."

Sam scooped up the half-eaten doughnut, bit off a piece and chewed it slowly. A defiant look on his pudgy face, he leaned back in his swivel chair, his protruding midsection straining the buttons on his blue-and-yellow plaid shirt. A chocolate-coated crumb dropped to his chest and he brushed it away, leaving behind a small brown stain. "Stress, that's what gives people heart attacks," he said. "Smart girl like you oughta be able to figure out nagging gives a man stress."

One of Sam's favorite ways of needling me is to call me a "girl," but today I refused to rise to his bait. Sometimes dealing with Sam Sherman feels like being back in my third grade classroom. Especially when it comes to getting him to take care of himself. How a man can have two heart attacks and still believe he's immortal is beyond me, but at least he's no longer smoking those putrid cheap cigars. Now he just chews them. "Truce," I said, sinking into the brown leather chair opposite Sam's desk. As the senior partner of Sherman and MacDonald, Private Investigators, Sam has the larger office, the one with the carpeted floor and the view of Grand Avenue. I could hear the traffic jammed in the street below.

"So who's the client who won't talk to Sam Sherman, twenty-seven years in the business?"

I smiled. "Now you know how I feel when somebody turns up his nose at me," I said. Sam was protective of his territory, the business he'd worked hard to build over the past three decades. I knew that, if it hadn't been for his health, he probably wouldn't have made me a partner. But he did and he's always treated me fairly, even if he does call me a "girl" too often. Since his second heart attack, he does most of the firm's sedentary research, spending a lot of time in public buildings—the State Hall of Records, the Ramsey and Hennepin County courthouses, and the St. Paul and Minneapolis City Halls—reading dusty old records while I do most of the legwork. It may not be the typical division of labor, but it works for us. Sam Sherman loves to bitch at me, usually

10

good-naturedly, but I know he'd step between me and a bullet without giving it a second thought. And I'd do the same for him. Maybe we're the odd couple of the private investigation business—a thirty-three-year-old, former schoolteacher who's a health food and aerobics nut and a sixty-year-old junk food addict who never finished high school and exercises by working his jaw—but we're genuine partners.

I drew a deep breath and told Sam about Dr. Levy and his son.

He shook his balding head. "I shoulda known it'd be trouble when the guy insisted on waitin' to see you, Devon. Soon as a kid's involved, you make as much sense as givin' a fish a bath."

"That's bullshit, Sam. You're just as big a pushover for a sob story as I am. Except with you it's usually a pretty face that does it. Here, take a look at this and convince me you would've turned Dr. Levy down." I tossed David's photo on his desk.

Sam picked it up and studied it in the gray morning light. Sounds of screeching tires and blowing horns drifted up from the wet street. Distant male voices shouted obscenities, followed by more blaring horns. After what seemed ages, Sam handed the picture back. "Like they say, the impossible takes a little longer. I just hope the kid's got that much time."

3

Benjamin Levy remembered little of value about the clinic where he'd donated sperm nearly two decades before. He thought its name might have had something to do with silver or gold and that it was located near the

11

medical complex of "the U," possibly on southeast Oak Street. Everyone in the Twin Cities calls the Minneapolis campus of the University of Minnesota "the U." That's not because it's the only college or university here—the metropolitan area has at least half a dozen others—but with more than fifty thousand students, it's by far the largest.

There was no listing in the Minneapolis phone book for a medical facility with either silver or gold in its name. I tried copper, lead, zinc, ruby, and diamond with the same results. The St. Paul book was equally unhelpful. The one useful detail Levy recalled was that he'd found the clinic through an ad in the campus newspaper when he'd been a medical student.

By the time I reached the U, the downpour had stopped and the only raindrops came from the tree branches overhead. I parked in the nearest ramp and walked across the soggy campus to Walter Library. The freshly washed air was heady with the scent of lilacs and lilies of the valley.

I descended the marble stairway to the library basement where the newspaper stacks are located. The newer West Bank Library has the same collection of the *Minnesota Daily* on microfilm, but I'd rather lug bundles of newspapers than subject my eyes to the strain of a microfilm reader. I spent over an hour poring over the classified columns from the early 1970s. The news sections of the old papers chronicled campus unrest far from today's student apathy, but the classifieds had changed little, except for the prices. Student apartments in Dinkytown, which bordered the East Bank campus on the north, were offered back then at less than a hundred dollars a month; today, with another twenty years' wear and tear having taken their toll, the same places bring five hundred or more.

The ad I was seeking appeared in the *Minnesota Daily* several times a week starting in 1971. "Sperm Donors Wanted," it announced. The Goldenberg Infertility Clinic, located on southeast Delaware Street, near the corner of Oak, offered young men who passed physical and mental examinations a quick and easy thirty dollars. At a library pay phone, I tried the number listed; it now belonged to a dress shop. Neither the white pages nor the physicians' listings in the yellow pages noted a doctor or clinic named Goldenberg.

On my way back to the office, I drove past the address where the Goldenberg Clinic had been located in 1971, but now that block had been swallowed up by an expansion of the University Hospital Medical Complex. I pulled into a space in the next block and plunked a quarter into the meter. My first stop was a barbershop dusty enough to have existed twenty years ago, but the proprietor assured me in a thick southeast Asian accent that he knew nothing about a clinic. After having the same luck at a drugstore, a copy shop, and a rental agency in the block, I drove back to the office.

Part of me had hoped for a quick conclusion to this case. It was remotely possible that I would find the infertility clinic Benjamin Levy had used and that the owner would tell me there was no way I could see the files without a court order. Then I could refer Dr. Levy to an attorney, bow out, and tell myself I had no reason to feel guilty. But life is never simple. At least not mine.

Two other cases-in-progress waited for me on my desk. A report on a traffic accident for an insurance company was due and I had six telephone interviews left for a firm of attorneys litigating a libel case. Tracking down the elusive Goldenberg Clinic would have to wait until tomorrow.

I had finished writing the insurance report, given it to Paula for typing, and completed two of the interviews by quitting time. The Honda coughed and died again as I left for home, but this time I was able to get it restarted. I resigned myself to having it serviced before the end of the month. Thank God for MasterCard.

At home, I made myself a salad for supper, tossing

together spinach, mushrooms, cauliflower, broccoli, mung bean sprouts, cheddar, and raisins, then topping the whole thing with homemade ranch dressing. I put on a pot of water for tea and carried the salad four feet to what my landlady calls a dining area.

My tiny one-bedroom apartment was once the third-floor servants quarters of a brick mansion in St. Paul's historic Ramsey Hill district. At the turn of the century, the neighborhood housed the city's elite—lumber, milling, and railroad barons. In the 1920s, F. Scott Fitzgerald lived only a few blocks away. But, like similar districts in many cities, Ramsey Hill fell on hard times. The wealthy fled to suburbs like Edina and White Bear Lake. Poorer families couldn't afford to heat the drafty mansions through the bitter Minnesota winters. Soon most of the great homes had been carved up into apartment buildings and rooming houses and the neighborhood's residents changed from pale-skinned Irish, Germans, and Scandinavians to blacks and Native Americans. Within the past few years, however, a resurgence of interest in Ramsey Hill has started and the area is well on the way toward regentrification. The yuppies have descended but, thankfully, so far my building has been spared.

This cozy walkup was all I'd been able to afford after my husband disappeared and I decided not to return to my teaching job. I tell people I stay here because it's cheap; even paying two eighty-five a month, I seldom have two dimes to rub together by the end of the month. The larger truth, however, is that the apartment's diminutive size appeals to me. It's clearly not big enough for two, so as long as I stay here, I don't have to deal with adding a man to my life, even on a temporary basis. Since my settled, middle-class life fell apart, I've felt safer alone; it's harder to get hurt that way.

As I munched on my salad and sipped herb tea, I tried to watch *The MacNeil-Lehrer Report* on TV, but I couldn't seem to concentrate on the news. While I struggled to focus on the threat of terrorism against

Americans in the Middle East, my mind kept going back to that photo of Benjamin Levy's eight-year-old son, smiling so bravely for the camera. Sick kids suffer their own kind of terrorism.

When the dishes were washed and put away, I read a paperback mystery for a while, then fell into an uneasy sleep on the sofa, dreaming for the millionth time of Danny. He'd awakened from his coma and was reaching out his short, plump arms to me, sobbing, "Mommy, Mommy!" As I bent to pick him up, his features twisted and changed and I found my arms encircling the bony, wasted body of young David Levy.

I awoke, whimpering.

— 4 —

"Place to start is the real estate records," Sam declared the next morning. "Find out who owned this Goldenberg Clinic place back in seventy-one and work from there." He sat tilted back in his swivel chair, his feet propped on his scarred oak desk. "Trade favors?" His mouth smiled at me around the unlighted cigar he clenched in his teeth.

"What?" I asked suspiciously. Too often Sam's favors eat up hours or require me to do things I hate.

"I'm gonna be downtown Minneapolis this morning. I'll look up this real estate stuff, you serve a subpoena for me."

"What's the case?" I fidgeted uncomfortably; after my fitful night on the couch, my back ached and my morning exercise routine hadn't helped.

"One of Billingsley's." Ambrose Billingsley is a Minneapolis attorney, one of our best clients. "Woman went to one of them hoity-toity France Avenue beauty shops—

you know, kinda joint where the limp-wristed hairdressers are called Mister Bruce and charge ten times as much. Treat the customers like shit and they can't get enough. Bill's client wanted her hair dyed to look like one of them TV broads . . . Linda Evans, somebody like that. Ended up balder'n me." Sam ran tobacco-stained fingers contemplatively over his fringed dome. "Bill wants the subpoena served on a witness works in the shop."

"Sam, all hairdressers are not gay and Linda Evans is not a broad."

"Coulda fooled me, sweetheart," he said, winking.

If I could simply ignore Sam's bigoted terminology, he'd probably clean it up. I tried that technique often with third graders who used profanity to get my attention and it worked on them. But Sam isn't a third grader and he usually manages to push just past the point where I can hold my tongue. He needs to liberalize his thinking; I need more patience. "It's a deal," I agreed. This favor sounded simple enough and I could understand why Sam didn't want to perform this particular chore. He'd be as comfortable in a chichi Edina beauty salon as I would at a cockfight.

In books and movies, private detectives' lives are filled with chasing criminals and fighting to the death. In reality, we spend most of our time doing the often tedious work of serving subpoenas, interviewing witnesses, performing surveillance duties, and examining public records. Still, the work appeals to me. It has more independence and variety than most jobs I'm qualified to do. After I left teaching, I painfully found out how rare those jobs are. I never learned to type decently and although I have a college degree, I don't have a business education. A bachelors in Elementary Ed. is good for teaching elementary school, period.

I was a waitress for a time, but I couldn't stand the bullshit the customers gave me. Then I tried clerking in a dress shop, but after a few months I'd had it with emaciated matrons trying to fill their empty days by spending money on overpriced and undersized clothing. My last stint was as a receptionist for a large local advertising agency. It sounded glamorous. I'd been working there three weeks when I punched a boozy director who put his arm around me, whispered an obscene invitation in my ear, and fondled my breast. I got fired. The director got a two-year contract to shoot all the national TV commercials for a Minesota-based brewery.

After a month on unemployment, I answered Sam Sherman's ad and went to work as a fledgling private investigator, operating under his agency license. Sam had had a succession of lazy or dull young men in the job—no male with both ambition and intelligence would work very long for the wages Sam paid, but I didn't have much choice, short of returning to the classroom. I simply couldn't take the thought of working with children again, not so soon after Danny. The money here wasn't any worse than at the other jobs I'd held. Sam is a good teacher and, despite his brusque manner, a decent man. And I like the work.

By the time I returned from Edina, Sam had called Paula with the information I needed. The Goldenberg Clinic building had been purchased by Dr. Agnes P. Leonard in 1955. In 1977 the property was condemned by the State of Minnesota and annexed to the University. Dr. Leonard's tenant during the entire time she'd owned the property had been Dr. Max W. Goldenberg. She had no idea where he was today.

I called the Board of Medical Examiners in St. Paul and learned that Dr. Max W. Goldenberg was no longer practicing medicine in Minnesota; he had died in 1983. Once again, I'd hit a dead end.

I ate lunch at my desk, a carton of yogurt and some

fresh local strawberries I'd bought at a country roadside stand the previous weekend. The flavored yogurt the grocery stores sell is loaded with sugar, so I mix my own at home. As I licked the sweet-and-sour concoction off my plastic spoon, I thought about what happens to medical records when a doctor dies. According to Sam's information, Max Goldenberg's name was the only one on the lease for the Delaware Street clinic. If he'd had partners, surely the property would have been leased to all the partners, or to a corporation they'd formed. I was inclined to think that he'd been a loner.

What, then, had happened to his records when he retired or died? I could think of two possibilities. One was that they were destroyed, which would end my search. The other was that they still existed somewhere, either sold to another doctor along with Goldenberg's practice or in storage. In either case, I'd have to find Goldenberg's survivors, assuming he had some. If anyone would know where those old records were today, they would.

I tossed the empty yogurt carton into the wastebasket and grabbed my notebook. At the reception desk, Paula was painting her nails magenta. Technically, she was still on her lunch hour, but I was certain it would take her more than her remaining fifteen minutes to finish applying the polish. Then there'd be another twenty minutes of drying time before she could actually use her hands to do anything useful, such as opening the stack of mail piled on the desk. Strenuous work like typing undoubtedly wouldn't be risked before late afternoon.

"Looks like you're planning to spend tonight catching up on your gardening," I said.

She glanced up and had the grace to look a bit embarrassed.

"I'll be at the library." I closed the office door a little harder than necessary.

By the time I reached the street, Paula's laziness was

forgotten. The weather was a typically humid day after an early summer rainstorm. On the plus side, the storm had washed the pollen from the air, which made my sinus passages happier. I often ask myself why I stay in a place where the weather is good maybe two months a year and I'm allergic to virtually everything that pollinates. The only time I can breathe decently here is in the late fall, before the weather drops below zero, and in the early spring, before the trees begin to bud. Surely some place like San Francisco, or maybe Phoenix, would be better for me, but somehow I never seem to pack my bags and move on. Maybe next year . . .

I drove down Grand Avenue hill and wound around to Exchange Street, then onto Kellogg Boulevard. I was able to park within a block of the downtown St. Paul Public Library. It was cool inside, the library's thick marble walls a fortress against the humid heat outdoors.

The index to the *Minneapolis Star* and *Tribune* directed me to the correct spool of microfilm and I soon found myself in the Periodicals Room reading a blurry version of Dr. Max Goldenberg's obituary notice. According to the *Star,* Dr. Goldenberg had been "a pioneer in infertility research whose work included first donor insemination and later experimentation with *in vitro* fertilization techniques." The final sentence of the obit stated, "He is survived by his widow and longtime associate at the Goldenberg Infertility Clinic, Elizabeth Walden Goldenberg of Minneapolis." I plopped four quarters into the microfilm reader and listened to the whirring sound as the machine copied the section of newspaper page I'd just read. After collecting my still-damp reproduction, I rewound the microfilm and returned the spool to the librarian. Now I had a name, someone to track down who might know what happened to the Goldenberg Clinic's old records.

I waited five minutes for a blond teenager to finish using one of the pay phones. The St. Paul phone directory chained to the phone booth listed neither an Elizabeth Walden Goldenberg, nor any other Goldenberg with the appropriate initials. Directory Information for Minneapolis was equally unsuccessful in yielding Mrs. Goldenberg. I checked my purse for coins, deposited a quarter, and dialed the Hennepin County Voter Registration office. Several minutes' waiting time later, I got lucky. Dr. Goldenberg's widow was a good citizen and, as such, had voted in the last election. Elizabeth Walden Goldenberg's registered voting address was 320 Lakeview Court, Minneapolis.

I smiled to myself as I hung up the phone. Finally I was closing in on the elusive clinic's treasure cache of information.

— 5 —

Three-twenty Lakeview Court was a two-and-a-half-story white frame house on a cul-de-sac off Lake of the Isles Parkway in Minneapolis. True to its name, the street offered a view of the lake with its two small islands, lazily swimming ducks, and encircling bicycle path. This neighborhood cost serious money—houses here ran well into the six-figure range—but there was paint peeling on number 320 and its lawn sprouted hundreds of dandelions in the final stages of going to seed. I doubted that Mrs. Goldenberg's neighbors, with their hand-polished Mercedes-Benzes, Jaguars, and Cadillacs parked conspicuously in flower-bordered circular driveways, were thrilled that she lived here.

I parked my ailing Honda in front of the house and rang the doorbell. There was no answer. I rang again. Just as I was about to give up, a security panel opened in the door and a disembodied voice demanded, "Who's there?"

"Devon MacDonald. I'm an investigator. I'd like a word with Mrs. Goldenberg about her late husband's clinic." I held up my photo ID to the security panel.

"What've you got there? I can't read that from here," the woman said. "Hand it through, please."

I did as I was told, then waited. I began to think I might never see my photo ID again. I'd have to write to the State Department of Public Safety, explain how I'd lost it, fill out endless forms, wait two or three months for some civil servant to respond . . .

Finally, locks were unlatched and the heavy oak door swung open. Inside stood a tiny woman, too short to look through the security panel. Her white hair was pulled carelessly into a chignon and she was wearing the thickest pair of eyeglasses I'd ever seen. "Come in, Miss MacDonald," she said. "I'm Betsy Goldenberg." She handed back my ID and we shook hands; hers felt fragile in mine, as though her bones would shatter if I gripped too firmly.

I stood in the marble foyer as Mrs. Goldenberg carefully rebolted the door, then followed her slowly through a long hallway, where a grandfather clock chimed the quarter hour, into the cluttered living room at the back of the house. A film of dust covered dozens of china figures and gold-framed photos and a multitude of fuzz balls hid under the chairs and sofa. She motioned me toward a brown velvet chair and perched on a beige satin one next to it. "I've never met a lady private detective before. What's it like?"

"There aren't many of us in the business. It's not very much like *Charlie's Angels*." I didn't want to be sidetracked into telling war stories. I plunged ahead. "Mrs. Goldenberg, the reason I've come here is that a child's life may depend on my locating certain medical records from your husband's clinic." I told her about the Levys and their son.

When I had finished, she was silent for a moment, gently stroking a pink-and-white china shepherdess on the table beside her chair. "I can't give you Max's records." She pulled her hand away from the figurine. "My husband promised his patients confidentiality. Medical ethics are involved, especially with the kind of clinic Max ran."

"I understand that, Mrs. Goldenberg, but this is a very special circumstance. Think of it like this—if your husband had found out one of his sperm donors carried a hereditary disease, he'd have notified the families."

"I suppose so . . ." Her brow furrowed.

"This is no different," I said. "This is a matter of life and death, too." I pulled David Levy's photograph out of my purse and handed it to her. "If I don't get your help to find this little boy's biological half-brother or -sister, he's going to die."

Squinting, she held the picture close to her face, then reached for a large round magnifying glass next to the shepherdess. "I'm afraid my eyes are just about useless these days," she told me. "I still manage to read a little with this glass, but it tires me."

She handed back the picture and sighed. "I'm not even sure where to find the records you want. I'm afraid my husband was never much of a businessman. He didn't take in a partner, even when he started getting on in years. By the time he retired, he could sell only part of his practice. His current files were sent to the Twin Cities Reproductive Medical Group. But Max's old records, the ones earlier than about 1975, are stored away in boxes, dozens of them. When we closed the clinic, we sold the office furniture and the movers just piled everything else into boxes and sealed them up. We never got around to sorting things out. My sight had started to go and Max didn't have the energy." She shook her head and a few more hairs escaped from the disheveled white chignon perched at the back of her neck. "I just don't see how I can help you, Miss MacDonald, even if it were ethical. It would take me months to go through those boxes. By then, that little boy . . ."

"Mrs. Goldenberg, do you have children?"

"I'm afraid not." Her voice was tinged with regret. "That's one reason Max decided to specialize in infertility problems. We hoped he'd find some way to help us. Today, they've got all kinds of things—fancy surgery for both men and women, artificial hormones, babies conceived in petri dishes, frozen embryos, surrogate mothers, every kind of miracle . . . or abomination, depending on your point of view. But all that came too late for Max and me."

"Still, seeing all those people desperate for a child, you must have some feeling for what it's like to lose one." I drew a deep breath. "I lost my little boy. He was only three. It was a hot summer day and Danny was splashing in the little plastic wading pool I'd put out in our front yard. He . . . he loved to play in water. I was watching him from the front steps. I knew kids could drown in a few seconds and I wasn't going to let anything happen to my baby. Suddenly a big gray Chrysler New Yorker came speeding down the street. It sideswiped a car parked across the street, bounced off and crashed into our front yard. A drunk driver, at three in the afternoon. Danny was hit straight on . . . never regained consciousness. He died four months later."

Without realizing what I was doing, I'd leaned forward and gripped Mrs. Goldenberg's hand. Now I felt it pull away from mine. I let go. "There's a reason I'm telling you this, Mrs. Goldenberg. I want you to know I didn't come here today just because I was hired to do a job. I won't let the Levys go through what I did, not if I have it in me to help."

She hung her head; her mouth narrowed.

"You talk about ethics, Mrs. Goldenberg. Can't you see, there's no easy answer to what's right in this kind of situation? You tell me . . . is it ethical to keep a secret if it means letting an innocent child die?" The world of baby making, of genetic engineering, had more than its share of muddy ethics, but certainly Mrs. Goldenberg knew that without my telling her.

The clock in the hallway chimed the hour. "Would you like a glass of iced tea, Miss MacDonald?"

"I'd love one."

We proceeded haltingly to the kitchen at the west side of the house. Mrs. Goldenberg bumped into things as she walked. I noticed that her arms and legs were dotted with bruises.

Like the living room, the kitchen was grimy. The countertops looked sticky, the floor had a dingy gray tint over the green vinyl tile, and dirty fingerprints smeared the edges of the white cupboards. Mrs. Goldenberg took a pitcher of iced tea from the refrigerator while I sliced a lemon. Then we sipped our tea and talked for half an hour . . . about everything but David Levy.

I learned that Mrs. Goldenberg lived here alone. Three days a week, she employed cleaning and yard maintenance help, who obviously were taking advantage of her near-blindness, but she valued her independence too much to have someone live in. She was acquainted with few of her neighbors—it wasn't a friendly neighborhood and her limited eyesight restricted her to the house most of the time. She was lonely. Sometimes you have to let lonely people talk a while to gain their confidence. I poured us a second glass of tea and we chatted. I didn't mind. I began to like Betsy Goldenberg.

Betsy told me she had worked in her husband's clinic for more than thirty years, keeping the books and scheduling appointments. Sometimes she even did a little counseling with the patients, trying to help them cope with the pain of childlessness and the humiliation of the fertility tests. She'd felt useful in those days, but that feeling had left her after Max succumbed to cancer and her vision deteriorated. Now, she often wondered why she had to go on living, yet she'd never worked up the courage to end it. At length, she set down her glass and said, "I should be ashamed, Devon. Here I am complaining I've lived too long and you're here about a dying little boy who just wants a chance at life. I suppose that's the difference between eight and eighty."

"You can make a difference to that boy, Betsy. If we get lucky and find a child who's David's biological relative, that little boy may survive."

She stood up too quickly, smacking her hip against the kitchen table, and carried her glass to the sink. She set it down precariously close to the edge of the drainboard. "There won't be many to find, you know," she told me. "Max was very fastidious about that."

"I'm not sure what you mean."

"The number of children conceived from a single donor's sperm. In those days, some doctors paid no mind at all to how many women were inseminated by one donor. The same donors might come to them once a week for years. But Max could see the risks."

"Risks?"

She ticked them off on her frail fingers. "First, what if a man turned out to have some hidden disease or to be passing on a defect we hadn't caught in his genetic profile? We didn't want a dozen children threatened. Second, there was always the danger that these children would grow up and intermarry, never realizing that they had the same biological father. The babies they produced would have an increased risk of being born defective."

She took my silence for skepticism.

"That's not as far-fetched as you might think, Devon. Say that one man's sperm resulted in twenty-five or thirty children born, which did happen with some less scrupulous physicians. They'd be about the same age and living in the same general geographic area. Their families would travel in fairly affluent, educated social circles. They might easily come to know each other. With donor insemination, the children's origins are almost always kept secret. So, unlike adopted children, they wouldn't even be aware that an incestuous relationship could be a possibility for them."

"I never thought of that."

"Max's strict limit was four children, and it wasn't often even that many were born from one father," Betsy told me. "Chances are no more than a couple of children exist with your Dr. Levy's genes."

"One could be all we'll need," I said, carrying my glass to the sink and surreptitiously righting Betsy's.

She squared her shoulders and tilted her chin upward. The late afternoon sun shining through the kitchen window caught the thick lenses of her eyeglasses and reflected into my eyes. "You seem like an honest person, Devon. Someone with the right motives. I don't know if Max would approve, but I'm going to take a chance. Maybe I just want to be useful once more before I die. I've decided to give you my permission to look through the clinic's records."

Betsy Goldenberg had not exaggerated the task at hand. She pointed me in the direction of the attic—she was reluctant to climb the stairway herself and I was relieved that the frail, nearly blind woman didn't attempt it—and told me the boxes I needed were located in the northwest corner. It was obvious that the attic had not been visited in years, probably since Max Goldenberg had died. A thick layer of dust coated everything, undisturbed by footprints, at least human ones. Closer inspection by the light of the single bulb hanging from the ceiling revealed tiny animals' prints. Mice? Squirrels? I tried not to think about what sort of creatures might be sharing the musty space with me.

The chamber was a hodgepodge of a long-married couple's cast-off belongings: an old metal trunk with hinges corroded by years of exposure to humid air; an old-fashioned wire dress form; a single-speed bicycle that dated back to the 1940s; stacks of outdated medical books; an open box filled with moldering paperback Westerns; at least half a dozen cobwebbed suitcases; a mahogany rocking chair missing its seat. The boxes I needed were stacked neatly in a corner, in piles five boxes high. I counted seventeen stacks.

I fashioned a work center for myself by placing a board over the frame of the rocking chair and positioning it under the light. Then I carried the files, one heavy box at a time, to the center of the room for inspection.

Most of the boxes contained records of patients who were not candidates for artificial insemination. Their problems were solved with hormone treatments or surgery. Others were victims of incurable infertility. Betsy had explained that the files I was seeking would be marked either AID, for Artificial Insemination by Donor, or AIM, for Artificial Insemination Mixed. AIM indicated that the husband was able to produce some sperm of his own, but had some problem, most likely a severely low sperm count. In such cases, the husband's sperm was mixed with a donor's before the wife was inseminated. Often these couples later convinced themselves that their child had resulted from a union of the wife's egg with one of the husband's sperm. The donor's contribution was suppressed and eventually forgotten. A third category, AIH, which stood for Artificial Insemination by Husband, would not concern me. Betsy explained that this procedure might be used, for instance, when a husband was facing cancer radiation treatments or surgery that could make him sterile. He could store his sperm at the clinic, where it was kept in a frozen state. As long as several years afterward, his frozen sperm could be thawed and used to inseminate his wife.

I spent two hours inspecting the files in three of the boxes before I found the first AID reference. By then my eyes itched fiercely and I'd had three sneezing fits from the dust I'd stirred up in moving the boxes. Since childhood, I've been plagued with breathing allergies and sensitivities to airborne pollutants, everything from perfumes to pollen to household dust. The Goldenbergs' attic was my equivalent of a torture chamber, but I could hardly carry more than eighty boxes downstairs to inspect them. Anxiously, I searched through this first AID file for the identity of the sperm donor involved in conceiving a healthy male infant for Joan and William Glazer. On the final page, there it was: Number B11-12-48. Damn! Old Dr. Goldenberg had made certain that no one with access to his files would find out easily who had fathered an AID child. I'd have to go after it from the other direction. Surely there was a box here that contained Benjamin Levy's file. That file would include his code number. Since the clinic's patients were either women or couples, I figured that any file carrying only a man's name must be a sperm donor's. I found them collected in the forty-seventh through fiftieth boxes, nearly two hundred of them. Ben Levy's code number was A6-9-44. I noticed that his birthdate was listed as June 9, 1944. So that was the code: the donor's date of birth preceded by a letter, perhaps to distinguish between two or more donors born on the same date. The grandfather clock downstairs chimed eight o'clock. I sneezed for the hundredth time, then heard Betsy's voice calling from the foot of the attic stairway.

She announced that she had prepared dinner for us. In a bathroom that smelled strongly of mildew, another of my allergies, I made a stab at washing off the attic dirt on my hands and face, then joined Betsy in the dining room. The meal she offered consisted of TV dinners: fried chicken, mashed potatoes and gravy, green peas, and a tiny square of cherry cobbler. Our two sectioned aluminum holders rested on chipped and cracked bone china plates. Betsy explained apologetically that frozen meals were all she could manage these days. The tears in my eyes were not entirely a result of my allergies. I set aside my prejudice against commercially processed foods and ate everything on my plate.

By four the next morning, I had searched through all of

the clinic's boxed files and set aside seven in addition to Ben Levy's. I was bleary-eyed and my sinuses felt as though they'd been subjected to a week in a mature ragweed field when I carried the files downstairs. Betsy had fallen asleep in her beige chair. She wore a faded pink chenille bathrobe and her white hair was now draped around her thin shoulders. I tiptoed into the dining room and turned on the chandelier, then spread out the files on the table.

Seven women had been inseminated by sperm from donor Number A6-9-44. Three of the women inseminated had failed to become pregnant. I set their files aside. Two others had miscarried. Their files joined the first three. The final two manila folders contained little David Levy's best—possibly his only—hope of survival. The first was marked AIM. On April 2, 1971, Ben Levy's sperm had been mixed with that of Tom Meyers and used to inseminate Sarah Meyers. A healthy female infant was born to Sarah Meyers on January 6, 1972. But was the biological father of that baby girl Benjamin Levy or Tom Meyers? Only sophisticated clinical tests would tell. The final file contained stronger promise for David. It was marked AID. Ben Levy's sperm had inseminated Myra Hoffman, wife of Gilbert Hoffman, on May 12, 1972. A male, four-weeks premature, had been born to Mrs. Hoffman on January 15, 1973. The infant had remained in the hospital for two weeks, then was pronounced healthy and sent home. Here the file was clear; the Hoffman child's biological father was Dr. Benjamin Levy.

I gathered up the Hoffman and Meyers files and set them aside, then returned the others to the attic and closed the boxes. I didn't have the energy to restack them, but doubted that it would matter. No one was likely to enter this room until after Betsy Goldenberg's death. Then someone else would have to figure out what to do with the clinic's files.

I left a note printed in large letters thanking Betsy, who

by now was snoring lightly, made a note of the number on her unlisted phone for future reference, and let myself out the front door, making sure it locked behind me. Clutching the files to my chest, I sucked in the clean air hungrily. A shower would wash the dust from my hair and body, but I felt as though it would take days to clear my head and lungs.

Exhausted, I climbed behind the wheel of the Honda and turned the key in the ignition. Nothing happened. Ten minutes later, I conceded that the battery was deader than Max Goldenberg and his clinic. I didn't have the heart to wake Betsy, so I picked up the files and hiked to Lake Street, where I found a public phone in a gas station and called a taxi.

It was nearly seven and the sun was rising before I fell into my bed. I needed a few hours' sleep before I could deal with the Hoffmans, Meyerses, and Levys. And my derelict automobile.

— 6 —

I slept until ten, then forced my tired body through my daily aerobic dance routine in my cramped living room. After a shower and some breakfast, I felt ready to face the day. By the time I'd had my car towed and a new battery installed—that set me back $129 plus tax—it was after two o'clock.

Sam was out when I arrived at the office, but I was scheduled to have dinner with him and Rose tonight. I'd bring him up to date on the case then. Paula was sitting at her typewriter, wearing a light blue outfit that buttoned within a few inches of her chin. She was actually typing. I gave her a warm smile of approval. Never let it be said that Devon MacDonald holds a grudge.

I plopped down the Hoffman and Meyers files on my desk, pushed my phone messages aside, and grabbed the Minneapolis and St. Paul directories from the row of telephone books on the shelf. There was no listing for either Tom or Sarah Meyers. I called the Voter Registration Offices for Hennepin, Ramsey, Anoka, Dakota, Washington, Scott, and Carver counties, but either Tom and Sarah didn't exercise their patriotic duty or they'd moved out of the greater metropolitan area. So much for easily locating the Meyerses.

I had better luck with the Hoffmans. Gilbert Hoffman still had a phone listed at the Pascal Street address where he'd lived eighteen years ago. I slipped the Hoffman file back into my briefcase and headed west on Grand, then south on Snelling. The Hoffman house was in an area of modest lower-middle-class houses in St. Paul, built mainly before World War II. It was a gray bungalow with a detached single garage and six blooming peony bushes along the front. An army of ants crawled on the mammoth pink-and-white blossoms.

A lanky young man in blue shorts and a Highland Park High School T-shirt answered the door. "Hi," he mumbled through a peanut butter sandwich he was chewing. His narrow face, ruffled dark brown hair, and pale blue eyes left me with little doubt that I was meeting Ben Levy's son.

"I'd like to speak with your parents, please."

"Just a minute." He dusted crumbs from his chin and yelled, "Mom! Somebody here to see you."

An extraordinarily pale, middle-aged woman in a housedress walked toward us. She wiped her hands on a gingham apron, frowning slightly. She reminded me of a farm wife, except that she was so colorless she obviously spent little time outdoors. "Yes?" she asked hesitantly. Her watery blue eyes gave her face a frightened look.

"Mrs. Hoffman, I'm Devon MacDonald." I handed her my card.

She squinted at it, turned it over, then looked up at me, her expression registering a combination of bewilderment and fear. "An investigator . . . What—?"

"There's something I'd like to speak to you and Mr. Hoffman about privately," I said, glancing uneasily at the boy, who was licking a smear of peanut butter from his fingers and listening avidly.

"I don't . . . if this has something to do with Gil, he's not home," she said.

"Perhaps you and I can chat a bit before he arrives. It's important."

She shook her head. "I don't know. My husband doesn't like me to let strangers in the house. He's very strict about that. You'd better come back after six, when he's home."

I didn't want to waste the rest of the afternoon. "It's rather urgent, Mrs. Hoffman . . . about Dr. Maxwell Goldenberg."

It was hard to imagine the woman growing paler, but the last trace of color left her cheeks. Her shoulders closed in on her chest, as though to protect herself. After a long pause, she said firmly, "I don't know what you're talking about."

"A long time ago," I said, "you were one of Dr. Goldenberg's patients."

"That's not true. I never—" She turned toward the boy and snapped, "Tyler, go do your homework. Right now! And don't get crumbs on the floor." The lanky teenager shrugged and started toward the other end of the small house.

I opened my briefcase. "I have your medical file from Dr. Goldenberg's office right here, Mrs. Hoffman. Here's your name, Myra Hoffman. You listed this address."

"I suppose you want money." She sounded resigned.

"No. I just want to talk to you. I'm not going to hurt you or your family."

There was silence as she weighed her options. Finally, sighing, she opened the door wider. "Come in," she said.

I walked into the living room, sparsely furnished with old blond wood occasional tables and a sofa and matching chair upholstered in nubby green nylon. After I entered, the woman peered anxiously into the street, then shut the door tightly.

"We can talk in the kitchen. Follow me." Mrs. Hoffman led the way into a room that had no more personality than the living room. It smelled of peanut butter and disinfectant and was immaculate, with dark-stained pine cupboards and a yellow tile floor. The yellow-and-white ruffled curtains on the single window overlooking the tiny backyard were straight out of the Sears catalogue, like the matching toaster cover and potholders. The sole personal touch was a framed needlepoint of a white cottage surrounded by pink flowers and a white picket fence; "God Bless Our Home" was cross-stitched across the picture's cloudless sky.

I pulled a chair from the table, sat down, and opened the medical file. Eyeing the papers, the woman took a chair opposite mine. "I'm sorry if I startled you, Mrs. Hoffman," I began.

"The doctor promised he'd never tell. . . . It all happened eighteen years ago. I thought my secret was safe." She was near tears. "I haven't got any money. I can't pay you."

Why are people so ready to believe PIs are crooks? "Please, Mrs. Hoffman. I don't want your money. I'd never have bothered you if a boy's life weren't at stake."

She gnawed her quivering lower lip. "Is it Tyler? Did Tyler inherit some terrible disease?"

"Nothing like that." Briefly, I explained about David Levy and his leukemia and why Tyler might be David's only chance for survival.

She picked at the hem of her apron, avoiding my eyes. "I—I can't. You can't make me do this. I could lose everything."

33

"Mrs. Hoffman, without Tyler's help, David Levy stands to lose his life. Thanks to Benjamin Levy, you have a fine, healthy son. Now Dr. Levy and his wife want a relatively small thing from you and Tyler, something that could give them a healthy son, too. Please at least think about it . . ."

She shoved her chair back and stood up. "No. It's impossible. I can't do it. It's too risky. I'm sorry, Miss MacDonald, you'll have to leave now."

I put the file back in my briefcase and closed it. "I'll come back after six, talk with your husband—"

"No! You can't do that." Her rabbit-like eyes widened.

"Maybe Mr. Hoffman will better appreciate the Levys'—"

"No! You don't understand. He'll kill me, he'll kill both of us."

"Mrs. Hoffman, nobody's going to kill you. I know it's not an easy thing to tell your son about his real origins, but surely you and your husband can manage it. Tyler looks like a fine young man. It'll be a shock at first, but he'll get over it. Adopted children do."

Myra Hoffman's chin quivered and her tenuous composure cracked. She pulled a tissue from her apron pocket, covered her eyes, and sank back into her chair. Suddenly she began to weep loudly and hysterically. I let her cry, battling my own feelings of guilt and hoping her son wouldn't hear her and come to investigate.

Sniffling, she began to reveal her story, a tale she'd spent eighteen years hiding. "He doesn't know," she began. "My husband thinks he's Tyler's father. If he ever found out, he really would kill me. He'd kill Tyler, too. You don't know him."

I didn't know what to say. I couldn't picture Dr. Goldenberg, the ethical physician Betsy had described to me the previous night, agreeing to artificially inseminate a married woman without her husband's knowledge. And I couldn't believe what Myra Hoffman was saying about her husband could be true. What kind of man could murder his wife and the boy he'd raised as his own son for seventeen years? "How could he not know the truth?"

"I was desperate. I tricked him." Her fingers shredded the tissue. There was a faint row of bruises on her right arm.

"But how?"

"I had all the fertility tests, every test Dr. Goldenberg could come up with. It took two years, but he couldn't find anything wrong with me, said it was probably Gil who—I had to beg him for weeks, but I finally got Gil to go to the doctor's office."

"Once your husband had a sperm test, he must have realized he couldn't be Tyler's father."

Myra shook her head. "You don't understand. I only got Gil to come to the doctor's office in the first place because he thought they'd found something wrong with *me*. When Dr. Goldenberg suggested he be tested, Gil exploded. He said some terrible things." Her face registered mortification. "He called Dr. Goldenberg a filthy, lying Jew. Then—then he dragged me out of there. That night Gilbert . . . beat me. He said he'd kill me if I ever went back to see Dr. Goldenberg again. I was so bruised I couldn't leave the house for six days." Briefly, the sterile kitchen was silent. "My husband meant exactly what he said."

"But you went back anyway."

She held her hand over her mouth, as though to prevent herself from saying anything more.

"Mrs. Hoffman," I pressed, "this doesn't make any sense. If you really believed your husband would kill you, how could you have returned to Dr. Goldenberg's office? Why?"

"What else could I do? I wanted a baby more than anything in the world." Two spots of color stained her cheeks. "And I knew Gil would never stay with me if I didn't give him a child, a son. You're a woman, you know how men are."

I made a noncommittal sound. She took it as an affirmation. "All that aside, Mrs. Hoffman, I can't believe Dr. Goldenberg would have agreed to inseminate you against your husband's wishes."

"You still don't understand. I forged Gil's signature on those papers. I swore to the doctor that Gil had calmed down and agreed to the procedure, as long as he didn't have to have any tests. Dr. Goldenberg had told me he always used a donor who looked like the husband. You know, the same height, weight, coloring, blood type. He'd promised nobody would ever guess Gil wasn't the real father by looking at the baby. I figured Gil wouldn't know, either. And he doesn't. He has no idea."

"But after Gil had insulted the doctor . . ."

"Don't you think I apologized for my husband's behavior a million times? I begged the doctor to forgive him, told him Gil's masculinity'd been threatened and he'd been sorry and ashamed the minute we'd got home. Dr. Goldenberg believed me. He said a lot of husbands saw it that way, even though fertility has nothing to do with manhood."

"It must have been hard on you, keeping quiet all these years," I told her. Sometimes playing sympathetic psychologist elicits the most information.

She raised her puffy eyes and dabbed at the corners with her tissue. "It was worse in the early years. When Tyler was first born, I'd be afraid of things like his eyes would turn brown. Gil's and mine are both blue. After a while, I just didn't think about it anymore. Tyler was my son, our son. Then, lately . . ."

"Lately?"

"Truth is, recent years I'm relieved Tyler isn't Gil's son."

"Why?"

She paused, rolling her tattered tissue between her index finger and thumb. "My husband is not well," she said. "He was always a hard man, but lately he's become . . . well, I suppose vicious is the word for it, and sort of obsessed. He has spells, times when he believes people are out to get him, 'specially Jews and blacks. Gilbert says Hitler had the right idea." The tissue shredded and she stuffed the remains in her apron pocket. "This Dr. Levy, is he a Jew?"

"I didn't ask him. Most people named Levy are."

She grimaced, looking around her immaculate kitchen. "Dr. Goldenberg sure got his revenge on Gilbert Hoffman, didn't he?"

I kept silent.

"People find out Gilbert Hoffman's son is really half Jewish," she said softly, "Lord help us. He'll torture me to death, he finds out about this."

I leaned toward her. "Mrs. Hoffman, if your husband is as brutal as you describe, why do you stay with him?"

She rose and walked to the window, staring out into the compact yard. "I don't go out much. Got no place to go anymore. If I left here, where would I go? How would I live? What would happen to Tyler?" She shook her head. "I could never do it. Gilbert would just come after me."

"There are shelters for battered wives. You could be with other women who've gone through this. They'd protect you and help you get a job."

She turned toward me, her eyes wide with fear. "I—I couldn't. I couldn't leave my home. Gil's not really so bad, 'specially now he's on his new medicine. It's just once in a while he sort of loses control. Usually it's because I did something to get him mad."

"What kind of medication is he taking?"

"Little red pills." She opened a cabinet drawer and pulled out a small bottle. "These. I pack one with his lunch every day." She handed me the bottle. The label read, *Nardil. 15 mg. One tablet four times a day as directed.*

"This stuff calms him down?" I asked, setting the bottle on the table.

"Long as he takes it on time and keeps off certain foods, he's a lot easier to be around. Says he feels better, not so depressed as he used to be. He's even been putting in a full day at work the last few months."

"Where's that?"

"Pearson's Meats. Gil's a master butcher. Bought into the business a couple of years ago. It's lucky meat's not one of the things Gil can't eat now he's taking those pills. Loves a good steak, a nice thick pork chop. As an owner, he can bring home the best. Gil's a real good provider."

She was becoming an apologist for her husband, suddenly realizing she'd told me too much. Was it possible that she loved the cruel bigot she'd described to me? Or maybe she was just terrified of losing the support he provided. "How often does he hit you, Mrs. Hoffman?"

"Not too—" She folded her arms across her chest and said, "Miss MacDonald, I'm never going to leave Gilbert. I'm never going to leave this house. I can't. I won't. The only reason I told you this was because . . . well, I wanted you to understand why I can't help your Dr. Levy. Why Tyler can't help. Gil would never be able to accept this. If it came out, he would suffer, I would suffer, Tyler would suffer. And the Levys' little boy still wouldn't get that transplant he needs. I'm sorry."

I opened my briefcase and removed one of my cards. Quickly copying Dr. Benjamin Levy's name and office phone number onto the back, I handed her the card and headed toward the front door. "Think about it," I said. "If you change your mind, please call either Dr. Levy or me right away. You could save Tyler's brother's life, but there isn't much time left."

As she opened the door for me, she cautioned, "Remember, if you don't keep my secret, you'll kill Tyler. And me. You do that, your Dr. Levy won't have any sons left."

I sat in the Honda for a few minutes in front of the house, making notes on my disappointing and depressing interview with Myra Hoffman. I would type them up later, leaving out her name and address, and give them to the Levys. It was a task I dreaded.

When I was finished, I started the car and glanced one last time at the nondescript house Myra Hoffman refused to leave. People have strange needs, strange priorities. As I shifted the car into gear, a curtain at one of the windows twitched slightly, as though someone had been watching the street, watching me.

— 7 —

I'd driven past Pearson's Meats hundreds of times. Since I almost never eat meat anymore, I was not a customer. Still, it was hard to miss the huge blue-and-red Pearson's Meats sign hanging over the Snelling Avenue shop, with its picture of a grimly smiling steer. I wasn't ready to give up yet. When Myra Hoffman had had time to get over the shock of my showing up at her door after eighteen years, she might change her mind and decide to help David Levy. In the meantime, I wanted a look at Gilbert Hoffman.

I pulled into the recently blacktopped parking lot, went inside, and took a number. It was nearing the dinner hour and the place was crowded as the two men behind the counter scrambled to serve the long line of customers. One was a well-built black man about six feet tall, in his early thirties. His once-white apron and shirt were smeared with blood. The lettering on his white plastic name tag identified him as Leon. The other was a good fifteen years older and six inches taller, a huge white man with dark hair and blue eyes that radiated as much warmth as a couple of marbles. I was not surprised to see the name Gil pinned to his immaculate white shirt. His sleeves were rolled to the elbow and there was a small turquoise coiled snake tattooed on the inside of his right forearm.

During the time I waited to be served, it became obvious why Gil remained tidy while Leon's clothing was thoroughly soiled. Gil weighed and wrapped pre-cut meats—steaks, chops, roasts—and collected money from the customers. Whenever anything needed to be fetched from the walk-in cooler in the back room or required any kind of special attention with a knife or cleaver, Leon was elected.

"Leon, pound this piece of round steak for the lady," Gil would bark. Leon would pound the slab of muscle with a tenderizing hammer while Gil supervised, continually prodding, "You about ready with that round steak? Lady's waiting and three more behind her." The black man's face remained immobile. He was silent whenever speech could be avoided.

When my number was called, I approached the counter. "Help you, ma'am?" Gil Hoffman asked as I handed him my cardboard ticket.

I'd been too busy observing him and his employee to think about what to buy. The irony of my eating carefully enough to live to be a hundred while working in a profession where I could risk having my brains blown out this afternoon hasn't exactly eluded me; I just prefer to ignore it. "Chicken," I blurted out. "You sell chicken?"

"How large, ma'am? Whole or quartered?"

"Uh, breasts. Make it four chicken breasts. Boneless, please."

Hoffman picked four chicken breasts from behind the glass showcase, weighed them, then plopped them on the cutting surface. "Leon, bone these for the lady and be quick about it." His tone was contemptuous. "Take just a minute, ma'am. I'll help the next customer while you're waiting. Number fifty-six!"

I watched as Leon bent over the chicken. As he slipped

the long boning knife under the bird's flesh, he silently mouthed the words, "Fuckin' honkie."

"You mean him or me, Leon?" I whispered.

Startled, the man's head jerked upright as though I'd caught him with his hand in the cash drawer. "I didn't "

I gave him a reassuring smile. "Don't let it bother you. I see your point." Relieved, he returned my smile.

When Leon had finished the boning job, Hoffman swiftly wrapped the chicken breasts in white butcher paper. I paid him and took the package. It would make a useful, if unusual, hostess gift for Rose Sherman tonight.

As I left Pearson's Meats, I heard Gilbert Hoffman apologize to the next customer, a man who wanted a whole filet mignon sliced into steaks two inches thick. "Sorry to keep you waiting, sir. The boy here's a little slow today."

Personally, I thought it a credit to Leon's patience that he didn't slice his boss into steaks.

— **8** —

Rose Sherman graciously accepted the wrapped chicken I offered her. "Dinner for tomorrow. You're so thoughtful, dear," she said, greeting me with a kiss.

"Not exactly flowers or fine wine, but it's a long story," I said. "I thought you could use it and it's on Sam's diet."

Rose served a meal of sole filets baked in white wine and tarragon, a mushroom and wild rice casserole, and French-cut green beans dusted with slivered almonds but without butter. She'd set the table with her best Japanese china and served a good Chardonnay in crystal goblets. Rose loved to be social, to give parties, especially now that she'd retired from managing a fabric shop and had time on her hands. Any excuse would do, even Sam's partner coming to dinner.

I told her the meal was outstanding, and I meant it. Sam complained that, with nothing to eat but "this fairy food," he was slowly starving to death. Rose and I surveyed Sam's portly figure, then caught each other's eye and laughed.

"Always something to kvetch about, that one," she scolded, but her voice was affectionate. I hoped she didn't know about the Twinkies and taco chips he ate at the office. Sam's health problems had caused Rose as much stress as they had Sam. Maybe more, because Rose had faced reality. She'd changed her lifelong cooking habits and learned to cook low-cholesterol, low-fat, low-calorie meals for him, a change that was a genuine sacrifice for her. Feeding people the rich, fattening goodies she once had baked, roasted, or fried was a significant part of the way Rose Sherman showed she loved them.

Rose had begun a morning walking program, too, solely because exercising with Sam was the only way she could get him to move his bones. She'd also insisted that Sam cut back his load at the office, which, along with her retiring to care for him, cut their family income sharply. It wasn't hard to tell Rose Sherman truly loved the old curmudgeon.

The irony was that Rose had stripped a good twenty pounds from her five-foot-two figure since Sam's first heart attack, while he hadn't lost an ounce. She looked ten years younger than when I'd first met her. Once rotund like her husband, she was now trim. Her hair was tinted a dark reddish brown that covered her natural streaks of gray, and her skin had a healthy glow. I once heard her tell Sam that she had to keep her looks to catch a second husband. The way he was letting himself go, she'd added, she couldn't count on his lasting much longer. I'm not sure she was kidding. At any rate, she made her point; not long afterward, Sam quit smoking his beloved cigars.

Over a dessert of honeydew melon slices topped with raspberries, Sam and I talked shop. "I can't explain why, but I'm not ready to throw in the towel on the Hoffmans, even if Gilbert is a total turd," I concluded. "I've just got to give it a little more time, find out as much as I can about Gilbert and Myra Hoffman, then maybe make one more attempt to talk some sense into her."

"Sounds like you're out to save the world again, Devon," Sam said. "I can hear the wheels grinding away in that stubborn head of yours; this one case, you figure you can save a sick kid and a battered wife both. Missed your calling, shoulda been a social worker."

"I don't like to butt in," Rose said, sipping her decaffeinated coffee, "but I'm afraid this time Sam's right, Devon. You won't get that Hoffman woman to leave her husband, not after she's put up with him all these years. Reminds me of Tessa Mahoney from my card club. Her husband Tim's a bigshot lawyer. Every time he loses a case—wham!—Tessa needs her bridgework repaired. Everybody knows about it. Once we girls decided to talk to Tessa about it. We begged her to leave the creep before he really hurt her. Even offered to let her stay with one of us until she could get a court order or whatever you need for that kind of thing."

"What happened?"

"Ha! Tessa swore she was clumsy, fell down the stairs a lot, walked into doors. That's why she's always so banged up. Tim? He'd never lay a finger on her. Practically walked on water, Tim did, according to her."

"So I suppose he kept right on beating her?"

Rose shrugged. "Don't know. Right after we had that talk, Tessa quit the club."

I finished my melon and refused a second cup of coffee. "I hear what you're both saying, but I can't give up this easily; not when a child is dying. I'll nose around a little, see what I can learn about the Hoffmans, then have a second go at Myra. If she says no again, I promise I'll tell the Levys I bombed out. Okay, Sam?"

"You've got one day. Meantime, I'll see what I can turn up on the Meyerses. You finish Vince Vinelli's libel case yet?"

"Four more interviews to go. Court date's not till September. They can wait a couple of days."

I retrieved my briefcase from the coat closet and gave Sam the Meyers file. "If they're still in the Twin Cities, they've moved, they don't vote, and their phone's unlisted. That's as far as I had time to take it."

Sam thumbed through the pages of the medical file. "Good, we've got birth dates on both Sarah and Tom. I'll try the DMV first thing tomorrow." With a name and date of birth, we could get the driver's license number, current address, and physical description of any licensed Minnesota driver from the Department of Motor Vehicles.

Rose walked me to the door. "I slipped a little something in your coat pocket," she whispered. "Just a little treat I baked for the grandchildren. Don't tell Sam. He can't eat it, so why should his mouth water?"

I kissed her good-bye and she watched as I walked out to the street and got into my car. She waved and closed the door. By the Honda's dome light, I examined Rose's "little something," a foil-wrapped package of sticky cookies spread with some sort of apricot jam. I tasted a corner of one and found it cloyingly sweet. The package would go in the trash as soon as I got home, but I appreciated it just the same. It made me feel loved. Lately I hadn't felt that very much.

— 9 —

I spent the next morning knocking on doors in the Hoffmans' neighborhood, posing as an insurance investigator. As in most city neighborhoods nowadays, few people knew their neighbors. "The people in the gray house, third from the corner," I explained to a frazzled young woman in a starched white uniform, who was about to leave for her nursing shift at Midway Hospital.

"Hey, sorry, I don't know them. My roommates and I, we just rent here. We work different shifts and we really haven't been friendly with the neighbors."

"How long have you been here?"

She rolled her green eyes skyward and thought, figuring on her fingers. "Gina and Faye had the place first. Then Faye got married and moved out two years ago last fall, and Susie and I moved in. . . . I guess altogether we've had the house maybe three years. I've been here almost two and a half."

I fared equally well at most of the houses where my knock was answered. At more than half, no one was home. This was a neighborhood of two-income families.

I was becoming discouraged when I saw a late-model Dodge pull to the curb in front of the house next door to the Hoffmans'. The driver was a crew-cut, sandy-haired man in his early forties. He was dressed in brown polyester pants and a mustard-gold short-sleeved shirt. As I approached him I guessed, without looking, that he'd be wearing white socks with dark loafers. I sneaked a look and gave myself half a point; he had on white socks, all right, but his shoes were tie oxfords. He had a broad, good-looking face, marred only by the thick scar that ran from his left eyebrow to his earlobe. He reeked of Aqua Velva aftershave and clutched a sheaf of papers to his chest.

I launched into my cover story, explaining that I was a private investigator hired by an insurance company with which his next-door neighbors had applied for a sizable policy.

It was a hurried interview. The man, who introduced himself as Herb Keller, said he was rushed for time, that he'd come home during his lunch hour to pick up something he'd forgotten that morning. As far as he was concerned, the Hoffmans were model neighbors, never any trouble. Keller had lived next door to them for five years. He knew Gilbert well, Myra less well; she tended to be reclusive. But Gil was a helluva great guy.

"Sorry, I've got to run," he said. "Tell you what, give me your card and I'll call you if I can think of anything about the Hoffmans that you should know." I handed Keller a card, thanked him, and walked back across the street, considering the possibilities. Myra Hoffman could be lying about her husband's brutality. Or maybe she managed to keep silent while being slapped around by the foul-tempered giant I'd observed at Pearson's Meats. Herb Keller certainly wasn't deaf. More likely, he was suffering from a disease rampant in our society: not wanting to get involved.

Despite his impatience, Keller was still watching me when I reached the opposite curb. As I rang the doorbell of the pink stucco house directly across the street, I turned and saw him disappear into his beige-and-brown bungalow.

An elderly man who leaned heavily on a cane opened the pink door just enough to peer out at me. "Don't you see the sign?" he barked, pointing a gnarled finger to the right of the door. "Says no solicitors, clear as your nose." The door swung shut. I stepped forward before it could close.

"I'm not selling anything, sir."

"Saw you going house to house. Don't want to hear about your religion, either."

I went into my insurance routine before the old man could slam his door in my face. "It's standard procedure that we learn as much as possible about the applicants before issuing this size policy," I told him.

"What for?"

"Well, sir, I'm afraid that not all people are as . . . well, candid with insurance companies as they might be. Human nature being what it is, the insurance companies get applications for life insurance from people with terminal diseases, from drug addicts, from people who misrepresented their occupations. For instance, if somebody tests experimental airplanes for a living, the company either won't insure him at all or they'll charge a higher premium. It'd obviously be to a test pilot's advantage to tell the insurance company his work was something less risky. Unless an investigator like me finds out the truth before a claim is paid, all the company's customers' premiums go up to pay it."

The man nodded, getting the idea. "You ever find situations where somebody's murdered?" he asked.

"You mean where the beneficiary murdered the insured for the insurance money?"

"Uh huh."

"Once or twice. Why?"

He opened the door wider. "This insurance policy on Hoffman or the wife?"

I hesitated. "I believe there's an application for insurance on each of them."

"They're each other's beneficiaries?"

"I would guess so. That's usual with married couples."

"Hmph. He's playing it smart. Makes it harder to pin anything on him."

"I don't understand, Mr.—"

"Norwalk. Melville Norwalk." He offered his hand and I shook it.

"I'm Devon MacDonald, Mr. Norwalk. Do you suspect something about Gilbert Hoffman?"

"Damn right, I do." He was warming to the theme. "The man's a wife-beater and a goddamned Nazi. Your company writes that policy, it deserves to get stung. Wouldn't be one bit surprised to see him murder her for the money. Probably's got it planned that way."

"That's just the sort of information I need," I said. Things were looking up. Many neighborhoods have one nosy person who likes to keep track of everyone else. I had a feeling I'd just met this neighborhood's. "I'd like to hear whatever you know about the Hoffman family."

"I can give you an earful. Lived here thirty-six years. Built this house myself. The Hoffmans been here a good twenty." Melville Norwalk's relationship with his long-term neighbors clearly had not been a friendly one.

Norwalk invited me into his living room. A round table and chair were placed facing the picture window. The street was clearly visible through the sheer white curtain; as I stood there, I could see Herb Keller drive off in his Dodge. Yet the same curtain kept anyone outside from realizing that he was being observed.

Old Melville proved to be a treasure chest of information. I wondered how much of it was true.

According to him, he'd often heard Myra Hoffman's cries. Once or twice, he'd called the police, but when they showed up, Myra insisted she'd fallen and hurt herself. That's the way she wanted it, he'd be damned if he'd stick his neck out again trying to save her. Let the big bully kill her, no skin off Norwalk's nose.

Myra no longer even left the house, he said. "Been a good three years or more since I seen her outside. Look for yourself." He gestured at the window, by which the Hoffmans' gray bungalow was framed. "They got just the one car, she don't drive. She wants to go someplace, she's gotta go on foot, don't she?"

I nodded.

"The Nazi and that kid of his, I see them together

sometimes. Usually it's the boy goes off on his bicycle, the father takes the car, and the mother stays home. The boy brings home the groceries. Never his old lady. If I didn't see her answer the door now and again, I'd say Hoffman'd already done away with her."

"What makes you call Mr. Hoffman a Nazi, Mr. Norwalk?"

He leaned forward on the cane as though to make his observation more confidential. "He's a big muckamuck in asp."

"Asp?"

"A-S-P. Stands for Aryan Supremacy Party."

"I've never heard of it."

He grimaced. "You will. It's one of them white hate groups want to take over Idaho, Montana, Washington, a couple other states, keep 'em all 'pure.' Won't allow no blacks, no Indians, no Jews in."

"How do you know Hoffman belongs to this ASP?"

"Belongs, hell. He's president of the local chapter, from what I heard. You seen that tattoo he's got on his arm? A snake, all wound up like it's ready to strike. That's an asp, old-fashioned word for snake. That's their symbol. Ask me, fits 'em good. They're poison, collectin' guns and money, sendin' out hate literature. I'd like to see 'em out of this neighborhood, all of 'em. Hell, I'd like to see 'em off the face of this earth."

What Melville Norwalk was telling me meshed with what Myra Hoffman had told me yesterday about Gilbert's treatment of Dr. Goldenberg all those years ago. His hatreds and prejudices apparently went back many, many years. I felt chilled. What I was learning merely confirmed that I was unlikely to change Myra Hoffman's mind or to engage Gilbert's cooperation to save David Levy's life.

As I left the Norwalk house, a vintage Cadillac with rust spots marring its white finish pulled into the Hoffmans' driveway across the street. The garage door opened on a radio impulse. A minute later, Gilbert

Hoffman emerged from the garage and entered the house. Apparently he was working a short shift today, or else he'd come home for a late lunch. Damn. I wouldn't be able to talk to Myra while he was there and, after hearing what Melville Norwalk had to say, I wondered whether I'd be wasting my time to talk to her at all. Still, I wasn't ready to admit defeat. Sam had given me twenty-four hours. I decided to return later and try my luck one more time.

In the meantime, I had a hunch that Leon, the young butcher at Pearson's Meats, could tell me a thing or two about his fascist boss, maybe something I could use to help the Levys. With Hoffman at home with his neurotic wife, it seemed as good a time as any to find out.

A bell jangled as I opened the door of the butcher shop and Leon entered from the back room, wiping his hands on his apron. This afternoon the place was deserted. "Hi, Leon," I said, "remember me?"

The black man wasn't about to be too friendly with a white woman until he saw what she wanted. Not in Gil Hoffman's store. "More boned chicken?" he asked impassively.

"Just want to ask you a few questions about your buddy, Gil Hoffman."

He made a spitting sound. "No buddy of mine. You a cop?"

I shook my head. "You expecting the police?"

Leon didn't answer.

I could see that I was off on the wrong foot. "My name is Devon MacDonald. I'm a private investigator working on a case that involves Gilbert Hoffman. I'd really appreciate it if you'd tell me what you can about him."

"What kind of case?"

"Sorry, I can't tell you that."

"You want me to spill my guts but you ain't givin' me a reason? Fuck that."

This wasn't going to be easy. "I'm honestly not trying

to be coy with you, Leon, but my profession has a strict code of ethics and I try to keep it. It doesn't allow me to tell you who my client is without his permission, and I don't have that. But I think I can tell you this much . . . that the case involves trying to help a young boy. Without that help, he's going to die."

Leon lined up an errant pork chop so that the tray was symmetrical.

"Just tell me this," I coaxed. "Gil Hoffman treats you like a slave, in public. You hate him. Why do you work for him?"

Leon flinched. Anger flared briefly in his eyes. He subdued it.

"I'm on your side, friend. From what I saw here last night, your boss is a racist pig. How come you put up with it?"

"This case 'bout a kid?"

I nodded.

"I got kids. I got two little girls and a baby son, another one on the way. My wife is sick. I got a prison record. If I could get another job, lady, I'd get it. I tell the man blow it out his ass, how I gonna feed my kids? Go back on the streets? A little B and E? Some dealin'?" He shook his head. "I ain't goin' back inside. I have to eat it awhile to be with my kids, I guess I eat it."

"Sorry," I said. "It was really none of my business."

"You gonna tell that fuckin' asshole what I tell you 'bout him?"

I smiled. "No way. It's between you and me." I extended my arm over the counter and held out my hand. "Do we have a deal, Mr.—?"

Leon hesitated, examined his hand, wiped it once more on his apron, and finally grasped mine. We shook. "Jackson. Leon P. Jackson, Junior."

"Pleased to meet you, Mr. Jackson." Leon glanced at the back of the store. He probably expected Hoffman to return any moment. I figured I'd better cut to the chase. "I'll try to take as little of your time as possible," I promised. "You ever hear of a group called ASP? I've been told Hoffman's a member."

Leon Jackson confirmed Melville Norwalk's story. "Some o' them assholes hang out here," he told me. "Place like a fuckin' KKK rally sometimes."

"Why did someone like Gil Hoffman ever hire a black butcher to work in his shop?"

"Weren't him. Pearson give me the job."

"The two of them get along?"

Jackson smiled. "Like Sugar Ray Leonard and Marvelous Marvin Hagler," he said.

According to Jackson, Hoffman kept his job only because he'd invested ten thousand dollars in the shop at a time when Roger Pearson was verging on bankruptcy. The money bailed out the shop and ensured that Gil Hoffman had a job. Hoffman was a lazy son of a bitch, spending his energy trying to get Jackson to do the work while he lazed around the back room eating his lunch and drinking out of his Thermos bottle. Whenever the shop got really quiet, like this afternoon, Hoffman would split.

"Is Hoffman a drinking man?" I asked. Alcoholism might explain his irrational behavior.

Jackson shook his head. "Keeps to a special diet 'cause o' some pills he's takin'. Can't drink no booze. Sucks some kinda fruit juice all day."

Jackson admitted that Hoffman had been calmer the last few months—since the time Myra said he'd started taking medication. At least during that time there'd been no flying cleavers, no slamming the Laotian cleaning help against the wall. The bigot hadn't changed his basic attitudes, however. "Ol' Gil still a pit bull," Leon said, his chin high. "'Cept now he a pit bull on downers."

I smiled and thanked Jackson for his time. This time he met my glance and shook hands without hesitation. His deep brown eyes added volumes to his comments about his boss; they told me that working for Gilbert

Hoffman was still a very special form of torture for a person of color.

I left Pearson's Meats feeling thoroughly depressed. I didn't see how I could succeed on this case. It offended me deeply that a slimeball like Gilbert Hoffman could keep an innocent kid like David Levy from living a full life, but I was afraid Myra Hoffman was right. Either way. If Hoffman were told about Tyler's origins, he might injure or kill his wife and son. Even if he didn't, it seemed certain he'd never allow Tyler to donate bone marrow to David. If Hoffman weren't told, I might as well never have found Tyler. David would get no bone marrow that way, either.

I drove back to Pascal Street, waited until I saw Gil Hoffman's car pull out of the driveway, and rang the doorbell at the Hoffman house. It was three o'clock. There was no answer.

From what I'd learned this morning, it was unlikely Myra Hoffman had gone out. She certainly hadn't been in the car with her husband. I pushed the button again. The chimes sounded within, but still no one opened the door. I stepped back. The draperies were closed, but the one across the living room picture window swayed almost imperceptibly. Someone was inside. It was obvious Myra Hoffman had no intention of speaking with me again.

With the taste of defeat in my mouth, I turned and headed back to my car.

— 10 —

My outer office was empty except for Paula, who was engrossed in a copy of *Dental Digest*. Three or four similar magazines were piled on her desk.

"Let me guess," I said. "Helen Gurley Brown is recommending dental bonding as the quickest route to the bonds of marriage."

Paula's gaze drifted toward the ceiling.

"Orthodontics for the smile men love?"

"Honestly, Devon. Give me *some* credit." Paula flipped the magazine shut and added it to the stack.

I refrained from reminding her that less than a year ago she'd had her formerly flat chest enlarged to a D-cup, and only last month she'd changed her naturally dark hair for a shade optimistically called Golden Girl. With her new sexier wardrobe and makeup and her cultivated, whispery voice, she barely resembled the old Paula Carboni. Which was precisely her objective. "Unless you're applying to dental school," I said, picking up a copy of *Dental Management* from the stack, "your choice of reading matter has to have something to do with a man."

She smiled sheepishly. "I met him night before last. Stuart Lindblom. He's a dentist, Devon."

"Give. Where'd you find this one?" Paula has researched where to find men more thoroughly than Sam and I research most of our cases, but somehow her efforts never seem to pan out. Last month she wrote thirty-seven letters in response to ads in a local singles publication. The only man to write her back turned out to be an inmate at Stillwater State Prison. He was serving fifteen to life for second-degree murder.

"The salad bar at Lund's." Lund's is a posh supermarket in Highland Park. "He was making himself a salad to take out. You know, lettuce, tomatoes, carrots, stuff like that. When he got to the bean sprouts, he asked me whether I thought they looked fresh." Her round face took on a dreamy expression.

"Sure sounds romantic."

"You can laugh if you want, Devon, but grocery stores are one of the best places to meet eligible men. They're definitely a cut above the ones you meet in Laundromats, too. You ought to try it yourself."

"Thanks, but I'm not exactly eligible."

"That's your own fault. Why don't you divorce that so-called husband of yours? You're just delaying the inevitable. You haven't lived together for years. Find another man, Devon. Might improve your—"

"So Stuart Lindblom is a dentist. Sounds promising." Somewhere I'd lost control of the conversation. "Sam in?" I asked.

"Yeah, he got back about half an hour ago."

"Thanks." I knocked twice and opened Sam's office door just in time to catch him stashing an Eskimo Pie wrapper in his metal wastebasket. Chocolate was smeared on his lower lip. I pretended not to notice; I'd had enough pointless confrontation for one day.

"Park it, Devon," Sam said, gesturing at a chair. My partner certainly has an elegant way with the English language. "Got some stuff on the Levy case for you."

I sat. "Shoot."

Sam bent his head over an untidy pile of papers on his desk. When he looked up again, his lip had been licked clean. "This Meyers family left the country," he said. "Moved to Israel in seventy-seven."

"You have an address for them over there?"

Sam tugged his earlobe. "Nope. Tried callin' the place

they had their mail forwarded, but no luck. Could try the American Embassy, but that goddamn red tape can take months. I understand right, the Levy kid don't have months. If the doc wants to pursue it, we can locate a PI in Tel Aviv. It's that or you go over there. Either way, he'll be runnin' up a bill."

"I'll lay it out to Ben Levy and his wife and see what they want us to do. What else've you got?"

Sam grimaced. "Some background on that bastard Hoffman."

"I hope what you've got gives us more hope than what I dug up today."

"Fat chance." Sam shuffled through his papers and drew out a yellow pad on which he'd made notes. "Property records show he owns one house, on Pascal Street in St. Paul. The wife's name's not on the deed." I wondered if Myra Hoffman realized that; it was probably just one more way her husband had of keeping her in line.

"DBA files show he's part owner of Pearson's Meat Market," Sam continued. "I ordered DMV records for both Gilbert and Myra Hoffman; should be in tomorrow."

So far Sam had told me nothing new. "What about arrests?" I asked. "Anything there?"

"Gilbert's got one conviction. Disturbing the peace."

"Domestic disturbance?"

Sam shook his head. "Jewish Community Center had a Holocaust Remembrance Day a few years ago. Hoffman's one of those bastards got arrested for picketing outside. You know, those 'The Holocaust Is a Hoax' boys. Asshole probably marched on Skokie, too."

"So Melville Norwalk was right."

"Who the hell's Melville Norwalk?"

I told Sam about my canvass of the Hoffmans' neighborhood and about what Melville Norwalk had told me of Gilbert Hoffman's membership in the Aryan Supremacy Party.

He rolled his green-flecked brown eyes until they nearly disappeared beneath his drooping lids. "You got as much chance of getting that creep to help as I got of being the next Miss America."

"Wish I could argue with you." It was obviously pointless to think Hoffman would change his stripes, and it could take months to locate the Meyers family. Once they were found, we had no guarantee they would—or even could—help David Levy. No doubt about it; I had failed. "I'll call the Levys and tell them we're ready to make a preliminary report."

Sam took a cheap cigar from his top desk drawer, unwrapped it, and tossed the cellophane wrapper into his wastebasket. "Tell them *you're* ready to report, kiddo. I'm outa here." He stuffed the unlighted cigar into his mouth and chomped down on it with tobacco-stained teeth. "Rose's got the grandchildren comin' over for supper."

"I can tell you're dreading it," I said. Delighted anticipation was written all over Sam's face.

"Did I tell you Debbie's playing first base on her Little League team? First girl. Damn good at it, too."

My spirits lifted a little. Despite its terrors, the world still has eight-year-old girls playing baseball. And proud grandfathers.

I went into my office and dialed Ben Levy's office number.

— **11** —

Dr. Benjamin Levy had appointments with patients until five o'clock, but he agreed that he and his wife would stop by my office at six-thirty. Although I warned him that my report would be disappointing, I knew he'd be expecting

57

some ray of hope, however dim. I hated giving people bad news, but I couldn't see any way I could make what I'd learned into anything else.

Sam and Paula left for the day and I spent the time before the Levys arrived at Paula's desk, typing up two summaries of the case. The first was for my files, detailing my interviews that morning as well as Sam's discoveries. The second was a briefer summary I would give to the Levys, one that left out names, addresses, and identifying details about the Hoffman and Meyers families. I totaled up the hours Sam and I had spent on the case, relieved that Dr. Levy's advance would cover our bill. At least I wouldn't have to ask for more money. When I had finished, I made a copy of the shorter report and put the paperwork in the manila folder that held my notes and the Goldenberg Clinic's medical records.

The day grew cooler. I shut off the rattling air conditioner and opened a window. Traffic sounds from Grand Avenue filled the room as I paced nervously, trying to prepare a speech that would let the Levys down easy.

They were ten minutes late. Ben apologized for keeping me waiting and introduced his wife. Gloria Levy was a surprisingly small woman, certainly no more than five feet tall and less than a hundred pounds. I wondered, as taller than average women often do, why so many short women end up with big men. Gloria's glossy black hair was pulled back starkly into a ballerina's bun; not a hair was out of place. Her face was carefully made up, eyebrows plucked and penciled to perfection and eye makeup tastefully subdued. Her crimson lipstick was so precisely applied that I was certain she'd used a lip brush. "How do you do, Ms. MacDonald," she said, extending a manicured hand. I locked the hall door after them and showed them into my office.

"Benjamin says I shouldn't get my hopes up," Gloria said, seating herself on the edge of the chair to avoid wrinkling the simple navy silk dress she wore. "But I can't help believing you can help our son. David's doctors want to send him down to the Mayo Clinic to begin treatment as soon as possible." Her fingers played with the opera-length strand of pearls she wore, the only break in her rigid physical composure. The jewels looked genuine.

"I'm afraid I can't offer you much hope." I explained that I'd found two possible bone marrow donors, but that neither seemed very likely at the moment. I told them the basic facts about the Hoffmans without naming them—Myra's eighteen-year-old secret, Gilbert's bizarre behavior, Myra's passive reaction to it. I told them our chances of locating the second family in time were slim at best. And in their case, we weren't even sure Ben was the biological father. Privately I thought it would take a miracle to save David Levy, although I didn't tell them that.

"I don't understand." Gloria's voice was low and cultured. "Surely this Family A, as you call them, can understand we're talking about a child's life. What kind of people are they?"

"The father is a violent man with severe mental problems, and he's an anti-Semite. As I explained, Mrs. Levy, he doesn't even know his son was conceived through artificial insemination. His wife tricked him. She's convinced he'll kill her and the boy if he finds out. From what I've learned about him, she may be right."

Ben stared silently at the report I'd handed him. Suddenly he crumpled it into a ball and looked up. "Maybe if we talk to them personally." The plea in his voice was naked.

"No. I can't put this boy in jeopardy. I explained that to you going in, Dr. Levy." I closed my folder and leaned across the desk. "Look, I know what you're feeling. But I'm morally certain that pursuing this family could result in harming, maybe murdering, two people. Even if I'm wrong about that, there's no way this man would ever agree to let the boy help David." Gloria Levy twisted her strand of pearls tighter and tighter. They became a noose around her neck. "The only lead we've got left—and you've got to understand it's a very long shot—is Family B. And that's going to require spending some money on Israeli detectives . . . unless we can light a fire under the American Embassy in Tel Aviv, get them to help us without the usual bureaucratic delays."

"I may be able to help there," Ben said. "An old friend from college went to work for the State Department. He should be able to grease some wheels for us."

Maybe there was hope for David after all. "Can you reach him?"

"I'll have to." Levy's face hardened.

"Ask him for the name of a contact in the embassy," I said, "and I'll call Tel Aviv first thing—"

Suddenly Levy choked, grasped his throat and doubled over. His wife gasped softly and got to her feet. "Get him some water. Please hurry."

I shoved my chair back and rushed into the outer office. As I filled a paper cup from the water cooler, the strangling sounds became louder.

"Here," I said, hurrying back into my office, the dripping cup held at arm's length. Gloria stood over her husband solicitously, her small hand patting his back. She was still composed, cool.

He grabbed the cup and gulped the water down greedily.

"You going to be all right?" I asked.

He breathed deeply before answering. "Yeah. Guess I breathed in some dust." He cleared his throat. "That's better. I'll be okay now." He rose to his feet. "We'd better be going. It's already late in Washington and I want to phone my friend tonight. I'll give you a call in the morning."

When they had left, I put the Hoffman medical file in

my briefcase. I would return it to Mrs. Goldenberg tomorrow, before I was tempted to do something stupid with it. I locked the rest of the paperwork on the Levy case in the black metal file in my office, closed the window, and locked the office door behind me.

The evening had begun to cool down nicely, and a slight breeze kept the voracious Minnesota mosquitoes at bay. I was too keyed up to go home to my empty apartment. What I needed was some exercise and something to eat. What I needed was a distraction from this impossible case. I decided to walk the mile to Zelda's, a popular restaurant named after Scott Fitzgerald's wife. It's in an old converted fire station over on Selby Avenue. I couldn't afford a dinner out, not with the recent cost of the repairs to my car. But neither could I afford not to do something for my battered psyche. So I kept walking, my briefcase under my arm, trying to keep my thoughts on the plate of steamed shrimp and glass of wine that awaited me.

— **12** —

It was dark by the time I left Zelda's, well fed and feeling infinitely more mellow with two glasses of Chablis under my belt. It didn't take long for me to realize that walking to the restaurant at dusk might have made sense, but walking back to the office in the dark was something else. Despite continuing urban renewal, this neighborhood was not one of St. Paul's finest; down Selby just a few blocks is an area frequented by prostitutes and their pimps. There's something, too, about night air that always makes my allergies worse. Tonight, the air was pungent with a mixture of sweet-smelling pollens and exhaust fumes from the cruising cars that made my nose itch.

"Hey, baby!" a deep male voice called from a souped-up Chevy that crawled by me. "Lookin' for a party?"

I kept walking.

"Come on, baby. Show you a real good time." The car came to a halt at the curb and I heard a door open. "Hey, bitch, don't be so cold."

I turned and looked at my propositioner, a burly kid probably ten years my junior. Orange and red flames decorated the sides of his noisy jalopy. "Listen, pal," I said, praying I wouldn't sneeze and ruin my tough image. They say a good part of self-defense is in your attitude, your body language. "There are a couple of things you ought to know. One, I'm not interested. And, two, this is a police officer you're harassing here. Now get your ass out of here before I bust it."

The young man's Adam's apple bobbed. He banged his car door shut and peeled rubber down Selby. I turned into a side street and tried to become invisible. A German shepherd growled at me, lunged at the chain-link fence that restrained him, and set off a cacophony of barking throughout the block. As porch lights flickered on, I ran the last quarter mile to the office.

I was seldom more grateful to see my Honda waiting in the parking lot, especially when it started right up. I pulled onto Grand Avenue, my thoughts now on antihistamine, a warm shower, and a good night's sleep. At least my evening's foray had taken my mind off the Levys.

It was dark at the back of my building. Not anticipating I'd be out so late, I hadn't left the yard light on, so I had to feel my way up the wooden staircase that leads to my third-floor digs. As I fumbled to find the lock with my key, I became aware of a lingering sweet odor. Were the roses blooming already? I stepped inside and sneezed.

As I reached for the light switch, there was a sudden

movement behind me. I turned toward it just as a heavy weight landed at the base of my skull. Pain shot through my head and I stumbled forward, dropping my purse and briefcase. I blacked out before I reached the floor.

I awoke in complete darkness. I could barely breathe. My first thought was that I'd been buried alive. I knew I was alive because of the searing pain at the back of my skull; surely death is pain-free. As I gradually regained consciousness, I realized I'd been gagged and that my head was swathed in fabric. I lay awkwardly on my left side, struggling for oxygen. My nose was stuffy, common for me in the summertime, and I was forced to draw choppy breaths through the rough cloth tied across my mouth.

I tried to raise my hands enough to free my head, but my wrists were bound together behind my back— loosely, with some sort of slippery-feeling tie, but I couldn't manage to free them. Don't panic, Devon, I told myself, choking back the bile that rose in my throat. I forced myself to lie still and breathe as deeply as the smothering cloth and my clogged sinuses would allow. I had to be rational. I had to make a logical plan to free myself and follow it carefully or I wouldn't survive.

I lay on a hard surface—the floor of my apartment? Or had I been carried somewhere else? Because I could see nothing, I didn't know whether I was alone, either. Wherever I was, it was quiet. I could hear nothing. Dared I hope that meant my attacker had left me alone? With some relief, I could feel that I was still clothed, a sign that I probably hadn't been raped. Yet I was cold, freezing cold, and unsure whether that was reality or merely my burgeoning fear.

Calm, stay calm. It could be days before anyone would find me. I work alone so often that Sam might easily assume I'd gone off to follow some lead on a case and would be in touch when I had a chance. How long would it be before he began to worry? Before he came looking for me? Would I still be alive?

I stretched my arms behind me as high as they would reach and dug my fingers into the fabric around my head. I yanked, but all I managed to accomplish was to draw it tighter across my face. My head seemed to be enclosed in some sort of bag. I let go and sucked in a shallow breath. I'd never get the bag off by tugging at it from behind.

Fighting pain in my head that throbbed with each tiny movement and a resulting wave of nausea, I painstakingly pulled myself to a sitting position, then even more slowly got to my feet. I teetered dizzily before I got my balance. Something to lean against, that's what I needed. With a table, a wall to support and balance me, I knew I could work my hands around to the front.

I carefully slid one foot after the other across the hard floor until I hit what felt like a wall. Leaning a shoulder against it for support, I bent forward dizzily and paused until my head cleared. I slid my manacled wrists underneath my buttocks, then my thighs, and, pretzel-fashion, raised my left leg and backed my foot slowly over my bound hands, blessing my daily morning workouts. I teetered sideways and nearly fell. Catching my balance before I hit the floor, I forced my body upright once more and concluded my bizarre acrobatics, backing my right foot over and free. There, I thought triumphantly, leaning my aching back against the wall for a moment. I'd like to see Jane Fonda try that one.

My hands finally in front of me, I pulled the suffocating bag off my head. Free of it at last, I could see by the dim light of the clock radio in my kitchen that I was still in my apartment. The clock read 12:31. With stiff fingers, I worked the gag out of my mouth and breathed deeply, greedily. My panic began to subside. I seemed to be alone, and I would live. One of the pillowcases from my bed lay at my feet, the bag that had covered my head, robbing me of sight and air. I looked down; my hands were bound with the sash from my green silk dress. It looked like the attack had been an unplanned one; my assailant had used materials he found at hand.

Clumsily, with my hands still bound, I pulled the receiver from the desk telephone and punched in 911. It took the St. Paul police less than five minutes to reach me.

Two uniformed officers had freed my hands and begun writing up a report when Sam's old friend, Lieutenant Barry O'Neil, barged through the door. Built like a brick wall, with a thick thatch of graying red hair, Barry had known Sam since they were kids together. He shares Sam's fatherly attitude toward me. Every once in a while, I actually appreciate it.

"Devon! I heard the report come over the air. For godsakes, girl, what happened?"

I shifted the ice pack I held against my throbbing head and tried to sort things out. It hurt to think. "I suppose it could've been the guy in the Chevy who gave me a hard time up near Zelda's, Barry. Maybe he followed me home. But I think I'd've heard him coming up the stairs behind me. More likely, somebody was inside waiting, but it happened so fast . . ."

The ice pack slipped from my fingers, my head throbbed so fiercely I couldn't bend to pick it up. Barry laid a beefy arm heavily across my shoulders, a clumsy attempt to comfort me. It felt good.

"Anything missing?" he asked.

"I dunno," I mumbled. "I haven't looked yet."

"Well, that can wait, kid. I'm gettin' you down to the hospital. We're gonna get that noggin X-rayed."

"Hell, Barry, I've got a hard head. I'll live."

"You comin' with me or you want me to call an ambulance?" Barry can be hardheaded, too.

"Okay, okay. I'll come. Just promise you won't call Sam. His heart doesn't need the stress."

Barry nodded, gathered up my purse and my keys, and told the two cops to wait there until he returned. Then he half-carried me down to his car. It felt good to let someone else take over for once. I leaned back against the car seat and closed my eyes as we raced downtown, siren blaring.

—— 13 ——

Doped up with painkillers, I didn't awake the next morning until after ten. I was back in my own room. Barry O'Neil had waited while I was X-rayed and sewn back together, then he drove me home and put me to bed. Luckily, I'd escaped a concussion, but the cut at the back of my head had required five stitches to close. What frosted me most was that the doctor had shaved a narrow strip of hair around the wound. I wouldn't be wearing my hair up for a while.

I made myself some decaf and decided against taking another codeine pill. I hate not being able to focus my thoughts. I swallowed four aspirin with a glass of orange juice and spent the next hour carefully inspecting my apartment. Nothing seemed to be missing or even noticeably disturbed. Even the twenty-seven bucks in my purse was intact. The contents of my briefcase, including the Hoffman-case file, were still there. My new supply of checks remained in the desk. And my few pieces of gold jewelry were still in the dresser drawer.

Black dust the police used to dust for fingerprints left a sooty film on the door and window frames and the kitchen counter near where I'd lain. Yet, even if these efforts raised some prints, they probably wouldn't be an immediate help in apprehending my attacker. St. Paul didn't yet have the costly and sophisticated kind of computer needed to check fingerprints against the hundreds of thousands on file. To check any prints found in my apartment manually against all those available could take longer than my lifetime. So, realistically, any prints lifted here would be held until we had a suspect's prints for comparison.

Neither the door nor the windows had been forced. Either the guy had been hiding on the dark landing, waiting for me to open the door for him, or he'd picked the lock. No one but me had a key to this place, except Helga Borg, my landlady. She's eighty-three years old and probably couldn't climb the stairs to the third floor if her life depended on it, never mind knock me out with a single blow.

Try as I might, I couldn't make sense of the situation. If I'd surprised a burglar last night, surely he'd have stolen something. Or else he'd have fled after bashing me. He wouldn't take the time to gag and bind me.

If the guy were a rapist, he wouldn't have stopped with simply knocking me out.

And if I'd been assaulted by someone with a grudge, what was the point of not letting me know who it was?

Had someone been looking for something specific in my apartment? If so, what? Nothing was missing. The idea that he hadn't found what he wanted, that he might return to continue his search, bothered me. I couldn't see how any of the investigations I'd worked on recently would lead to violence. Sherman and MacDonald hadn't taken on any criminal cases for at least a year. Even Vince Vinelli's libel case was a tame one—his client was a small southern Minnesota weekly being sued by a farmer it had accused of using illegal toxic chemicals on his crops. Hardly the stuff of danger and intrigue.

It even crossed my mind that it could be my husband, Noel, who'd hit me. If he'd been crazy enough to walk out without so much as a good-bye, and to stay away for all this time, could he be crazy enough to pull a stunt like this? No, Noel had no real beef with me. In my heart, I'd often suspected he was dead, an unidentified suicide in some faraway town. Wherever he was, he'd left because he couldn't cope with his life—our life—because he was weak, not because he hated me. If Noel wanted something from me, all he had to do was ask. I could see his taking his own life, but never his hiding in the dark and batting me over the head.

I vowed to look into a home alarm system. Maybe Helga Borg would pay half the cost; it would surely improve her property. In the meantime, I would leave the outside light on twenty-four hours a day—the Northern States Power bill be damned—and add a second deadbolt lock.

I showered, carefully keeping my hair dry; I couldn't get the stitches wet for five days. At least I'd kept my hair long and I managed to pull it back into a low ponytail that partially covered the bandage. I spent an extra ten minutes on my makeup in an attempt to cover the bruise on my cheekbone I'd gotten when I fell. I don't usually wear much makeup, and covering purple spots was not exactly my forte, but looking in the mirror when I'd finished, I felt I'd done a credible job. Donning a pair of comfortable jeans and a loose-fitting red blouse, I felt almost ready to face the world. I grabbed my things and double-locked the door behind me. It was after one.

"There you are, Devon," Paula said as I entered the office. "Sam's been looking for you and he's really getting pissed. I didn't know what to tell— Hey, you look gruesome!"

"Balm for my battered ego." So much for my careful makeup job.

"What happened to you?"

"I sort of got mugged."

"You okay?"

"I'll live. It just won't be much fun for a couple of days. So what's stuck in Sam's craw?"

"That Dr. Levy was waiting outside at eight o'clock when I got here. Something about calling Israel this morning and an eight-hour time difference. When you weren't here by nine, I sent him in to talk to Sam. He's trying to balance the checkbook and you know how he gets." Math is not Sam's strong suit, but he refuses to hire an accountant to do the books. Too cheap. The result is several mornings of hell around here every month.

Paula pulled a makeup case out of her handbag. "Here, Devon. Try some of this on that bruise." She held out a white plastic cylinder. "It's a little dark for your complexion, but it should help."

"Thanks," I said, gratefully accepting her offering. If anyone would know how to use cosmetic methods to alter a woman's looks, it'd be Paula.

I tiptoed past Sam's closed office door into my own smaller space, took a hand mirror from my desk drawer and gently rubbed Pancake Number Eleven onto my nose and left cheek. The purple disappeared under a patch of fake suntan.

"Goddamn it! Balance, you sucker!" Sam was bent over the agency check register, viciously punching the buttons on his pocket calculator, when I entered. A Minnesota Twins game blared from a portable radio. With Sam's grasp of numbers, he probably was adding somebody's batting average into accounts receivable and then fuming when the total came out wrong.

He quickly turned his irritation on me. "So! The queen of Sherman and MacDonald finally decided to show up. Good thing I was here to deal with your client . . . Say, what's that crap you got all over your face?"

That was the final straw. I burst into tears.

Of course, Sam was instantly contrite. By the time I'd managed to choke out my story and calm down, most of the Pancake Number Eleven had been transferred to the shoulder of his striped shirt. I pictured Sam trying to convince Rose the makeup all over his shirt had been acquired innocently and began to giggle. Which spurred another round of tears. When I'd finished, I must admit I felt infinitely better. Maybe what I needed was a good cry more often.

Sam and I batted around what had happened to me the previous night without coming to any new conclusions. Neither of us could suggest a plausible villain or motive. Still, the pattern wasn't that of a random attack, unless tying up women was the way some nut case got his kicks.

Sam told me he'd managed to reach the American Embassy in Tel Aviv before closing time there, but the bureaucrat Ben Levy's friend had recommended, Walter Hempstead, had gone to Haifa for the day. He'd be back tomorrow. Sam had assured Dr. Levy that I would follow up at the first opportunity and sent him on his way. In the meantime, I'd get back to searching out illicit sources of DDT for my libel case and Sam would resume his tirade over the account books.

I pulled the Levy file, clipped the embassy phone number to it, and laid it on my desk so I wouldn't forget to phone first thing in the morning.

I didn't realize until hours later that I hadn't needed to unlock my file cabinet. Someone had already done that for me.

— **14** —

Five days later, I'd made no headway in discovering who had attacked me or what he'd been seeking. The contents of my file cabinet appeared to be as intact as the contents of my apartment. I was at a loss to explain what had happened to me, or why, but at least it hadn't happened a second time. As I stepped into the shower this morning and held my head under the warm water, I was feeling better. The recurrent headaches had been a nuisance, but I'd just had the stitches removed and this was my first shampoo in nearly a week. At least I'd look human again. My hair is that nondescript color halfway between red and blond, and it doesn't hide dirt well. I squirted on some shampoo and rubbed it into a lather, then rinsed it off and repeated the process.

I'd been busy the past few days. Twice I'd phoned Walter Hempstead at the American Embassy in Tel Aviv. I explained that it was urgent we locate Tom and Sarah Meyers and their seventeen-year-old daughter and he'd assured me he'd "get right on it." Somehow that didn't fill me with confidence.

I tried to put little David Levy out of my mind. He was not, after all, my child and I'd done the best I could. Now his fate was in the hands of the U.S. Government. I had to move on.

On Sunday, I'd driven to Lake of the Isles to return the Hoffmans' medical records to Betsy Goldenberg. It was my turn to supply the meal, so I took her out to brunch at the Hotel Sofitel in Edina, where they bake a heavenly loaf of real French bread. I added a takeout loaf so Betsy could have it with her supper and put the whole thing on my agency credit card. We didn't mention young David.

By Monday, I was feeling well enough to plunge full-time into Vince Vinelli's libel case, so I drove southwest to spend some time in Minnesota's fertile farmlands. I returned feeling triumphant. I'd obtained a signed affidavit from a farmhand who swore that the plaintiff in my libel suit had ordered him to spray a field of tomato plants with contraband DDT. My witness hadn't told his story before because the farmer had threatened him. Once he knew about the lawsuit, he said, his conscience began bothering him. Probably more significant, however, was the fact that the farmer hadn't rehired him for this season's planting. With a little luck, my affidavit would halt the lawsuit before it ever reached the courtroom, saving the defendants thousands of dollars in court costs. I had visions of a nice fat bonus check from Vinelli and his newspaper client, maybe enough to finance a week's vacation at Gull Lake later in the summer. Even Sam congratulated me when I told him the news.

The morning was already a steamy one. By afternoon, it would be well into the nineties—the temperature vying with the humidity for the higher figure. I poured myself a glass of iced tea, plugged in my hair dryer and sat down at the dining room table to dry my hair while I read this morning's *Pioneer Press.* I always read the obits last, half dreading I'll find a friend or acquaintance listed there. I seldom do. The Minneapolis and St. Paul area is home to nearly two million people, few of whom I've ever met.

Today, however, I got lucky, if recognizing a name in the death notices can be called luck. There it was, on page 9B:

Hoffman

> Gilbert J., age 48, after a sudden illness. Survived by wife, Myra, and son, Tyler. No visitation or reviewal. Funeral services 1 P.M. Tuesday at ROSE HILLS VISTA.

I was back on the Levy case.

— 15 —

"It's *you!*" Myra Hoffman's words were filled with such raw hatred that I unconsciously stepped back from the open door.

"I've just come to offer my—"

"I know why you've come." She spat the words at me. "First you kill him, then like a vulture you come to pick his carcass clean. Don't think you can fool me."

I was stunned. What was the woman talking about? Her normally pale face looked worse than my own had a few days ago, a mass of yellowing bruises. Even in the day's oppressive heat, she wore sleeves that covered her arms and long pants, probably to hide any traces of her husband's brutality. Had a severe beating unhinged her mind? "I don't know what you're talking about, Mrs. Hoffman. I didn't kill anybody. The newspaper said—"

"Damn the newspaper! You killed my husband same as if you stuck a knife in him and you know it. Now what's to become of me . . . and . . . and Tyler. How will we survive?" Her face crumpled.

It took me ten minutes to calm her down, minutes in which she alternated between shrieking invectives against me and indulging in crying jags. She allowed me into her house only after I convinced her that Melville Norwalk was probably gleefully observing our clash from behind his lace curtains across the street.

Leaving her weeping in the living room, I went to get her a glass of water. Unlike the last time I'd visited her, the house was cluttered and dirty. A leg of the old blond coffee table in the living room was splintered so that the top leaned to the left. A section of drapery was ripped from its hooks, as though someone had grabbed it to break a fall. Dust streaked the floors. The kitchen faucet was spotted and the sink was caked with tiny pieces of food.

"Here." I handed Myra Hoffman the glass and a couple of tissues. She blew her nose, then sipped. "Now," I said, "how about telling me what I'm supposed to have done to your husband?"

She sniffed and set down the water glass. "I *warned* you not to tell Gilbert, to keep your mouth shut about Dr. Goldenberg, about Tyler. I *told* you what would happen. But you wouldn't listen—"

"I honestly don't know what you're talking about, Mrs. Hoffman. The only time I ever even saw your husband was when I bought some chicken from him. I certainly never told him anything about Dr. Goldenberg, or about Tyler." Unbidden, I sat down on the sofa next to her.

"Then you must've blabbed it all over," she insisted shrilly. "Somebody told Gil and it sure wasn't me."

"Mrs. Hoffman . . . Myra . . . the only person I told is my partner and he certainly didn't tell Gilbert anything. Sam's not even working on this case anymore. You've got to believe me."

"No! Somebody came into the butcher shop the other day and told Gilbert flat-out that he wasn't Tyler's real father. Told him your Dr. Levy was. That's a fact. You can't deny it. Why do you think Gilbert did this?" She opened her mouth and jabbed her index finger inside. I saw the raw space where two teeth were missing and flinched.

"He really hurt you this time, Myra."

"He never would've if . . . if you hadn't come along. If you'd've gotten out of our lives when I told you to, Gil never would've found out about any of this. He'd be alive today and I wouldn't be stuck with less than five hundred

74

dollars in the bank and a son to raise." She began to whimper. "What am I going to do now? Maybe I should've admitted it was all true, let Gil kill me then and there. I'd've been better off dead."

"You're not being logical, Myra," I said. "You insist somebody told your husband that Tyler was conceived through artificial insemination. So he came home and beat you. But you're not the one who's dead, Gilbert is."

She wiped away her tears and turned toward me, her pale eyes bloodshot but cold. "Gil died the day after. The stress killed him. He was still all riled up when he went to work. He'd been at me all night long, hardly slept. Along about noon or so, his blood pressure went sky high and next thing you know he got convulsions. They called the ambulance, the men at the shop, but the doctors couldn't do anything. Said he had a brain hemorrhage." Her gaze rested on the sagging draperies. "I couldn't believe it. One day he's raging around here, yelling, screaming, hitting. Next day he's gone. Just like that."

A wave of guilt swept over me. Myra Hoffman was right. Somehow somebody had found out the information I'd dug up and presented it to Gilbert Hoffman. If Gil had been a more reasonable man, of course, he wouldn't have reacted as he did, and he wouldn't have died. But that didn't absolve me. To some extent, I was morally responsible for the man's death.

As Myra droned on about how worthless her life had become, I tried to make sense of what she'd told me. I had tried to keep the truth about Tyler Hoffman's origins secret, but obviously I'd failed. Somebody had found out and told Hoffman. Ben and Gloria Levy were the obvious candidates. I thought back to my last meeting with them. Had I said something to them then that had given away Hoffman's identity? I knew I hadn't; I'd been extremely careful. Still . . . I could picture my file on the Levy case sitting on my desk. I recalled Ben's choking spell, my rushing to get him a glass of water. The file folder had been closed when I hurried out of the room, but either Ben or Gloria could have had enough time to peek inside, glance at the essential name and address, and close it again. A few seconds would suffice.

If they hadn't gotten the information then, they could have done so later that night. When I left the office, I took the Hoffmans' medical file with me, intending to return it to Betsy Goldenberg. And that night was when I was assaulted. Maybe, I realized reluctantly, it was Ben Levy who did it. Maybe my own client had tied me up and read Myra and Gilbert Hoffman's medical file while I lay unconscious on the floor.

Then there was the file cabinet in my office. I was virtually certain that I'd locked it before I left that night, yet it had been unlocked the next morning. Had Levy or his wife also broken into my office in search of information? I didn't want to think about their being responsible for any of this. Ben was an ethical physician, certainly not the type to commit burglary and assault. As far as I knew, Gloria was a good woman, a fine wife and mother. Still, their son was dying. I knew better than anyone how desperate that could make a parent.

Yet their obvious motivation and my suspicions didn't make them guilty. Was there an alternate scenario? If I accepted the premise that I'd been attacked and my office invaded because someone wanted a look at the Levy file, all sorts of new possibilities opened up. Maybe it wasn't the Levys. Perhaps it could even have been Gilbert Hoffman himself. Just because he told his wife that someone came into his shop the other day and gave him the facts about Tyler's birth didn't make it so. I had given Myra my card, with Dr. Levy's name and phone number written on the back. Had Gil found it and sought to satisfy his curiosity? Had a neighbor told him I'd been asking around about him? Somehow I could see—I preferred to see—bullying Gilbert Hoffman bashing me over the head much more easily than I could picture Ben

Levy in the same role. Hoffman was used to hitting women.

Or maybe it was someone else I'd talked to on the case. Leon Jackson looking for something to use against his boss? Maybe . . . maybe . . . it could be anybody. And maybe the break-ins and my assault had nothing to do with this frustrating case whatsoever.

". . . I can't go to work," Myra Hoffman whined. Her self-pity was beginning to get on my nerves. "I'm not trained to do anything. I'm not good with the public; people make me nervous. How am I going to pay the bills without Gil?"

"Didn't he leave any insurance money?" I asked.

"I . . . I don't know. He never said anything about insurance. Gil never talked to me about money. I only have the checkbook because they gave me Gil's things after he died. I don't know what to do. I don't even know how I'm going to pay for the funeral." She clutched her tissue and sniffed noisily.

"Let me talk with Dr. Levy, Myra," I said. "He mentioned helping Tyler with college expenses if he'd agree to the bone marrow transplant. Maybe he could find a way to help you out until you get on your feet."

Her rabbit-like face displayed its first ray of hope. I could almost hear her thinking that maybe she'd found another meal ticket. Well, I could work out that problem later. My job now was to get that transplant for David Levy, and fast. But she hesitated. "I . . . I don't know. It just doesn't seem right. And Tyler doesn't know Gil wasn't really his dad. Now's not the time to tell him, with Gil's dying and the funeral."

"Promise me you'll think about it, Myra." I rose to go. "Gil won't know the difference now and the Levys need your help. It sounds like you're going to need theirs, too."

She didn't answer. She was thinking it over, weighing her options, comparing her late husband's wishes with her own desperate need to be taken care of, her ingrained desire not to bear too much adult responsibility. "How . . . how much would it be worth to them?" she asked.

I shuddered involuntarily and headed for the door. "I'll talk it over with them and let you know," I said, escaping into the steam bath outside.

—— 16 ——

It rained overnight, cooling the air to a pleasant seventy-eight degrees. Thursday remained overcast, but I wasn't complaining. I couldn't say the same for Sam, who grumbled all the way to Gilbert Hoffman's funeral service at Rose Hills Vista, north of the Twin Cities. I hadn't wanted to attend alone, so I called in a favor and talked Sam into going with me. I wanted a chance to observe Myra Hoffman and her son in new surroundings. They held the life of my clients' child in their grasp and the more I learned about them, the better I felt I could do my job.

It was obvious that Myra had opted for the budget package, a short graveside ceremony and a pine box for Gilbert, who now was beyond caring. A cheerful gray-haired woman in a black dress directed us from the parking lot along a damp footpath to a hillside where three rows of folding chairs had been set up on the grass. The spartan coffin, a single bouquet of white gladiola on top, hung suspended by a series of ropes and pulleys over a freshly dug grave.

Sam stubbornly plunked himself down in the back row. His face clearly betrayed his thoughts. I might be able to strong-arm him into coming with me but that sure as hell didn't include his extending condolences to some

78

widow he'd never even met. Didn't I know funerals gave him the creeps?

I made my way to the front of the gathering. Myra Hoffman stood there, flanked by Tyler and her next-door neighbor, Herb Keller. In a short black A-line dress and pillbox hat that had been in style when JFK was President, Myra looked miserably out of place. "I'm sorry for your trouble, Myra," I said, reaching for her hand. It was icy; I could feel her trembling. The widow looked at me. Her lips moved slightly as she breathed rapidly through her mouth, but no words escaped. She was beginning to hyperventilate, balanced precariously on the edge of panic. I turned to her son. "I'm Devon MacDonald, Tyler. I never actually knew your father, but I am sorry for your loss. I'm sure you'll miss him."

"Yes, ma'am. Thank you for taking the time to come." Tyler's narrow, serious face and rigid posture made it clear that he was in charge here.

I walked back to Sam as others made their way forward to speak to Myra and Tyler. It was an odd gathering. Besides Myra and me, there were only two other women present, a young blonde who stood close to Tyler, frequently touching his arm and whispering in his ear, and a middle-aged woman with dyed black hair who periodically commented to the man sitting next to her in the front row.

At least a dozen men were there, however, most of them looking uncomfortable in their ill-fitting dark suits, a group of Archie Bunkers in cheap dress clothes. Several stared openly at Sam and me. I stared back at one until he dropped his gaze and turned around again.

Absent was Leon Jackson. Apparently he saw no need to fake respect for his late boss. Or maybe he was manning Pearson's Meats today. Melville Norwalk wasn't there, either. His curiosity about his neighbors evidently didn't extend as far as attending their final services.

An unsmiling young man in a black suit and clerical collar began what passed for a eulogy, speaking of "Mr. Huffman" as a loving husband and father, a good provider, a decent man who would be sorely missed by his family and friends. His speech was generic; the minister undoubtedly gave it whenever he was called upon to bury someone he didn't know. I hoped he generally got the deceased's name right.

As the young minister was explaining why it was God's will that "Gilbert Huffman was cut down in the prime of life," a sandy-haired man in his middle thirties hurriedly slipped into the seat next to me. He was wearing faded jeans with a gray corduroy blazer and a dark sport shirt.

"I miss much?" he whispered in my direction.

"Stick around for the next funeral and you'll get the same script all over again," I said.

He flashed me a grin. "I wonder why that doesn't surprise me." His eyes were the same color as his hair and the trace of freckles across his nose. He nodded to Tyler, who'd been turning around every few minutes to survey the gathering. The boy gave him a subtle high sign and his rigid shoulders relaxed slightly.

The minister led the assembly in prayer and the service was over in less than ten minutes. "Are you a friend of Tyler's?" I asked the man next to me.

"One of his teachers. Rodman Caldwell. Call me Roddy," he said, extending his hand. "That's why I was late. I'm in the middle of giving my final exams."

"I'm Devon MacDonald, and this is Sam Sherman. What do you teach?"

"Biology and chemistry. Ty's my best student, sort of a protégé."

"He seems like a fine young man. Bright?"

Caldwell nodded. "He's got an exceptional mind. Maybe now he'll be able to develop it."

"What do you mean?"

The teacher seemed suddenly embarrassed. "Sorry. That's a failing I have. I shoot my mouth off first, think

80

later. Old Gilbert's funeral is hardly the place to criticize him."

"It's all right by me," I said. "He was no friend of mine. Are you saying he was holding his son back?"

"You know the type. Macho, minimal education himself, thinks of intellectuals as sissies. 'What's good enough for me is good enough for my son' sort of attitude. I think he was threatened by the boy's brains. Ty wants to be a research biologist and I think he's got what it takes. But old man Hoffman wouldn't hear of that. Wanted the boy to become a butcher like him, waste his intelligence chopping up animals instead of discovering ways to prolong their lives."

Chalk one up for the Levys, I thought. With Gilbert Hoffman out of the way, the scholarship they could offer Tyler might well be an irresistible lure. "Who's the blond girl?" I asked.

"Marietta Tilsen, another one of my students. She's a bright kid, too, broke fourteen hundred on her SAT."

"Tyler's girlfriend?"

"Uh-huh. Ty's old man didn't approve of her, either. Thought she gave the boy fancy ideas."

"Did she?"

Caldwell flashed his contagious grin again. "Damn right." I grinned back. The crowd began to disperse. "Excuse me a minute," he said. "Got to say a word to Tyler and his mother."

"Nice meeting you," I said. I watched Caldwell walk over to Tyler and Myra, who was gripping her son's arm with one hand and Herb Keller's with the other. Her eyes radiated terror. I wondered what ghosts she imagined were closing in on her.

Sam tugged on my sleeve. "Let's get out of here."

A small cluster of men preceded us across the damp grass toward the parking lot. My shoes were soaked and a mosquito bite on my left ankle began to itch. One of the men, a tall guy with fair, close-cropped hair, glanced back at Sam and me. I had the strong impression they were talking about us. A shorter man in a heavy black suit nodded, then loosened his tie and removed his jacket. He wore a short-sleeved white shirt underneath. A tattooed turquoise snake coiled on his right forearm.

Sam picked up his pace and I hurried to keep up with him in my soggy shoes. "Next time," he declared, "I'll wear my yarmulke and prayer shawl. Really give these assholes something to gossip about."

— 17 —

I phoned Ben Levy at his office to bring him up to date and caught him between patients. Quickly, I outlined what had happened. "So I think there's a good chance now that the mother will go along with the bone marrow transplant, Ben. She needs financial help badly and, with her husband dead, her reason for keeping her secret no longer exists."

Levy's voice was filled with hope as he said he'd have his attorney draw up a letter of agreement immediately. He thought the woman might be more likely to cooperate if she could see, in writing, just how much her boy's help with the bone marrow transplant would mean to her. Gloria would bring it to me first thing the next day and I promised to present it to my contact as quickly as possible.

I didn't use Myra Hoffman's name, nor did Ben. I wondered whether he knew who she was, if he'd been the one who approached Gilbert Hoffman with the facts about Tyler's parentage. But I didn't ask. If Ben Levy had bashed me over the head the other night, somehow I didn't really want to know.

* * *

I was in the office early next morning, expecting Gloria Levy to arrive with the letter of agreement. Congratulating myself that I was close to pulling off the seemingly impossible task of getting a bone marrow transplant for David, I expected to greet a happier, more hopeful Gloria. But hour after hour crawled by. Finally, Gloria phoned.

"Miss MacDonald, I must request a favor." Her voice was low and controlled, as it had been the other night, yet today it had an eerie, almost hollow sound. "I am home alone with David and I simply can't leave him to drive to St. Paul. I'd appreciate your coming to my house as soon as possible."

"To pick up your attorney's letter?"

The line was dead for a moment. Then Gloria spoke. "That . . . and I have something else to discuss with you."

"Is there a new problem?"

"I don't want to talk about it on the phone. We'll discuss it when you get here," she said.

I checked the address and told Paula I'd be back sometime this afternoon, after I'd taken the letter to the Hoffman house.

The Levys lived in South Minneapolis, in a handsome English Tudor two-and-a-half-story place overlooking Minnehaha Creek. Scarlet geraniums bordered the concrete steps leading to the oak paneled front door. Gloria Levy opened the door before my finger reached the doorbell.

"Come in, please," she said, with a sense of urgency. Once again, she was immaculately groomed, every ebony hair in place, pulled back and held with a tailored bow at the nape of her neck. She wore ivory linen slacks and a pale pink silk tunic. The string of rose quartz beads around her neck matched her teardrop earrings. Her makeup was expertly applied. She made me feel inordinately sloppy in my khaki skirt, yellow striped cotton blouse, and comfortable sandals. My jewelry was limited to the fake gold expansion-band Seiko I wore on my left wrist.

Gloria led me through an oak-framed arch into the living room, which opened off the foyer. It was a large room with a bay window that took advantage of the creek view. Patches of sunlight lay in pale trapezoids on the carpeting, yet the room remained cool. The furnishings here were all in shades of ivory and beige, an attractive contrast to the dark oak woodwork. Yet I couldn't help wondering how one could keep near-white carpeting or cream-colored upholstery clean with a small boy in the house, even a sickly small boy.

We sat in matching Italian provincial chairs, a low pecan coffee table between us. I waited for Gloria to speak.

"Miss MacDonald . . . Devon, I— We need your help. Badly, I'm afraid." Her facial expression remained impassive, unreadable, but in her lap, her manicured fingers were closely intertwined and her knuckles were white.

"Something's happened to David." My heart sank.

She gnawed her lower lip. "No, it—it's not David. It's . . . you see, Benjamin's in trouble." Her eyes dropped to her lap. "He's been arrested."

"Arrested! Mrs. Levy, what happened?"

She raised her dark eyes and stared past me. "The police came and took Benjamin away this morning. He didn't . . . They didn't even let him say good-bye to David."

"The police took your husband? But why?"

"You're the only one who can help us, Devon. I want you to promise." A small tremor appeared at one corner of her mouth. She raised her hand and covered it.

"Of course I'll help, Mrs. Levy."

"Call me Gloria, please."

"Gloria. I'll do whatever I can, but you've got to tell me what you're talking about. Start at the beginning and tell me exactly what happened."

Still avoiding my eyes, she said, "It's that awful Hoffman man. They think Ben murdered him."

Hoffman. Murder. I froze. From the woman's cool demeanor, I'd expected something minor—a traffic offense, maybe driving under the influence. Certainly nothing as serious as murder, the murder of Gilbert Hoffman. An old suspicion crept back into my mind. "Gloria," I demanded, "just what has Ben to do with Gilbert Hoffman?"

"Please don't be angry, Devon. We didn't mean any harm. We were only trying to save David. You've got to understand—"

My neck muscles stiffened in anger. "What I understand is that you violated our agreement. You assaulted me, you could have killed me. Hell, you *did* scare the shit out of me. You invaded my home, snooped in my private files—"

The look she gave me said I'd taken leave of my senses. "I haven't the least idea what you're talking about. All Benjamin and I did was find the man's name in your folder when you left your office, when you went for that glass of water. Nothing more."

"No. I don't believe that. Later that same night, somebody—it must have been Ben—came to my apartment and bashed me over the head—"

"Benjamin did no such thing! He is not a violent man."

"But—"

"Why would he? We already *had* Hoffman's name."

"Somebody hit me, tied me up, left me near suffocation. If it wasn't your husband, who was it?"

She smoothed nonexistent wrinkles from the knees of her slacks. "I honestly don't know, Devon. But that doesn't matter now. All that matters is the police think Benjamin murdered that horrible man. You've got to prove he didn't, that he couldn't have. He's a doctor." Her tone implied that her husband's occupation was all the alibi he needed.

"Gloria, Hoffman died of a stroke, a brain hemorrhage. How could the cops possibly accuse Ben?"

"It's got something to do with pills, medicines . . . mixing one kind with another is what killed Hoffman. I don't really understand it all, but they're accusing Benjamin of giving Hoffman some kind of medication that caused his death."

"But how would he have had the opportunity?" I groaned. "Don't tell me he was stupid enough to contact Hoffman directly? Not after everything I told you." I was furious. I felt betrayed by the Levys. I hadn't wanted to take their case. I'd been playing Charlie Nice Girl, out to save the world. Now, unwittingly, I might have helped set a man up to be murdered.

Gloria Levy rose gracefully, crossed to the window, and stared out at the street and the creek beyond. "We both went to see him," she said quietly. "We went to his butcher shop. It was the night after you told us you'd done all you could to save David . . . except for a slim chance you'd find that other family in time. We felt so hopeless. You were right, you know . . . about Hoffman, I mean. He was a pig, a monster. Benjamin begged him to help us, but Hoffman just called us filthy names. He hit my husband in the face, nearly broke his nose. If it hadn't been for those other men in the shop, I think he might have killed Benjamin."

"And now the cops believe just the opposite happened." I suppressed a spiteful urge to rub it in, to say, "See? You should have listened to me."

Gloria turned to face me. Her voice was icy. "The police are wrong. I know it looks bad for Benjamin. He was there. He'll even admit he went back the next day."

"The cops must have more than that on him, to press charges."

"Only that they claim to have found some of the same pills that killed Hoffman in Benjamin's car. But my husband's a doctor. Just because he had some pills is no proof he killed anybody. He is innocent, Devon. All I can think is that somebody's trying to frame him. We—you have to find out who, prove Benjamin's innocent, before it's too late for David. Please promise you'll do whatever—"

"Mommy! Mommy, come here," called a small voice from the back of the house. "I need you."

A hundred occasions when I'd heard the same childish request raced through my mind, and I felt a nearly overwhelming desire to turn and run. With still-fresh guilt, I realized how many times I'd resented my own little boy's interruptions for taking me away from some task or conversation I'd once thought important. Now I'd give anything just to hear him call "Mommy!" once more.

"Come with me," Gloria ordered, striding gracefully toward the back of the house.

"Oh, no tha—"

"Come on, Devon! I want you to meet David." Gloria would accept no argument. I lagged behind as she led the way down a carpeted hallway. I didn't want to meet her son, to risk becoming attached in any way to another dying child. But still I followed, slowly.

"What is it, David?" Gloria asked, entering the child's room. Unlike the living room, here was a riot of color: wallpaper studded with pictures of red and blue racing cars; a multitude of stuffed animals; royal blue scatter rugs on a polished oak floor; two red lacquered dressers; a color television set and VCR on a gleaming white cart. In the middle of a double bed topped with a red, white, and blue striped comforter sat a thin, wide-eyed boy wearing a Twins baseball cap.

"The movie's over," he said to his mother. "Can I see *Hoosiers* again, Mom? Puh-leeze? Can I?"

Gloria bent over the VCR and removed a videocassette. "This is Miss MacDonald, David. She's trying to help the doctors make you well."

Damn! I didn't want that billing. I flinched as the boy's blue eyes darted toward me. They lighted his narrow face. "Hi," he said, smiling eagerly.

"Hello, David. Pleased to meet you."

He wore pajamas styled like a baseball uniform. The top of a rubbery chemotherapy catheter inserted in his chest peeked above the garment's V-neck. When Danny was in the hospital, I'd seen plenty of kids with leukemia who had those contraptions. I quickly raised my eyes to his face. "You like sports?" he asked me.

"Sure, some, anyway. I like to swim. And I always watch the Olympics on TV."

"I don't know how to swim yet. I like basketball best. Someday when I'm big like my dad, I'm gonna play in the Minnesota State Basketball Tournament. Maybe I can score the winning points for my school . . . like in *Hoosiers*." With broomstick arms, he feigned a basketball shot. "*Hoosiers* is my favorite movie. You ever get to see it?"

"Yeah, I think so. Gene Hackman and Barbara Hershey, right? Hackman plays a small-town basketball coach who turns a losing high school team into Indiana State champions."

"Hey, yeah! What's your favorite movie?" He shot me a crooked grin.

"Usually whatever movie I saw last." Just forget about the baldness hidden by the baseball cap, that catheter, this child's touchy prognosis. I smiled at him.

Gloria inserted a fresh videocassette into the VCR and pushed some buttons. The titles for *Hoosiers* flashed onto the television screen. "There you go, David. Need anything else?" she asked.

"Uh-uh." He turned back toward the TV, quickly engrossed in the story he knew so well.

"Bye, David," I said.

"Bye."

On the way back to the foyer, I heard myself assuring Gloria Levy that I would do whatever I could to help her son and her husband. She handed me the letter of agreement their attorney had drawn up for Myra Hoffman. I took it and stuffed it in my purse, knowing today wouldn't be the day to deliver it. We shook hands at the door. Gloria's was still cool. There was something about the woman's incredible control that made me uneasy. Yet, there was no way I could turn my back on that child vicariously playing basketball in the back bedroom. She'd known that, of course. That was why she'd called me here to the house, to manipulate me into helping Ben beat that murder charge. No matter how angry I was with young David's parents, Gloria Levy had correctly predicted that I wouldn't be able to desert him . . . especially after meeting him. I hurried down the steps to my car.

I walked around the back of my Honda toward the driver's door. Feeling used and cursing myself for the thousandth time for ever being suckered into taking this case, I kicked angrily at a tire. I succeeded only in stubbing my sandaled toe. "Shit," I muttered under my breath. My foot hurt, but at least this pain was physical.

The mess Ben Levy had presented me with a couple of weeks earlier had turned out to have everything I didn't need complicating my life. I wanted to walk away, to leave it to the cops and the lawyers and the doctors to sort out. But I knew I wouldn't.

Part
2

— 18 —

Sam sat with his feet propped against his desk, watching me pace. As the senior partner of Sherman and MacDonald, he gets the only office big enough for pacing. Mine won't accommodate more than an occasional pirouette.

"So you gotta face the fact that our man coulda done it," Sam said. "Hoffman was taken out by a pretty sophisticated method. Not something your average schmuck off the street dreams up. I can see what Levy'd be thinking—chances are it goes down as natural causes, one less asshole in the world, his kid gets the transplant, and nobody's the wiser."

"But Sam, the fact that Gilbert Hoffman was taking medication for his mental problems was no secret. His wife told me about it, even showed me the pill bottle." I leaned against Sam's desk and leafed through my file on the Levy case. Sam's stomach growled, but I pretended not to notice. "Here," I said, pulling out a page of my report. "I even wrote down the name of the stuff he was on—Nardil. Leon, who works in the butcher shop, said he knew about Hoffman's medication, too."

"Sure, maybe the fact he was on pills." Sam checked his watch. "Maybe the whole town knew that. But how's that add up to murder? How many people know what you'd hafta mix with this Nardil stuff to bump the guy off? A couple aspirin ain't gonna do it."

"I—I don't know," I said, grasping. "Leon Jackson knew Hoffman wasn't allowed to drink alcohol. I'll bet a lot of people knew that. And . . . and if they knew the name of the stuff Gilbert was taking, they could look it up in the library, see what drugs could cause a fatal reaction if they were taken together with Nardil."

"And then hold up a pharmacy to get what they needed."

"Damn it, Sam," I said, exasperated. "You know how hard it is to get drugs these days. Hang around any schoolyard in town for half an hour, you can get anything you want. Whose side are you on, anyway?"

"Yours, sweetpea. Your people admit they tracked Hoffman down, went to see him. Hoffman punched out the doc. Don't kid yourself there ain't enough o' both motive and opportunity here. I just think you gotta admit what you're up against." He inspected his watch once more. "Right now, we're both up against lunch hour. How 'bout a bite at Mickey's? I'll pop for a hamburg and fries."

"For God's sake, Sam. Don't you ever think about anything but your stomach? I don't see how you can even think about food at a time like this. Diner food, yet."

"At a time like this?" he asked, feigning innocence. "Lunchtime?"

"We need a game plan on this case and we need it now."

"Okay, girl. Don't get your Irish up. We'll divvy up the work, then I'll go to lunch. You wanna starve, I'll save a couple bucks."

I plopped down in a chair opposite Sam's desk and picked up a yellow legal pad. "How about you check with the coroner and find out exactly what killed Hoffman while I start interviewing likely suspects?"

Sam nodded. "Okay. I'll hit up Levy's attorney, too, let him know we're workin' with him. Who's representing him?"

"Charlie Hazelwood. You know him?"

"Yeah. He's good. Expensive, but good. Who you gonna talk to?"

"I'll make up a list of people who knew Hoffman was on medication and might have wanted him out of the way. People other than Ben and Gloria Levy."

"Frito to hold you over?" Sam pulled a yellow-and-red bag from his desk drawer, ripped it open noisily, and shoved it toward me.

I shook my head. "First there's Myra Hoffman," I said. I wrote down her name.

"Thought you said she never went outa the house. Old Gil was killed at the meat market, remember."

"So maybe she drugged the lunch she packed for him. Besides, I'm not so sure she's really agoraphobic. Could be a convenient cover story so nobody suspects her. She's certainly got as much reason to want Hoffman out of the way as anybody. More. The jerk used her for a punching bag."

"And 'The female of the species is more deadly than the male,'" Sam quoted, crunching on a corn chip.

I grimaced. "I'll bet that little gem's your entire repertoire of Kipling."

"Hell, no. I learned most of . . . 'Gunga Din' in the seventh grade. Miss Waterston, English Lit. Used to crack us across the knuckles with a ruler when we messed up."

"Sounds like a good idea to me. I wonder if Rose has thought of it."

"You're a laugh a minute, Devon. What about the schwartzer works in the butcher shop?"

"If you're referring to the black gentleman, Sam, his

name is Leon Jackson and, yes, he hated Hoffman's guts."

"He was around when Hoffman had his attack, too."

"Right."

"Then there's the kid," Sam mused.

"Tyler?"

"Yeah. That good-lookin' schoolteacher you were flirtin' with at the funeral said the old man wouldn't let the boy go to college."

I squared my shoulders. "I was not flirting with anyone, Sam Sherman."

"Well, he was flirtin' with you. Maybe you been outa harness so long you can't even recognize a race anymore."

I felt myself blush and lowered my head over my notes so Sam wouldn't notice. This was getting too personal, even for my irreverent partner. I concentrated on writing down Tyler Hoffman's name. The boy showed a talent for biology and chemistry. He'd seen his father abuse his mother more than once. And lately his own future had been threatened by the bully he called Dad. No, Tyler couldn't be overlooked as a suspect.

"Hey, Devon, I didn't mean to hurt your feelings. Guess I get testy when I'm starving to death. Maybe I got low blood sugar or something."

"It's not your blood sugar that's low, Sam, it's your impulse control," I said without smiling. "You want the Aryan Supremacists or should I take them?"

"With a face like mine and a middle name like Mordecai, I'm not gonna get shit outa them, honey. They're all yours. I'll stick to the public records. Like I always say, that's where you find your best clues."

"It's okay with me if you want to breathe dust all afternoon. I'll take the legwork."

"Sure you don't wanna go to Mickey's with me?" Sam shoved the Frito bag back into its hiding place and got to his feet.

"Not today, thanks. I'll head over to Pearson's Meats

and see what I can find out about Hoffman's last day. We'll touch base later."

As I passed through the outer office, Paula was sitting at her desk, savagely cutting a magazine into tiny pieces. "I'm afraid to ask," I said.

She looked up from her task. "I'm getting my anger out." Her face was rigid. "Either I make *Dental Digest* into confetti or I make Dr. Stuart Lindblom into confetti."

The dentist from the salad bar. "The paper's the better choice," I said. "It cuts easier." She started on a second publication. "Want to talk about it?"

"What's to talk about?" Paula kept slashing. "We had a dinner date tonight. I called his office to say I'd like to make it half an hour later, give me time to get my hair done after work. A woman answers the phone. I say I want to talk to Dr. Lindblom. She says he's tied up with a patient."

"So?"

"So . . . she says this is *Mrs.* Lindblom, can she take a message, please."

"Oh."

"Yeah."

"Did you leave a message?"

"I was tempted to, but there's laws against using that kind of language on the telephone. Besides, it's not *her* fault. I just hung up."

Paula's "in harness," as Sam puts it, twenty-four hours a day. Look what it's gotten her. "Paula, I'm really sorry," I said, meaning it. "Here." I handed her two more magazines. "Chop up a couple for me."

I headed out to Pearson's Meats.

— 19 —

When I arrived at the butcher shop, Leon Jackson was working as industriously as ever, doing something I'd rather not think about to a gelatinous slab of liver. How people can eat that stuff is beyond my comprehension. The way it looks raw is a big enough turnoff, but when you think about how many chemicals lodge in an animal's liver, you really have to be a meat freak to enjoy it. Still, some people can't understand what I see in tofu. To each his own, I suppose, although I take a certain comfort in the fact that a soybean can't look me in the eye or lick my hand.

Today there was a second man behind the counter, a stocky middle-aged man with thinning salt-and-pepper hair and long sideburns. I recognized him from Gilbert Hoffman's funeral. He'd been with the woman with the dyed black hair. The white plastic name tag on his shirt said "Roger."

I waited until Leon and Roger finished with the three customers ahead of me and then I approached the counter. "Hello, Mr. Jackson," I said. He nodded in my direction. "Mr. Pearson?"

"Yeah?"

"I'm Devon MacDonald. I'm investigating the death of your partner, Gilbert Hoffman. I'd like to talk to you and Mr. Jackson for a few minutes."

The door to the shop opened and a young woman toting a squirming toddler entered and began inspecting the various cuts of meat in the glass case. Pearson became visibly uneasy. "We already talked to three different cops," he said brusquely. "That oughta be enough reports to last you."

"This one a rent-a-cop," Jackson said, smiling faintly. "She here before."

The customer's attention left the meat counter and she stared openly at us. "Poke chop, Mommy?" the child asked.

"Sure, honey. Mommy'll buy you a pork chop. Just be patient."

"I wasn't even here when it happened," Pearson complained. "Hell, I got a business to run here."

"How about you, Mr. Jackson?"

"I was here. I call nine-one-one but it don't do no good."

"If Leon wants to go over it all again, that's up to him. I'll mind the store." Pearson was abrupt, unfriendly. "Take her in the back, Leon." He turned to the woman with the child. "What'll it be today, ma'am?"

Leon ushered me into a room at the back of the shop. It held a massive walk-in cooler, a stained butcher-block counter with a partially dismembered quarter of beef on it and, in the corner, a small white table with two metal stools. Two brown paper sacks, an electric coffeepot, and an overflowing ashtray occupied the center of the table.

Jackson motioned me to take a seat and pulled a pack of Marlboros out of his pocket. "Smoke?"

"No, thanks. You mind going over things once more for me?"

"Not on comp'ny time. They pay me, I shoot the shit all day, that what they want." He lit the cigarette with a Bic and the scent of smoke mingled with the odors of dried blood and refrigerated air. "You workin' for the guy come in here the other night. The dude did Gilbert."

"I don't believe he did it."

Jackson shrugged and exhaled a long stream of smoke. I averted my face to avoid it.

"Tell me what happened that night," I said.

"Tall, skinny guy come in with a tiny little woman. He come up to Gilbert, and say he want talk private, somethin' 'bout their kids." Jackson settled onto the other stool. "Gilbert bring 'em back here. Next thing, I hear shoutin', ole Gilbert's yellin' something 'bout motherfuckin' Jew bastards, that sorta shit. His favorite subject. I got a customer, so I try not to hear. But, she-it, after while it sound like Saturday night in a downtown bar back here, things slammin', the woman whimperin'. So I come back. Tron—he the janitor—he come up from the basement."

"What did you see when you got back here, Mr. Jackson?"

"The skinny guy, he on the floor layin' 'gainst the cooler door, lookin' shit-scared. He holdin' his nose, blood all over. The woman, she standin' there, pleadin', 'Don't! Please don't hurt him!' An' ole Gilbert, he reachin' for a cleaver off the table here." He gestured toward the cutting table with his cigarette. Ash dropped to the concrete floor.

"What did you do?"

"Grab that cleaver 'fore the motherfucker lay his hand on it. Tron get the phone." He indicated a black wall phone near the cooler. "We say we call the cops, they don't cool it. We tell the skinny guy and the woman get out fast. They go like they sittin' on dynamite with a lit fuse."

"What night was this?"

"Night 'fore old Gilbert die." He took another long drag on his cigarette, making the tip glow. My sinuses throbbed.

"What happened after the man and the woman left?"

Jackson smiled ironically. "Gilbert throw a fit, pound the table, hit the wall. I hang on that cleaver till he stomp outa here."

"When was that?"

"Ten, fifteen minute later."

"What about the next morning? What happened then?"

"I open up, eight o'clock, like always. Hoffman come 'round nine, quarter after. Look like shit."

"What do you mean?"

"Wild eyes. Bitchin' 'bout he don't sleep all night. On my back right off, do this, do that, hurry it up, boy."

"Sounds like enough to make you reach for that cleaver again."

"Ole Gilbert tempt a saint to use a cleaver on 'im. But it weren't me wasted him, lady. I got plenty reason 'fore now and I never do it. His ass not worth the time."

"Who else was in the shop that morning, before Hoffman got sick?"

Jackson leaned back on the stool and gave me a slow grin. "'Sides your man?"

"Everybody."

Pearson's Meats had been busy that morning, according to his recollection. A dozen or more customers came in, although none of them ventured behind the counter. It was just Leon and Gilbert minding the store, although Roger Pearson came in briefly to pick up some account books. There was a beef delivery to the back room from the South St. Paul stockyards, and a UPS truck delivered several cartons of freezer paper.

"You said that Dr. Levy was here that day, too. Do you remember the circumstances?"

Jackson shrugged. "Man don't learn. He come in the back door. I back here on break, havin' a smoke like now. The man say maybe Gilbert think over what he say, change his mind. I say how many stupid kids his mama raise 'sides him."

"You don't keep the back door locked?"

"Nah, not during the day. It usually stay open for deliveries."

"So Dr. Levy came in that way and you spoke with him. Then what did you do?"

"I get Gilbert."

"I take it Hoffman was less than hospitable to the doctor?"

Jackson grinned. "Threw your man out on his ass. Ole Gilbert say he come back again, he chop off his balls, grind 'em up, sell 'em fer ground round."

"That message seems clear enough," I said.

Roger Pearson appeared in the doorway. "Leon," he said. "I need you up front for a few minutes. I'm gettin' backed up out here."

"Wait here," Leon told me. "I be back." He laid his burning cigarette on the edge of the ashtray. A filter from an extinguished butt began to smolder. I reached over and snuffed out the whole stinking mess.

As I waited for Jackson, I looked around the back room of the butcher shop. It did nothing to convince me to go back to eating meat. Opposite the table was a large white-enameled sink with two dirty white coffee mugs in it. Under the sink was an aluminum garbage can partially filled with meat scraps that were beginning to smell. Flies buzzed against the unlocked screen door leading to the alley behind the shop. I realized that, while Pearson and Jackson were busy in the front of the store, I could easily walk out the back without their knowing. And anyone could walk in.

When Jackson returned, I pointed toward the table with the paper bags and asked, "Is this where Hoffman kept his lunch?"

He nodded.

"He drink from this coffeepot?" If it was the coffee that had been drugged, I wondered why it hadn't affected Jackson.

"Uh uh. Gilbert quit coffee when he go on them pills. Say no caffeine. His old woman pack a metal Thermos bottle with juice. He drink that."

"Apple juice, orange juice, that sort of thing?"

"Uh-huh."

So anyone who knew the bottle was Hoffman's could

have tampered with it here in the back room. Or Myra could have added a little extra something to her husband's lunch before it left her kitchen. "Anyone else come back here that morning?"

Jackson thought for a moment. "Just Keller, he come in, shoot the bull. Say he look for Roger."

"Keller?"

"Herb Keller, Roger's brother-in-law."

"Is that the same Herb Keller who lives next door to the Hoffmans?"

Jackson nodded. He lighted another Marlboro and inhaled. "Same dude. Gilbert come to work here 'cause o' Keller. He know the shop need cash, Gilbert need work."

"So Herb Keller was the one who introduced Hoffman to Pearson? Got Hoffman to invest his money in this store and come to work here?"

"They asshole buddies, Keller and Gilbert."

"Pearson, too?"

"Nah. Roger okay. He no honkie racist like them mothers. Roger need money, keep the store open, Gilbert got it. That all that is. He find out they holdin' them meetings here, Roger tell 'em get out, don't come back."

"Keller's part of ASP?"

Jackson nodded. "Should be A-S-S, not A-S-P." Another reason Keller had extolled Hoffman's virtues when I'd asked him about his neighbor. They shared a common philosophy, a common organization, in addition to their neighborhood.

"On that day, Mr. Jackson, what time did Gilbert Hoffman begin to feel ill?"

"Say his head ache . . . 'bout two, two-thirty. He stay back here. I work up front. Maybe a hour later, I hear a crash. Come back here, Gilbert on the floor, thrashin' 'round. He hot, too. I feel his skin, he burnin' up. I call nine-one-one."

"How long did it take for the paramedics to get here?"

"'Bout four, five minute." They put Hoffman on a

stretcher and took him to the emergency room at St. Paul–Ramsey Medical Center."

"What did you do?"

"Stay behind, mind the store. 'Fore I go home, I clean up ole Gilbert's things, wash out his bottle, throw out what left o' his lunch."

"Are you saying you destroyed the evidence, Mr. Jackson?"

His eyes flashed. "Shit! I helpin' the man. I think he jes sick, work hisself up, have a fuckin' heart attack."

By the time the cause of Hoffman's death was determined and the police began their investigation, the back room of the butcher shop had been thoroughly cleaned and the Thermos bottle handled not only by Jackson but by Tron, the janitor, as well. Clearly, without an eyewitness or even fingerprints on the Thermos, the police were relying solely on motive and some pretty flimsy circumstantial evidence in charging Benjamin Levy with murder.

I thanked Leon for his candor and willingness to tell his story one more time. By the time I was ready to leave, Roger Pearson was frantically trying to handle the afternoon trade single-handedly. He greeted Leon's return with undisguised relief.

"I appreciate your patience, Mr. Pearson," I told him, handing him one of my cards. "I would like to talk to you, too, but I'll come back another time, when the shop isn't so busy."

He nodded unenthusiastically. To refuse would require our discussing the situation in front of his customers, and Roger Pearson wasn't about to risk that. I had the feeling that he wasn't so much grieved by his partner's death as embarrassed by it. If the customers found out a man had been poisoned in this store, would they still come in to pay $5.98 a pound for rack of lamb?

I stopped at Country Club Market a few blocks up Snelling from Pearson's Meats and bought a ripe California peach, a package of Armenian string cheese, and a small bottle of unfiltered apple juice. I drove west to Mississippi River Boulevard, parked the Honda, and hiked down the bluff to Hidden Falls Park. I had it to myself today. Sitting on the riverbank in the shade of a tree, I ate my lunch and watched the great river wind its way toward New Orleans. Whenever I need to gain perspective, to clear my head, I find I'm drawn to water. Rivers, lakes, the sea—all are so substantial, so enduring, that they help me realize my own insignificance. The mighty Mississippi's water level was down this year despite the rains of recent days. It had been an unusually dry winter and the Midwest farmers were having a hard time of it.

As I ate my fruit and cheese, I watched dragonflies and mosquitoes swarming above the serene water. Periodically, a fish would surface and nab one of them, as though to keep me from having to eat alone.

It was tempting to hide here in this peaceful green haven for the rest of the day, but I had a client. Reluctantly, I gathered up the remains of my meal and started back up the hill.

— **20** —

Highland Park High School is not far from the Mississippi. It was only three-thirty, but the tan brick complex next to the junior high school was nearly deserted by the time I arrived. I parked around the corner on Edgecumbe Road and found my way to the school office. Two student workers were behind the counter gossiping and giggling. "So he goes, 'That's a really cool dress you're wearing,' and I'm like really freaked out," a girl with purple streaks in her light brown hair was telling her companion, a brunette with an unfortunate case of acne she'd tried to cover with too much makeup. I asked where everyone was.

"It's like finals week," the girl with the streaks said, leaning across the counter. Her thick eye shadow matched her hair. I wondered if it all would wash off. "Everybody splits early, ya know?"

I knew. "I'd like to see Rodman Caldwell, please."

"Mr. Caldwell?" The girl sneaked a glance at her co-worker.

"He teaches science here," I prompted.

"Yeah, I know, I had him for biology. I haven't seen him around this afternoon. Have you, Tiffany?" The brunette shook her head and giggled.

"Is there some way you could find out whether he's still here?" I asked.

"Uh, okay, I guess so," purple streaks said. "I'll see if he's like signed out." She ventured into an inner office.

"You a friend of Mr. Caldwell's?" the brunette named Tiffany asked me.

"No, I just met him once. I need to see him on business."

"He's like real cute, isn't he?" Her face took on a dreamy expression. So that was it. Roddy Caldwell was the object of adolescent affections here at Highland Park High. I'd almost forgotten about schoolgirl crushes and students' curiosity about their teachers' personal lives. There'd been a little of that even at Linwood Elementary when I taught there. I remember eight-year-old Terry Warnowski had a crush on me for a whole school year. He even saved up his allowance and brought me a heart-shaped box of candy for Valentine's Day.

"I hadn't really noticed Mr. Caldwell's cuteness before," I told the girl, smiling. "I'll be sure and take a closer look next time I see him." Her cheeks turned crimson under the heavy makeup.

Purple streaks came back, unwrapping a stick of gum. "Sorry, he signed out. Wanna like leave a note or anything?"

With unexpected thoughtfulness, she handed me a piece of paper and a stubby pencil. I wrote, *We met at the funeral the other day. Please call me as soon as possible. It's very important. Thanks, Devon MacDonald.* I folded the note over my business card and handed it to her.

"I'll like put it in his mailbox," she assured me. Tiffany looked at the note longingly.

"Like thanks," I said, and left. I was certain the girls would have my note read before I reached the school's front door.

I fought the start of rush hour traffic as I drove downtown on Shepard Road. Luckily, I was heading against most of it, so I was able to reach the library before it closed.

It took me twenty minutes to locate the story I was after in the microfilm records of the *St. Paul Pioneer Press.* It was a 1981 account of a group of about twelve men who had demonstrated with anti-Semitic picket signs outside a Jewish community center. According to the report, the demonstration had become violent when several members of the Aryan Supremacy Party began yelling taunts and trespassing on the center's property. A handful of men attending a Holocaust memorial event there attempted to remove the ASP members and a fight broke out. The accompanying photo depicted a muscular man poised to strike a smaller, white-bearded man, with a picket sign that read, HITLER WAS RIGHT. Even though the microfilm reproduction of the photo was muddy, the look of raw hatred in the ASP member's eyes was unmistakable. I've seen it before in fanatics of all races and religions and it always sends a shiver down my spine.

Besides Hoffman, the men arrested were listed as Orville Voss of Minneapolis and Paul Mueller of Bloomington, along with Eldon Bergmann and Herbert Keller, both of St. Paul. So Leon Jackson was right when he described Herb Keller as an asshole buddy of Hoffman's. They'd even gone to jail together, if only for a night.

— **21** —

"Coroner says methylphenidate hydrochloride is the drug that killed Hoffman," Sam reported, reading from his notes, on Monday morning. "Interacted with the antidepressant stuff he was takin' and bingo. End of Hoffman." He finished eating one of the banana walnut muffins I'd baked this morning from my favorite recipe; it uses whole wheat flour and honey. I'd had a couple of them hot for breakfast and brought the rest into the office to share. "This shit's not bad," my partner admitted reluctantly, licking his fingers.

"Methyl what?" I asked.

Sam spelled methylphenidate hydrochloride for me. "It's an upper, some sort of stimulant," he said. "Mix it with that Nardil stuff Hoffman's shrink put him on, and the coroner says you can end up with high blood pressure, a runaway fever, convulsions . . . even death, if you take enough of it." He reached for a second muffin and began to peel off its pleated paper wrapper. "Whoever gave it to Hoffman made sure he took enough." He pushed a button on the intercom and bellowed into it, "Any of that coffee left out there, Paula?"

Sam had spent some time over the weekend talking with Charleton Hazelwood, Ben Levy's attorney, and following up on the coroner's report. What he'd learned fleshed out the details Leon Jackson had given me.

Paula entered, carrying an unplugged electric coffee-pot. Her eyes were puffy. She filled Sam's mug without speaking and turned to leave. "Have a muffin, Paula," I urged. "They're healthy and even Sam says they're good."

"No, thanks, Devon." She sighed dramatically. "I'm not hungry."

"At least take one for later, before Sam wolfs down the whole batch."

She floated out of the office as though she hadn't heard a word I'd said.

"What's with her?"

"Romance problems."

Sam rolled his eyes. "I was hopin' it was somethin' new. Next time I hire an unmarried secretary pushin' thirty, have me committed."

I smiled. "Tell me what the lawyer told you," I said.

"Hazelwood's pretty sure he can get the doc off. The evidence against him is circumstantial, what there is of it. The problem is time. It's gonna take a couple more days before he can get Levy out on bail and then we're lookin' at months before this thing hits the court."

"In the meantime, Ben Levy's life is a nightmare. Honestly, Sam, I really don't understand why they charged Ben. Just because he's a doctor—"

"That's just part of what they got . . . or what they *think* they got." He drained his coffee mug, grimacing. "Dregs. Christ, this stuff's bitter."

"So give. What else is there except so-called expert knowledge that anybody with an IQ could get out of the *Physician's Desk Reference?*"

Ticking the points off, one at a time, on his fingers, Sam began to chronicle the police case against Ben Levy. "Levy was there at the critical time. In fact, he was there the night before, too. Got a chance to look over the joint. Then he comes back the next morning with the pills. There're witnesses say the two men fought. You and I both know the dandy motive Levy's got, and now the county attorney knows it, too."

"Still—"

"Hey, kid, I'm on his side, too. Don't argue with *me*. Save it for the opposition, huh? I ain't through."

"Sorry."

"According to Hazelwood, the clincher comes when the cops get a search warrant and fine-comb Levy's car, the one he took to Pearson's Meats that day. They find some of them pills that killed Hoffman under the driver's seat."

"So Ben's a doctor. Doctors carry pills. You know, like in their little black bags."

Sam turned his sticky palms upward. "The guy's a goddamned *skin* doctor, Devon. This shit we're talkin' about here don't cure acne or athlete's foot. It's shrink medicine. The cops' stance is, Ben Levy's got no more legitimate reason to be schlepping around this stuff than you or I do. Doctor or no doctor. Fact is, his bein' a doctor works against him. Gives him the necessary medical knowledge, plus easy access to drugs."

I sighed. "What does Ben say?"

He shrugged. "There were just a couple of pills, loose, lying under the seat of his car, like somebody accidently dropped 'em there, maybe while gettin' outa the car. Levy tells his lawyer he don't know how they got there, they ain't his."

"The cops find any record that Ben Levy ever wrote a prescription for methylphenidate hydrochloride?"

"They're still workin' on that. Figured they had enough to charge him without it. Even if they don't come up with that kinda record, who's to say Levy couldn'ta got 'em from a drug salesman? Doctors get free samples all the time."

"So what do you think, Sam? You think Ben Levy killed Gilbert Hoffman?"

He leaned back in his chair, his green and yellow

striped shirt straining at the buttons. "What I think is what you think. Ben Levy's a fall guy. Somebody wanted Hoffman out, and Levy showin' up when he did gave 'em a method and a suspect to take the heat off."

"Anybody who was at the meat market that morning could've put the pills in Hoffman's food —"

"Coroner thinks it was dissolved in grapefruit juice. That'd cover any bitter taste."

"Okay, grapefruit juice then. Hoffman had a Thermos bottle filled with juice that he carried from home every day. So somebody drugs the juice, knowing it's Hoffman's, then plants a couple of pills in Ben's car, figuring the cops'll find them."

"So our job," Sam said, "is to find out who—who wanted Hoffman dead, who set up the doc to take the fall. And why."

"And, if we're going to do it, we'd better get off the dime," I said, rising from my chair. I picked up the plate with the remaining three muffins.

"Hey, leave those. I ain't finished yet," Sam said.

I grimaced and put the plate back down. Rose would kill me. I picked up one of the muffins. "I'm taking this one for Paula," I said, walking out.

Paula stood at the window, looking forlorn. I set the muffin on her desk. "Did you have it out with your dentist friend?" I asked.

She shook her head listlessly. "I'm never going to speak to him again. There's no point."

"You might feel better if you told him what a bastard he is."

She turned her soulful glance in my direction. "You know I'm not good at that kind of thing, Devon. I'd rather just not see him again."

"What about your date last night? How did you break it?"

"I just didn't answer the door. When he called later, I hung up as soon as I heard his voice."

"So the poor jerk doesn't even know what you're pissed about." Paula equates femininity with passiveness and it drives me crazy.

"He ought to be able to figure it out—"

The phone rang. Paula stared at it. It rang a second time. "It might be Stuart," she said, her eyes widening. "I don't want to talk to him."

"Oh, for Christ's sake." I picked up the receiver. "Sherman and MacDonald, may I help you?"

"Devon MacDonald, please."

"Speaking."

"Hi, Devon, this is Roddy Caldwell. I got your message."

"Oh, hi. I hope you remember meeting me at Gilbert Hoffman's funeral."

"Sure. You're the strawberry blonde with the irreverent attitude."

"I'm afraid that's me."

He chuckled. "Hey, that's okay. I'm into irreverence. What can I do for you?"

I explained that I was working on the murder of Tyler Hoffman's father and would like to ask him some questions about the Hoffman family.

"Great. We can talk about it over dinner tonight."

"Oh, that's not necessary," I said. "I could come over to school today—"

"I know it's not *necessary*. Can't a lonely guy ask an attractive woman to dinner anymore?"

My hands began to sweat. "But this is business—"

"Besides, I'm tied up all day with testing and a faculty meeting. Dinner's the only time I've got free."

Shit, I thought. Why did this sound so much like a date? I didn't want a date. All I wanted was to do my job and be left alone.

"Are you trying to tell me that looking at me would spoil your appetite?" Caldwell asked.

"No, that's not it. It's just that I don't like mixing business and pleasure."

"So we'll call it a business meeting."

"And I'll pay for it, put it on the expense account."

"Dutch treat."

"Deal." I agreed to meet him at the Lexington at six-thirty and hung up.

The phone immediately rang again. Paula stared at it. I picked up the receiver and handed it to her. "Talk, damn it."

"Sherman and MacDonald," I heard her say as I grabbed my purse and left.

22

Myra Hoffman was vacuuming her living room when I arrived. Her activity had stirred up a cloud of dust motes. I sneezed. She did not bless me.

"Now what do you want?" she asked, standing aside reluctantly as I entered the room. She was wearing a pale green housedress and had her hair hidden under a blue bandanna. Dirt was streaked across the left side of her face.

What I wanted was to see how quickly she was recovering from her husband's death. She had the strongest motive for wanting him dead, despite all her moaning about his demise. She also still held the key to David Levy's survival. I was painfully aware that Ben's arrest didn't lengthen little David's lifespan; it didn't give me so much as an extra hour to find the boy some transplantable bone marrow. "The other day," I told her, "I promised you I'd talk to the Levys about getting you financial help if you and Tyler would cooperate with David's doctors. I came to tell you I talked to them."

She let go of the ancient Hoover's handle; it struck the

wall, making a small dent. She didn't seem to notice. "Yeah, well things have changed since then. You think I'm gonna help the man murdered my Gilbert, you got another think coming."

"Mrs. Hoffman . . . Myra, the police have made a terrible mistake. I know Ben Levy and I swear to you he is not responsible for your husband's death. He just happened to be in the wrong place at the wrong time. As you well know, there's a long list of people who wished Gilbert were dead."

She stepped back as though I'd struck her. "That's not true. Gil had respect."

The woman was unbelievable. "The man evoked *fear* in people, Myra. That's not the same as respect. Hitler aroused fear, but not very many people respected him. Gilbert Hoffman was a hateful man. He was a tyrant at work, and a tyrant at home, and it isn't going to do you a damn bit of good to start deifying him now that he's gone." I knew I was being cruel, but I couldn't stop. "Myra, you admitted to me that you were afraid of him. You'd have been a fool not to be. Look what he did to you, and to your son.

"Isn't that true? Weren't there times you wished Gilbert were dead so he couldn't beat you anymore?"

Myra's mouth worked spasmodically, but no words emerged. I continued to push her shamelessly. "I'd have wished him dead if he'd beaten me the way he beat you. That's only human."

Her nod was barely perceptible.

"Myra," I said softly. "Face it. You're in just as much trouble as Ben Levy. The fact he's in jail right now is the main thing that's keeping you out. And I'm going to see that he doesn't stay there."

Her bandanna-covered head jerked upward. "What do you mean?"

"You had just as much motive and opportunity to poison Gilbert as Ben Levy did. Once the police realize that Ben didn't do it, who do you think they're going to pin it on?"

"But—" Unconsciously, she pulled at the soiled skirt of her housedress. "I—I didn't kill Gilbert. I swear I didn't. I wasn't even there."

"You packed his lunch, and the coroner says the medicine that killed him was in his Thermos bottle. You filled that bottle, didn't you?"

"I filled it, sure, but all I put in it was juice. I already told the police that. I did that every day. I never even heard of that stuff they say poisoned him."

"That's pretty hard to prove, Myra. You knew that Gil's diet was restricted while he was taking Nardil. You knew he couldn't drink alcohol, he couldn't take drugs."

"That's ridiculous. Where would I get the stuff even if I did know it would kill my husband?" Her words spilled out and her voice rose.

"If somebody wants to get drugs," I said, "it isn't very hard nowadays."

"It is if you don't leave home."

"Prove you never leave. Have you got somebody here watching you twenty-four hours a day? Somebody who can vouch for you?"

"Of course not. That's ridiculous." Her hands began to shake and she loosened the grip on her skirt.

"The police may not think it's so ridiculous. As an alibi, it's pretty thin. Look, Myra, this is an election year. The county attorney doesn't want unsolved murders haunting him at the polls. That's bad politics. So he's going to lay this one on somebody and, if I have anything to say about it, it's not going to be Ben Levy. Now, if you don't want it to be you, you'll help me find the person who murdered your husband. Unless it really *is* you."

"No, no, it's not. I swear. Maybe Gilbert was a hard man, but at least he supported us, he paid for this house." She stumbled across the room, gesturing around her as though her spartan dwelling were a palace. "I

115

never wanted him dead, believe me. Without Gil, Tyler and I . . . I don't know what we're gonna do. I got a bill from the city yesterday, for the paramedics that took Gil to the hospital. Three hundred and twelve dollars! I don't know how I'm gonna pay it." Her pale, watery eyes registered panic.

"So isn't it pretty foolish to dismiss the Levys just because the police have made a dumb mistake?" I asked.

"I—I guess . . . Oh, I don't know what's right and what's wrong anymore. I never had to decide anything by myself. I—I'm scared." She sank onto the sofa and I sat beside her. "My father kept me and my sisters on a pretty short leash when we were kids." Her voice became barely audible. "And I was only nineteen when I married Gil. He was a lot like my father."

"Myra," I said, reaching to pat her hand, "you're not a little girl anymore. Your father's gone. Your husband's gone. There's nobody left to tell you what to do. It's all up to you now. You have to live your own life, make your own decisions. They'll be good ones if you just follow your head and your heart." I shrugged. "That's all anybody else does."

"But what if I'm wrong?"

"Gil never made a wrong decision?" I asked her.

"Well, sure, but—"

"Your father never made a mistake?"

"I suppose he must've."

"So you've got the same right. Besides, refusing to decide is just another way of deciding . . . except you lose control. By not deciding to help me solve this case, Myra, you may be making a decision to go to jail. You may be making a decision to keep Tyler out of college. You may be making a decision to let David Levy die. Are those things you can live with?"

The low growl of a car passing on Pascal Street filled the silence. Myra Hoffman stared at her skirt, her fingers alternately pleating and smoothing the green fabric. Finally, she spoke. "What do you want me to do?"

"I need to know the truth about your husband," I said. "Everything. His work history, who his friends are, who loved him, who hated him, his membership in the Aryan Supremacy Party. Everything."

"I—I can't—"

"You *must*. Unless you want to end up in jail."

Her panicked eyes darted around the room. She didn't find whatever she was seeking. "I don't. I'd die first."

"Then tell me everything you can about Gilbert."

"I—I suppose I haven't got much choice." Her shoulders sagged. "All right. I—I'll try."

Over the next couple of hours, Myra Hoffman painted a portrait of a man with severe personality problems, a man disappointed with life, who could never admit his failures were his own fault. Gilbert Hoffman was a man who needed scapegoats. If he was fired from a job, it wasn't because of his vile temper; it was because the market where he worked was owned by Jews who wanted him out so they could hire their own kind. If he had a traffic accident, it wasn't because he was a poor driver; it was because another driver, a black or a woman, cut him off. If his credit record was spotty, it wasn't because he failed to pay his bills on time; it was because Jews ran the banks and they had it in for people like him. If he hadn't fathered a child in the first few years of his marriage, it couldn't be his fault; there had to be something wrong with his wife.

Myra often served as Gilbert's whipping boy and, later, so did Tyler. Hoffman's adult years repeated the pattern of his own childhood. He had been an unhappy, abused boy. He became an unhappy, abusive man.

"Tell me how Gilbert came to work at Pearson's Meats," I prodded.

Myra poured me a cup of coffee. It tasted much better than Paula's, even if it was full of caffeine. "He was out of work," she said. "Laid off for the third or fourth time in a couple of years. Had a fight with his boss down at the Maximart. Things were gettin' pretty desperate around here. Then Herb next door tells Gil his brother-in-law, that's Roger Pearson, needs a business partner to invest some cash; maybe the two of 'em can work something out."

"So Gil bought into the business?"

"Yeah. That was his dream, to own his own business, be his own boss. He always said that's the only way you've got any security. Then there's nobody can fire you."

"But he never did it before Herb Keller told him about Roger Pearson's shop?"

"Couldn't afford it. Costs too much to open your own place. That's why Roger was havin' trouble. Gil said Roger had the cash to open his market but not enough left over to get him through a bad spell. Came close to going bankrupt."

A second mortgage on the Hoffmans' house supplied both the ten thousand in cash to bail out Pearson's Meats and a secure job for Gilbert. With the help of his medication, Gilbert had been holding down the job with little trouble. In the past year, the meat market had picked up business and it was now doing well. Still, now that Gil was dead, Myra had no idea what the success of Pearson's Meats might mean to her and her son. Gil never discussed money with her. I made a mental note to check whether there had been a business life-insurance policy on Gilbert Hoffman. If so, Roger Pearson might have had a strong incentive to murder his partner, and Pearson certainly wasn't grieving noticeably over Hoffman's death.

According to Myra, her husband's social life had centered around the Aryan Supremacy Party. As a couple, the two of them had no friends in recent years. "Herb and Susannah used to come over for supper," she said with a trace of wistfulness. "I'd make a pot roast or sometimes a turkey if it was a special occasion. Somebody's birthday, something like that. But I haven't seen

Susannah now since she and Herb got divorced." Myra's
life had to be an incredibly lonely one. "Stevie came to
see me sometimes when he was visiting his dad," she told
me. "Stevie's Susannah and Herb's little boy. But he
hasn't been around in a few months now. People move
away, you lose touch." Especially if you expect them
always to come to you.

Myra knew little about the workings of ASP, just that
Gil had been president of the local chapter at the time of
his death and Herb Keller had been treasurer. "They
don't let women in. I wouldn't've wanted to belong
anyway. Gil said I'd just be bored." Women weren't the
only people ASP excluded. Gil's life outside his job had
been filled with his hate group and their activities. Myra
tried to justify it as a harmless men's club, although she
had to admit that Gil had served a night in jail and spent
six months on probation after the incident at the Jewish
community center. "He told me it was all a big misunderstanding, that the Jews attacked the ASP people when
all they were doing was upholding free speech."

As long as you didn't count trespassing and incite-
ment, I thought.

She could not give me a list of members, although she
remembered the names of a few of Gil's old cronies.
"There was Herb, of course, and Eldon Bergmann, he
was here a few times. Then there was a guy called
Boomer—tall, red-haired fellow, nice looking. I don't
know his full name."

"What about Orville Voss or Paul Mueller?" I asked.

Myra rested her chin on her hand. "Names sound
familiar, but I can't put a face on 'em."

"They were arrested with Gilbert back in eighty-one."

"That's where I heard of 'em, then. Can't say I ever
met either one. Herb Keller'd know everybody in the
group, but I don't know if he'd give you their names."

Before I left, I extracted Myra's promise that she
would talk to her son about his true origins and a

potential bone marrow transplant. "I s'pose it's time he knew the truth, now that Gilbert's dead," she admitted, "but it ain't gonna be easy to tell him."

No, it wouldn't be easy, I thought as I drove away from Myra Hoffman's bungalow. Yet somehow I felt she might well find the truth a helluva lot easier to deal with than the lie she'd been hiding most of her adult life.

—— **23** ——

Roger Pearson agreed to talk to me, but insisted that we not do it in the meat market. That would provide too many opportunities for customers and delivery men to overhear our conversation. Spreading the news that a man had been poisoned at Pearson's Meats could only hurt his business; no one would care that Hoffman's death had nothing to do with the meat sold there.

I waited while Pearson signed for a delivery and carried it into the walk-in cooler. He removed his stained apron and plastic nametag and we walked down the street to the St. Clair Broiler, the metal cleats on his polished black shoes clicking on the pavement as we went.

We slipped into a booth in the back of the diner. Pearson ordered a hamburger with fries and a chocolate malted from a red-haired waitress in a hairnet; I settled for a glass of iced tea with a wedge of lemon.

"I really don't know what you wanna talk to me for." Pearson stroked one of his long salt-and-pepper sideburns with his index finger. I wondered if he grew them longer each year as nature further depleted the hair on his head. "Like I told you the other day, I wasn't even there when Gil keeled over. I don't know nothin'."

"I've got to explore every angle, Mr. Pearson. Besides, it looks like the actual moment Hoffman collapsed isn't nearly as critical as the time somebody put a handful of pills in his Thermos."

"Well, I don't know nothin' about that, either," he said, lining up his silverware precisely on the table.

"You were in the shop that morning," I pointed out.

"Just for a few minutes, when I come in to pick up my ledger book."

"How long would you say that took?"

The waitress delivered the hamburger. Pearson quickly covered it with catsup, then closed the bun and squirted an extra mound of the red sauce onto his plate, next to the french fries. "Ten, fifteen minutes at the most," he said.

"What happened at the shop during the time you were there?"

"What d'ya mean, what happened? Nothin' happened. I told you. Hoffman didn't get sick 'til later." He bit off a chunk of the hamburger and chewed it.

"I mean who was working that morning? Who did you talk to?"

"Oh," he said, swallowing some of his defensiveness with the bread and meat. "Well, lemme think. It was Gil and Leon workin' the morning shift that day. When I come in, Gil's in the back room, sittin' on his stool like he does, er, did, starin' off into space. Hardly notices me come in."

I poked at the lemon wedge in my tea with my straw. Two men in work clothes slipped into a booth near ours. They ordered black coffee. "Did you talk to him?" I asked.

Pearson glanced at the pair nervously. "Yeah, I says hello, but he's in one o' his moods. He don't respond too polite; just sorta grunts. I ask him what's got his goat, but he don't say nothin'. I figure, the hell with him, he's gonna pout. I ain't got the time for it. I got a business to run."

"So what did you do?"

"I go up front, say hello to Leon, get the ledger, and go home."

"That's all you said to Leon? Hello?"

He swirled a french fry in catsup and brought it to his mouth. A blob of catsup dropped onto his chin; he wiped at it with a paper napkin. "Asked him what's ailin' Gil, that's all."

"And what did he say?"

"Said there'd been some trouble the night before. Told me about that fella who come in and handed Gil some crazy line about bein' Tyler's real father. Leon said Gil punched the guy out and that was the end of it, but Gil was still pissed off. That's pretty much it."

So Leon had heard more than Gilbert Hoffman's threatening shouts that night. He'd listened in on what Ben Levy had told Hoffman about Tyler, too.

"What kind of business partner was Gilbert Hoffman, Mr. Pearson?"

Wariness crept into his eyes again. I could hear the low rumble of conversation from the men in the other booth and the whirring sound of the malt machine behind the counter. "Gil had ten thousand bucks I needed," Pearson told me, "so he bought in. I agreed to give him a job and twenty percent of the profits. If you mean were we friends outside the store, the answer's no."

"I understand your brother-in-law introduced you to Hoffman?"

"Keller's my wife's brother." He shifted in his seat. "They're different as night and day, Herb and Anne, but Herb's her baby brother and she dotes on him."

"I take it you don't."

"Anne says I should be grateful. If it wasn't for Herb, my business probably wouldn'ta made it."

"But you don't like him."

"We're different men. We don't think the same."

"What does Herb do for a living?"

"Runs a little printshop—does small jobs, Xeroxing,

flyers, brochures, that sort of thing. H&S Printing, up on University Avenue."

"Is he successful at it?"

"Does all right. Works pretty long hours now that his wife's out of it."

"Susannah?"

"That's right. She's the S in H&S. Stands for Herbert and Susannah. But they got divorced a while back and Herb hadda buy out her share. Can't say as I blame Susannah, though."

"Why's that?"

"Herb's a strange guy. Keeps strange company. Susannah's a decent enough girl, just got fed up with the whole lot of 'em."

"You mean the Aryan Supremacists?"

Pearson's eyes darted to my face, then to the men in the next booth. He swallowed hard, then took a breath and spoke quietly. "So you know about them."

"I know both Herb and Gil were officers in ASP. I know there was a time they held meetings in the basement of your store. Are you a member of the club, too, Mr. Pearson?"

There was a long pause. Pearson sipped his malted milk noisily and looked up. His jawline was rigid. "No," he said. "I'm not a member of that so-called club. I kicked 'em the hell off my property, soon as I found out they were meetin' there. You ask me, there oughta be a law."

The men in the next booth threw some bills on the table and left. I watched them walk out onto Snelling Avenue, then turned to Pearson. "So Hoffman was moody," I said. "He had a violent temper. He used your property for meetings of a group you think ought to be outlawed. Nobody claims he was much of a worker. I saw for myself how he treated one of your employees with public sarcasm and contempt. I don't think I'm wrong in suggesting, Mr. Pearson, that Gil was not exactly the world's most desirable business partner."

His smile was mirthless. "Truth is, I shoulda known better than to listen to my jerk of a brother-in-law. I can't blame anybody else; it was my own damn fault. I'd probably been better off borrowin' the ten grand from a shark than teamin' up with Gil Hoffman."

"Gil was more trouble than he was worth?"

"You can say that again. The man was an A-number-one pain in the ass. You want the truth, Miss MacDonald? I can't say I'm a bit sorry that doctor fella poisoned him. All I wish is he hadn'ta done it in my store."

I stirred the slivers of ice in my glass with my straw. "What was your financial arrangement with Hoffman?"

"Like I said, he put in the ten grand, he got twenty percent of the business and a job. He got a salary, same as me, then we split the profits at the end of the year— providin' there was somethin' to split—the same way. Twenty percent for Gil, eighty percent for me."

"And if one of you died?"

Pearson looked confused. "Whaddya mean?"

"What happens to Hoffman's share of the business now that he's dead?"

"I s'pose it goes to his wife, Myra. Her and their kid. I'm hopin' she'll let me buy her out. Had my fill of business partners."

"There was no provision for the surviving partner to inherit?"

Pearson shook his head.

"What about insurance?"

"That's what I'm gonna use to buy out Myra's share." Pearson wiped his mouth with the paper napkin. "I suppose she'll want to make a little profit. That's okay. I can afford to put in some extra, providin' she don't get greedy. Pearson's Meats is doin' okay . . . if this business with Hoffman don't ruin a good thing."

"There was a policy on Hoffman's life with you as beneficiary?"

"A small one, ten thou. There's one on me, too, with

Gil as beneficiary. That reminds me, guess I'd better do somethin' about changin' that now he's gone."

The purpose of the insurance policies was to provide whoever survived with ready cash to use toward buying out his partner's heirs, providing they were willing to sell. It was a simple arrangement worked out without the assistance of an attorney.

"Tell me about Leon Jackson," I said.

"What about him?"

"Could he have killed Hoffman?"

"Leon?" Pearson was incredulous. "Leon Jackson?" He laughed. "Leon wouldn't hurt a fly. You should see him with those little kids o' his."

"Mr. Pearson, Jackson himself told me he has a prison record. And he admits Hoffman rode him mercilessly. Under those circumstances, a lot of men might commit murder. Especially an easy one where all you've got to do is put a few pills in somebody's drink."

"Well, not Leon. I know the man. He's worked for me a long time now and he's been clean the whole time, not a lick of trouble. Best employee I ever had. Leon appreciates havin' a job, not like most of 'em you see these days. He don't call in sick, he don't steal from the cash register or the meat counter. . . ."

"Then he didn't deserve to be treated the way Hoffman treated him."

"A dog deserves better'n that. Used to bug the hell outa me. I told Gil a dozen times if I told him once, lay off, leave the guy alone."

"And what did Gil say to that?"

Pearson lowered his eyes to his plate. "Can't repeat it to a lady."

I smiled. "That's okay, I get the idea. What was Leon in prison for?"

"You'll have to ask him about that, Miss MacDonald."

Fair enough. I drained my iced tea. "What about Myra Hoffman? You know her well?"

Pearson pushed his plate away and signaled the waitress for the check. "Met her once or twice when I had to go to Gil's house for some reason or other. She never once set foot in the store that I know of."

"Why's that?"

"Beats me. Mousy woman, afraid of her own shadow."

The red-haired waitress set down a green and white check on the table. "You have a good day now," she said, smiling and walking back behind the counter.

I opened my purse. "You think Myra Hoffman could have poisoned Gilbert?" I asked Pearson.

"I'll get yours," Pearson said, pulling a roll of bills from his pocket.

"Thanks, but I'm not allowed to accept favors." I placed a dollar bill and two quarters on the check.

Pearson shrugged. "Have it your own way. I couldn't say about Myra. Like I told you, she seems like a scared rabbit, but you never know. Maybe poison's the way that kinda woman'd get rid of her old man, if she was inclined to. God knows how she stood bein' married to him." He peeled off a five-dollar bill and added it to my contribution. "Say, is it true that this Levy guy is really Tyler's old man?"

"You'll have to ask Mrs. Hoffman about that, Mr. Pearson."

"Yeah, well, I guess that's her business, ain't it? I gotta get back to the store, give Leon a hand till I can hire on a new man."

"That going to be a problem?" I asked. "To hire a new butcher?"

He shook his head. "Gonna be a pleasure," he said, sliding his portly figure out of the booth. He nodded good-bye and I watched him walk into the bright midday sun.

I stopped at the Lund's market in Highland Park and made myself a quick lunch at the salad bar. I stood in line with six or eight people in office attire, more women than men. None of the men tried to pick me up. I wasn't sure whether to be grateful or offended. If this was really the trendy meet market that Paula had described, the pairings must be decidedly discreet. I didn't even notice any signals being passed between the marketers but, then, my receiver has been out of commission for a long time now.

I sat in my car in the Lund's parking lot and ate my salad with a plastic fork while I listened to the CBS network news on WCCO-AM. Detective work sure can be glamorous. When I'd finished eating, I drove up Cleveland Avenue to University, then turned left toward the U. My route took me through an ugly industrial district, then past the KSTP-TV studios, perched on the line dividing the cities of St. Paul and Minneapolis. H&S Printing was a brick storefront a few blocks into Minneapolis, wedged between a seedy Laundromat and an appliance repair shop.

I parked in a one-hour zone and approached the store. The plate glass windows across the front were grimy and plastered with signs: COPIES 10¢; BUSINESS CARDS PRINTED; SMALL JOBS OUR SPECIALTY; WE PICKUP AND DELIVER. Lights were on inside, but the front door was locked. On its glass hung a sign reading BE BACK AT. The well-worn black cardboard hands on the clock face below were positioned at four o'clock. So much for Herb Keller's long working hours, I thought, unless he was out on one of his WE PICKUP AND DELIVER routines.

It was almost three and my list of subjects to interview was not diminishing very rapidly. I wanted to talk to Keller before I approached his ASP colleagues. I would need to talk to Tyler Hoffman, too, but I didn't want to do that before his mother had told him about his biological connection to Benjamin Levy. That kind of news shouldn't come from a stranger. I felt, too, that my dinner meeting tonight with Rodman Caldwell would help me decide how best to approach Tyler; the boy's teacher obviously knew him well and had earned his friendship.

No, Herb Keller should be next, but if I waited until four, I might be late for my dinner appointment. The hell with it, I decided, turning back toward St. Paul. I'd get back to Keller in the morning.

I decided to wear my aqua print dress with the short sleeves and pleated skirt to the Lexington. When I returned to Ramsey Hill, I showered, washed and styled my hair, and spent a few extra minutes applying eye makeup. By the time I finished, I had discernible eyebrows and lashes. I even broke down and put on a pair of pantyhose. I hoped Roddy Caldwell would be suitably impressed.

The Lexington was beginning to fill up when I arrived ten minutes early for my appointment. This old St. Paul restaurant includes among its clientele a large number of older people who liked to eat early. I asked for a table for two in the nonsmoking section and chose a chair that allowed me a clear view of the entrance. Caldwell was right on time. I caught his eye as he searched the room and he grinned when he spotted me. Tonight he wore a blue tweed sportcoat with tailored jeans, a button-down-collar shirt, and a dark red tie. As he sat down, I noticed his hair was damp and he smelled faintly of soap.

"I hope you don't smoke," I said. "The smoking section is always blue and I try to avoid it."

"I quit ten years ago," he told me. "It's hard to justify

calling yourself a scientist if you ignore the evidence of what the filthy weed does to people. Unless you're suicidal, of course, and I'm pretty sure I've got that licked. Except for an occasional lonely Saturday night." When he smiled, the corners of his eyes crinkled. His eyes were an unusual shade of light golden brown.

I handed him a menu. "I appreciate your taking the time to meet me," I said. "I've got to interview Tyler Hoffman and I could use your help in deciding how to approach him."

"Hey, no problem. This evening promises to be the highlight of my week." Caldwell signaled the waiter. "I may have given up smoking, but I have yet to conquer demon alcohol. Join me?"

"A glass of white wine would be nice." The waiter nodded and looked at Caldwell.

"Make that two," he said.

As we sipped our wine, I explained that I was working for the man charged with killing Gilbert Hoffman and that I was convinced he was innocent.

"This Levy guy," Caldwell asked, "he's Ty's biological father, right? The sperm donor?"

My mouth fell open. "Who told you that?"

"Ty did. He told me all about your coming to see his mother and asking that he donate bone marrow to his half-brother. The kid's got leukemia or something, right?"

"When did Tyler tell you this?"

"I don't know. I guess it's been, what, ten days or so now." Caldwell shook his head in confusion. "I thought you talked to him. That's the impression he gave me—"

I took a long drink of my wine and set the glass down, my thoughts spinning. Only that morning Myra had obviously been agonizing about how to tell him the truth. Had she been putting on a show for me? I didn't think so. "Tyler must have eavesdropped while I was talking to his mother," I said. Myra had sent him to his room while she and I talked in the kitchen, but that didn't mean he'd stayed there. "What a rotten way to find out the man you thought was your father really isn't," I said. "I feel awful."

"Don't. Listen, Devon, Ty wasn't upset by the news. Honest, he was excited. And, I think, more than a little relieved."

"I can see where Tyler might be relieved to find out he didn't carry Hoffman's genes. Still, the man was the only father he'd ever known."

We were silent while the waiter delivered our dinners—I had sautéed scallops and Caldwell had the pike fillet. "I guess you've got to know the dynamics of the Hoffman family to understand," he said. "Ty's been confused and disturbed by his relationship with his father—Hoffman, I mean, not Levy—ever since I've known him. Truth is, he hated his old man's guts. But that made him feel guilty. Honor thy father, and all that crap."

I nodded my understanding, squeezing lemon juice onto my seafood. "The two of them didn't get along."

"Listen, Devon, I've been teaching adolescent kids for a dozen years now. They all have conflicts with their parents. They wouldn't be human if they didn't. But Tyler Hoffman and his father were different."

"How?"

His brow wrinkled. "Theirs was more than the usual —you know the kind of thing, fights over curfews, using the car, dating. It went far beyond the Oedipal stuff, too. It was more like Ty truly hated his old man, was contemptuous of everything he stood for. And yet, the guy had Ty scared silly. That was obvious."

"Did you say you teach psychology?" I asked.

"Biology and chemistry. But psychology fascinates me. Kids fascinate me. People fascinate me."

"Me, too," I said. "I love trying to figure out what makes them act the way they do."

"In your business you must see the worst of them," Caldwell said.

"The best, too. I see people in crisis and that's when their true colors show."

Caldwell ordered more wine. I drained my first and handed the empty glass to the waiter. "You and Tyler must be close for him to tell you all this."

"The kid needs somebody. I suppose I've become Ty's mentor, more or less. Kind of a substitute father or big brother. He's extremely bright, one of the best students I've ever taught, the kind who make being a teacher worthwhile. I've encouraged Ty to go to college; he could get a scholarship anywhere in the country. But when he brought the notion home, his old man crapped all over it. Called him a sissy for wanting to use his brains instead of his brawn. That was a big issue between them, the old man's preoccupation with making Ty more macho."

"Gilbert Hoffman was a strange man."

"No lie. According to Ty, his old man was one of these crazy guys who're into guns, survivalism, sending the blacks back to Africa. A real certified weirdo."

"And the boy couldn't accept that."

"I think one of Tyler Hoffman's problems has been the fear that blood would tell—"

"What do you mean?"

"That somehow he'd turn out to be as cuckoo as his old man. When he learned that Gil Hoffman's blood wasn't flowing in his veins after all, he was damn near elated."

"And to think I was worried about the boy's being psychologically devastated by the bad news."

Caldwell grinned. "Not to be too crass about it, Devon, that 'bad news' is probably the best news Ty Hoffman has had in his life. He doesn't even seem particularly upset that Gilbert is dead. Relieved is more like it. All I hope is that your Dr. Levy isn't guilty. The kid doesn't need to lose one father who was an asshole only to have the replacement turn out to be a murderer."

As we finished our meal, I tried to process what Caldwell had told me. In one way, I was relieved. I felt certain now that Tyler would agree to donate the bone marrow for David, if medical tests determined the half-brothers were a close enough match. But I was also disturbed. Inadvertently, Caldwell had built a case for Tyler's murdering his father. The boy had hated Gilbert. As of my first meeting with his mother, Tyler had felt freed of any blood ties with the man he so despised. And the boy was a near-genius at chemistry and biology. He certainly knew about the medication Gilbert had been taking; it would be easy for him to learn what chemical combinations could cause his death. Tyler had plenty of opportunity, too. He could have drugged the Thermos before it left the house, knowing his father would drink from it at work. It also seemed significant that Hoffman had been murdered the day after he'd had a violent row with his wife. Where was young Tyler while Gilbert was beating his mother? Had these scenes finally become more than the boy could bear? Had he decided to end them the only way he knew how? I shivered. In some ways, my interview with Tyler Hoffman might prove even more difficult than I'd feared.

"Enough about the Hoffman family," Caldwell said, pushing back his plate. "I want to hear what it's like being a detective."

Most people who ask me that question specify "lady" detective. "It's part psychology, part research, part tedium." I fingered the still-tender spot on the back of my head. "Once in a while it can be dangerous, but, believe me, not often."

I spent the next half hour answering Caldwell's questions about my work, describing some of the cases I'd handled, telling him about my partnership with Sam.

"I'm very impressed," he said. I ordered a cup of tea and Caldwell asked for coffee, apple pie, and two forks. "You'll have to help me eat it," he told me. "I don't really want anything else, but I needed an excuse to sit here and talk with you a while longer."

I laughed, feeling absurdly flattered. "Your turn. Tell me about yourself. Why did you choose high school teaching?"

Like me, Caldwell had become a teacher out of idealism, feeling he could make a valuable difference in young people's lives. "I've had those ideals punctured on dozens of occasions," he admitted wryly. "I guess I had this dumb image of myself as a knight in shining armor, a guy who would so impress these kids that they'd be inspired to learn what I had to teach them. Instead, I found most of them bored with life, dependent on drugs, or preoccupied with material goods. Most of the kids in my classes are there for one reason—because they have to be. If they learn anything, it's sheer coincidence."

"Except for the ones like Tyler Hoffman," I said.

"Right. When I get a student like Ty, I almost forget how dismal the others are. This kid's bright, he's interested. He actually comes in after school to discuss genetic engineering, how bacteria attack organisms, nuclear physics . . . you name it, Ty wants to know all about it. It's exciting to be around a hungry young mind like his, to watch it soak up everything I've got to teach." Caldwell's enthusiasm was contagious. I could see why he'd become a teacher and why he inspired kids like Tyler.

"So you plan to stay with teaching?"

He shook his head. "I don't know. I ask myself that question two, three times a month at least. Sometimes I decide yes, I'll stick it out, other times I think no. The pay stinks, the emotional satisfaction is minuscule compared to the frustrations. It becomes repetitious, teaching the same thing semester after semester. Still . . ."

"What would you do if you changed careers?"

"That, Devon, is the sixty-four-dollar question. My ex-wife wanted me to go into her father's business—he's a real estate developer near Lake Minnetonka. She didn't like living on a teacher's pay. I didn't like the idea of working for my wife's old man. There you have it. Truth is, I still don't know what I want to be when I grow up." He laughed. "Maybe I'll become a private eye. That sounds exciting." Deftly, he shifted the focus of the conversation back to me.

I found myself describing my own teaching career and why I'd left it; Danny's death; Noel's departure. There was something comfortable about Roddy Caldwell. He really listened to what I told him and gave the impression he cared. I learned that his wife, Lisa, had found a man who made more money than he, a stockbroker who could support the sort of life-style she wanted. Theirs was a short marriage, only three years, and they'd had no children.

"I've been pretty gun-shy the past few years," Caldwell admitted. "Once burned . . . To tell the truth, sometimes I think part of my dissatisfaction with my work is really displaced from my private life. You know . . . if I had a happy homelife, maybe I wouldn't need so much from my work. Lately I've been thinking maybe I should find another woman, get married again. You know what I mean?"

"Maybe you should consider becoming a shrink," I said. "You seem to have a natural talent for it." I looked at my watch. It was nearly ten. We'd stayed for more than three hours while diners at the tables around us had come and gone. The waiter had refilled Caldwell's coffee cup twice and long ago laid the check discreetly on the table. "I had no idea it was getting so late," I said, reaching for my purse. Suddenly I had to get away. I was attracted to this sensitive man, but things were progressing much too quickly for me. Here he was, already talking about finding a new wife. "I've got to get home."

"Now I've scared you off," Caldwell said, reading my mind. "Listen, Devon, I know I have a big mouth. And a tendency to bare my soul too quickly. I make women nervous, but I don't mean to, honest. I'm not pushing anything, but I'd really like to see you again sometime. When the *entire* evening can be social. How about it?"

I folded my napkin and placed it on the table. "I—I'm not very good at this sort of thing. My work takes up almost all of my time."

"Your work can't be your whole life, Devon."

It could if I had anything to say about it. I felt my face grow hot.

"Just think about it." Caldwell reached across the table and placed his hand over mine. "I'll call you in a few days."

I nodded, not trusting my voice, then pulled my hand away and searched in my bag for my credit card. We divided the bill, signed our receipts and walked together to the parking lot across the street.

"I really enjoyed this." He held the door of the Honda open for me as I climbed into the driver's seat.

"Me, too," I said, meaning it.

"I'll call you."

I smiled and nodded, then backed my car out of its space. I turned and waved as I exited the parking lot. Caldwell was still standing there, watching me as I drove off.

— 25 —

I awoke early the next morning, feeling rested and optimistic for the first time in months. The sun was shining, a cool breeze was blowing, and life definitely seemed worth living.

I pulled on my leotard, put an upbeat Pointer Sisters album on the stereo, and did my dance routine until I was panting and sweaty and my muscles ached. I had a shower and a bowl of granola with strawberries and made it into the office before eight-thirty.

Sam had beat me in. His office door open to the reception area, he sat at his desk, his feet propped on the desktop and a self-satisfied smirk on his face.

"Was the canary tasty?" I asked, sticking my head in his office door. "You sure look like you enjoyed it."

"We found 'em," he said. "Devon, we goddamn well found 'em!"

"Found who?"

"The Meyers family. Hempstead just called from Tel Aviv. He found 'em living in Haifa, he's already talked to 'em, and they're gonna send their kid's medical records over on the first flight to the States." Sam was as excited as a little child at Christmas. So much for the blasé, world-weary image he tries so hard to convey. "Hempstead figures the docs here can tell whether it's worth involving the kid in medical tests after they take a look at her records—blood type, that sort of thing. The Meyerses promise to tell their daughter what's what if it looks like she can be any help to David."

"Hey, all right! Nice work, partner." I'd been right about it's being a promising day; David Levy's chances for a successful bone marrow match had just doubled. "I'll call Gloria Levy and tell her the good news. She and Ben can use some."

I grabbed the phone on Sam's desk and dialed the Levy house. A phone machine answered; I left a message and asked Gloria to call me back when she returned.

"What's on your schedule for today?" I asked Sam.

"Got a subpoena to serve for Billingsley, downtown Minneapolis. Vinelli wants to talk to me about a new case he's got comin' up, too. Figured I'd spend whatever time I've got left in Public Records, digging up background on the Levy case. You got some names for me?" I nodded. He picked up a ballpoint pen and a yellow legal pad and balanced them against his thigh. "Shoot."

"I talked with the owner of the butcher shop where Hoffman worked yesterday. His name's Roger Pearson. Wife is Anne Keller Pearson. See what you can find on them. Pearson hated Hoffman's guts. He admitted to me that he regretted ever taking the guy on as his partner."

"Wouldn't be the first time somethin' like that led to murder." Sam frowned and jotted down Pearson's name.

"Check out Leon Jackson, too, the other guy who works there. He's got a prison record. Pearson claims Jackson is a pussycat these days, but he won't tell me why the guy was sent up. I have a feeling Jackson'll be tight-lipped about it, too. It's possible Pearson and Jackson collaborated to get rid of their least favorite co-worker."

"Right." He nodded, adding Jackson's name to his list. "Anybody else?"

I added Myra Hoffman's name and those of the ASP members who had been arrested with Gilbert Hoffman: Eldon Bergmann, Orville Voss, Paul Mueller, and Herbert Keller. "Keller is divorced," I added. "Might be some interesting information in his divorce file. The ex-wife's name is Susannah, and they have a kid, Stevie."

Sam had filled a page with notes. "This oughta keep me outa mischief for an hour or two."

I laughed. "Even you are not that good, Sam. I'll get back to you tomorrow." It was almost nine. If I hurried, I could make it to H&S Printing shortly after it opened.

—— 26 ——

The door of the printshop was propped open. A buzzer sounded as I stepped across the black rubber mat at the entrance. Inside, the front room was jammed with copy machines of various sizes, a small offset press, a shelf stacked with completed printing jobs, and a battered old metal desk and chair. Samples of printed pages were taped to the dirty buff-colored walls. The place smelled strongly of ink, copy machine fluid, and a sweet scent I couldn't quite identify.

Keller came forward from a room at the rear of the shop when the buzzer sounded. "Hello. I was just putting away—" He stopped in midsentence. "Well, hello. Damned if it's not the insurance investigator."

"Devon MacDonald. You have a good memory, Mr. Keller. I have a few more questions to ask you about your late neighbor."

As he came closer, I recognized the sweet smell lingering in the air as the Aqua Velva after-shave Keller was wearing. It made my nose itch. "You always attend funerals for people your company insures, Miss MacDonald?" he asked. So he'd noticed me at the cemetery, too. "Or wasn't there ever any insurance policy . . . or insurance company?" His eyes riveted me and I felt my face redden. I'm always embarrassed whenever someone catches me in one of the lines we private investigators tell while trying to do our jobs.

I shrugged and flashed him a smile. "You caught me," I admitted.

Keller did not return my smile. "What are you really after?" he asked.

"I needed some information about the Hoffmans for a client of mine. Sometimes, when you can't reveal why you want the information, it's just a lot easier to give people a plausible story. Sorry about that, Mr. Keller. Now, I've been hired to look into Gilbert Hoffman's murder and I need to find out what you know about it."

"What I know is that the cops already have the murderer in custody."

"I don't think so."

"Well, *I* do."

"Mr. Keller, all I want is to ask you a few questions. You were at Pearson's Meats on the morning Gilbert Hoffman died. You might have seen something. Besides, how could it hurt you to talk to me? The police could be wrong about Dr. Levy, and I'm sure you want the person who really killed your friend caught."

He perched on the edge of the desk, making room to sit by pushing back a stack of papers. "The guilty person has been caught," he said coldly. "All I've got to say about it is I'm sorry Minnesota doesn't have capital punishment."

"My questions will take only a few minutes."

"Questions about what?"

"Why don't we start with the Aryan Supremacy Party." His eyes registered fleeting shock. I pressed my advantage. "I understand you're an officer in ASP, Mr. Keller. Just what office do you hold?"

His face froze and he didn't answer.

"Maybe we should start with some history," I said. "Did you recruit Gil Hoffman for the party or did he recruit you?"

Keller pushed himself up off the edge of the desk and stood, bringing us a few inches closer together; I repressed an impulse to step back. "That's confidential information and it's none of your damn business."

"If you don't want to tell me, Mr. Keller, I'm sure I can find out from some of the other members. Maybe Eldon Bergmann, Orville Voss, Paul Mueller . . ."

"Where the hell—" He paused, then snapped his fingers. "Of course! It's that damn picketing arrest, isn't it? That's where you got those names."

"It's hard to keep your organization private when you publicly picket people because of their religious beliefs, Mr. Keller. Or when you get yourself arrested for assault." His fist clenched. I began to wish there were more foot traffic on the street.

"You want to know, do you? Well, I'll tell you, lady. I am an officer in ASP, all right—treasurer. Gil was president. And we were a helluva team until that asshole Jew of yours poisoned him, like the slimy, sneaky bastards all his race are. If the courts don't take care of him, I give you my word ASP will."

I didn't flinch. "Is that so?"

"You're gonna hear more about the Aryan Supremacy Party, too." Keller shook his fist in my direction. He began to pace. "Next election, we're gonna be in office all over this country. The mood of the people is right for it. We've got more of 'em joinin' ASP every day—farmers, steelworkers, miners, all kinds of people. People whose lives've been ruined by the moneymen, the Jews. People who're sick and tired of blacks gettin' their jobs or keepin' their kids outa college. They've had it with this affirmative action bullshit; all it ever was is discrimination against the whites who built this country. ASP wants this country the way it was before the kikes and the niggers and the slant-eyed illegals started takin' over and we're gonna get it back."

I wondered how much of Keller's rantings were based in fact. I had read newspaper reports about hate groups popping up among those hardest hit by recent economic hard times—the farm crisis, the steel industry cutbacks. The numbers of homeless Americans were mushrooming daily. Still, my vision of America was a place where people of all religions and all colors could coexist peacefully and learn from each other's cultures. Certainly the majority agreed with me. "The way my history books told it, Mr. Keller," I said, "in the beginning there was nobody in America but the Indians. How'd you and your cronies like to go back to that?"

He laughed humorlessly. "That's just the kind of thing I'd expect from a Jew-lover like—"

The buzzer sounded and I turned to see a tall young woman in a navy business suit enter. "Hello, Marian," Keller said to her. "Be with you in a minute."

I smiled ingratiatingly. "I don't mind waiting," I said. "Please, Mr. Keller, take care of your customer."

Keller flashed me a begrudging look. I gambled that he'd dare not let Marian witness him throwing me out.

"I want to pick up those flyers I left yesterday," she said. "And I've got another one here, for the summer schedule of classes. I thought maybe a bright yellow paper would be nice; yellow's always cheerful and summery. What do you think?"

As Keller fetched paper samples from the back room, I wandered around the shop, casually inspecting the materials he had printed. Keller did a quality job. There was an announcement for a rock concert at Powderhorn Park; a bright green brochure outlining a cooking course; a large poster advertising an exhibit by a modern artist. Across the surface of the desk was a variety of forms and receipts, spread out randomly, as well as the stack of printed letters that Keller had shoved aside. I positioned myself on the edge of the desk as though I were tired of walking and surreptitiously read the letter on the top of the stack. My ability to read upside down serves me well as an investigator.

"Dear Fellow ASP Members:" the letter began. It called for "increased unity in the wake of Gil Hoffman's tragic death at the hands of the Jewish enemy." This guy wasn't kidding; I'd never encountered bigotry quite so blatant. The letter called for an emergency election to replace Hoffman as president with . . . who else? . . . Herb Keller. "My dear friend and colleague would want me to take over in his place," Keller had written. "He

141

and I shared a vision for the future of ASP, for the success of our candidates in the upcoming congressional elections, for the future of the country toward which we all work. Your vote for Herb Keller will assure the continuity of leadership that ASP needs if we are to reach our sacred goals."

Marian finally settled on goldenrod paper and left her order for two thousand flyers. She wrote Keller a check for the order he'd already completed and left the shop.

"So you're planning to be ASP's new president," I said when the door closed behind her. "That's quite a campaign letter you wrote."

Keller's eyes blazed. "I think you'd better leave before your snooping buys you more trouble than you can handle, lady."

Keller started toward me. My spine tightened and I stood. He followed close behind as I headed toward the door. "The police might see your campaign as a motive for murder," I told him. "You were in the shop that day. There are witnesses to that. Now you're after Hoffman's position. Maybe you wanted him out of the way so—"

Suddenly Keller stopped in his tracks and began to laugh. "Hah! That's a good one. I killed my best friend so I could move up from treasurer of ASP to president. I've been president, lady. I've been vice-president, secretary, membership chairman. There's not an office I haven't held sometime. The idea that I needed Gil dead so I could be president is a load of bullshit and you know it." His laughter died. "Now get out of here before I throw you out. And take your phony theories with you. They're not gonna save your beloved kike doctor. Like I told you before, if the cops let him off, I'll personally see to it ASP takes real good care of him. Nobody kills one of our people and lives to brag about it."

— 27 —

As I drove south toward Bloomington, I couldn't get
Herb Keller out of my mind. His fanaticism and ASP's
"holy war" displayed the kind of mentality that kept
getting people killed in Beirut and Belfast, in Iran and
Iraq, and on a dozen other blood-soaked battlegrounds.

I took Cedar Avenue south toward Bloomington, missing at least half of the traffic lights as I slowly made my
way through a series of old Minneapolis neighborhoods.
Traffic thinned at the green belt surrounding Lake Nokomis and, after I made it to the point where Cedar Avenue
widens into a divided highway, I was able to make some
decent time.

Roger Pearson's house was a modest split level with a
single attached garage on East Eighty-third Street. The
house was newly painted pale yellow with dark green
trim. A lush lawn and beds of marigolds bordering the
sidewalk picked up the color scheme. The place was
certainly not palatial but it was easy to see the people
who lived here loved it. The garage door was open and a
late-model tan Chevrolet station wagon was parked
inside.

A jet taking off from nearby Minneapolis–St. Paul
International Airport roared overhead, rattling the glass
on the front door as I rang the bell. There was no answer.
I pushed the button again and could hear the bell ringing
inside the house. Still no response, although the open
garage indicated someone was home. I walked across the
front yard and around the side of the house, calling
"Hello . . . anybody home?" When I reached the back-

yard, a middle-aged, slightly overweight woman kneeling in a vegetable garden got to her feet. I recognized Anne Keller Pearson from the Hoffman funeral.

"Oh, hi," she said. "I'll bet you've been ringing the bell."

I nodded.

"Sorry. I can't hear it when I'm out in the yard. I've been meaning to put a bell on the outside of the house for years, but I never seem to get around to it." She smiled apologetically and pulled off her gardening gloves.

I introduced myself and told her why I had come.

"My husband told me you talked to him yesterday," she said, patting her permed and dyed black hair, "but I don't know why you'd want to talk to *me*." She said it as though no one ever wanted to talk to her.

"It won't take long," I assured her. "You never know where something valuable will crop up, so I'm trying to talk to everyone who knew Gilbert Hoffman." Although I didn't tell her, I hoped Mrs. Pearson, as the wife of one man and sister of another who were at Pearson's Meats on the morning Gil Hoffman was killed, might be able to give me some insight into their personalities.

She set down her gloves on the grass, next to her gardening tools. "I was just about ready for a break anyway. Come on in."

Anne Pearson ushered me in the back door, through a modern kitchen decorated in shades of brown and yellow, and into the living room at the front of the house. She offered me a glass of lemonade. I accepted. While she returned to the kitchen, I looked around her living room. An L-shaped sofa occupied the corner opposite a brick fireplace that still held the ashes of a fire. The end tables were decorated with tiny framed photographs of relatives and a bookcase along one wall was filled with Reader's Digest Condensed Books. Several objects on the fireplace mantel seemed to be souvenirs from family vacations: a small cedar statue with "Sequoia National Forest" lettered across its base; a sand sculpture from the American

Southwest; an Indian totem pole; a seashell clock from Florida. In stark contrast to the Hoffmans' place, this home had dozens of personal touches.

Mrs. Pearson returned with two tall glasses of pink lemonade, a sprig of fresh mint floating in each. "The mint's from my garden," she said. I complimented her on her attractive yard. "Gardening is my hobby," she told me. "I know it sounds corny, but it always gives me a thrill to plant a few seeds, water them, and watch them grow into something wonderful." She laughed shyly. "Guess I shoulda been a farmer." She took a package of Salems from the pocket of her red cotton smock and offered me one. When I declined, she lighted one for herself and discarded the spent match in an ashtray that said, "Expo 86 Vancouver."

"What can I do—" Another jet passed overhead deafeningly. "—for you, Miss MacDonald?" she asked. "I hope the planes don't bother you. We've been here twenty years and we're used to them. We just turn up the TV or talk louder when the flight pattern passes overhead."

"Did you know Gil Hoffman well, Mrs. Pearson?"

She took a drag on her cigarette. The smoke drifted toward me. "He came for dinner once, when he and Roger were first setting up their deal. I saw him in the store, too, whenever I stopped by. But, no, I couldn't say I knew him very well."

"What about his wife, Myra?"

She shook her head, her jet-black curls bobbing. "No. I never even met her until Gilbert's funeral. My husband and I invited her to come to dinner that time, so she and I could get to know each other, but she didn't come. Said she wasn't feelin' well, as I recall. I think I asked her over once or twice more, but she never did make it. Come to think of it, I don't think she ever set foot in the shop, either. To tell the truth, it sorta hurt my feelings. I had the impression Myra Hoffman thought she was too good for us."

I sipped my lemonade; it was homemade and delicious. "I understand that the business partnership between your husband and Gilbert Hoffman was not exactly a happy one."

"I guess you could say that. Of course, Roger never really wanted a partner, but we needed the money. I don't suppose anybody really could've pleased him. There was trouble between Gilbert and some of the help workin' in the shop, too, and things got off to a pretty bad start."

"You mean the conflict between Hoffman and Leon Jackson?"

"Yeah, Leon didn't like Gil, but nobody really did. There was Tron, the janitor, too, and Roger had another man working behind the counter in the beginning, Jeff Noucharian. Jeff left maybe a month after Gilbert started, said he wouldn't work with Gil." She bit her lower lip and frowned. "Roger was stuck with Gil, so he had to let Jeff go."

"Nearly everyone I've talked to says Gil Hoffman was a real tyrant, Mrs. Pearson," I said. "It's no surprise he had trouble getting along with people at the shop. The man was a blatant bigot. Yet . . ." I paused for effect. "He was your brother Herb's best friend. Herb helped set your husband up in business with Hoffman. How do you account for that?"

"I don't think it's up to me to explain how or why my brother chooses his friends," she said.

"Of course not, Mrs. Pearson, but I thought you might have some insight into why Herb might have put your husband together with a man he knew was a hatemonger."

"I don't think Herb knew any such thing, Miss MacDonald. Gil Hoffman lived next door to Herbie. He was a butcher by trade. He was out of work. I suppose my brother thought he was doing everybody a favor by introducing Roger and Gil. There was nothing sinister about it. Herb's just got a big heart." Privately, I thought

Herb Keller had managed admirably to keep his "big heart" hidden that morning. "Maybe Herbie saw only the good side of Gil," she said. "Everybody's got some good in them."

"Mrs. Pearson, Gilbert Hoffman was a member of the Aryan Supremacy Party. Your brother is an officer in that organization."

She shook her head. "The orion what?"

"Aryan Supremacy Party. A-r-y-a-n. Its members believe whites are superior to other races, that Christianity is superior to other religions. They want to get all the minorities out of America. They harass Jews on their way to synagogue. They want to take the vote away from blacks. They believe women are inferior to men."

"You're mistaken. Herbie would never get involved in something like that. My brother's a decent man." Her expression turned wistful. "He was such an adorable little boy."

So was Charles Manson; I've seen photos. "I saw your brother this morning, Mrs. Pearson. He admitted to me that he's the party treasurer. Hoffman was president and Keller's planning to run for that job himself, now that Hoffman's dead. Your husband even told me Herb and Hoffman tried holding party meetings in the meat market and he threw them out."

Sighing, she stubbed out her cigarette, took a tissue from her pocket, and blew her nose. "Roger never said a word about it to me. I honestly don't know what's going on with Herbie lately. He's been upset, I'll admit that. He hasn't been himself . . . ever since he and Susannah split up." She shuddered. "It was awful. They fought over everything—the printing business, their house, Stevie. The darned lawyers practically bankrupted Herbie. The whole thing hit him very hard. Roger and I loaned Herbie a few thousand to help out. That's one of the reasons Pearson's Meats ended up in trouble a year or so later. We didn't have the extra cash to keep going when the business didn't grow as fast as Roger'd figured."

"Herb must have felt pretty guilty that he owed you money while your own business was in trouble."

"Sure, he felt terrible. Any decent person would. But there wasn't much he could do about it back then. The only way he'd've been able to pay us back would've been to sell his printshop, and I don't even know if he'd've been able to sell it fast enough to do any good. I'm positive that's the main reason Herbie introduced Gil to my husband. He figured it would help all of us out of a bad fix."

I drained my lemonade and set the glass on the table. "Where does your former sister-in-law live now, Mrs. Pearson?"

"She and Stevie live in South Minneapolis. Susannah does free-lance art work, but Herb really still supports both of them."

"I'd like her address if you have it."

Anne Pearson stiffened and her eyes darted to my face. "What for?"

"She used to live next door to the Hoffmans. Myra Hoffman says they were friends, all four of them. She might be able to give me some information about the Hoffmans."

"Oh." She thought it over. "I guess that'd be all right," she said. She went to an Early American desk in the corner of the living room, took a small leather address book from a drawer, and wrote something on a piece of yellow note paper. "Here," she said, handing it to me. "It's on Colfax, near Forty-eighth. An old duplex. Susannah and Stevie have the upper floor."

I thanked her for the address and the lemonade. "Mrs. Pearson," I said, as I rose to go, "what did your husband plan to do about the partnership with Gil Hoffman?"

"What do you mean?"

"The two of them didn't get along. Hoffman was hurting the business more than he was helping it. I was just wondering whether Roger had a plan to buy out Hoffman's share, something like that."

"We talked about it, sure. But we didn't have enough money in the bank. We figured Gil would want what he paid for it, plus. But if you're implying that Roger would kill Gil to get rid of him, you're crazy."

"I'm not implying anything," I said. "Just asking questions. By the way, did your brother ever pay back the money you loaned him?"

"Sure did," she said, happy to be on safer ground. "He paid back every penny, plus interest. Herbie's always been an honorable man. He always pays what he owes."

28

I stopped for a spinach salad at Lee's Kitchen in Highland Park and called Myra Hoffman from the restaurant's pay phone. As promised, she had spoken with her son about his genetic history. "He took it pretty well," she told me, "and he's willing to go along with the bone marrow transplant." Although my evening with Roddy Caldwell had pretty much assured me of Tyler's cooperation, I breathed easier now that it was confirmed. Now all we needed was medical tests showing a good genetic match between David and Tyler. Myra had sent Tyler to the grocery store, but she expected him back shortly. I told her I'd be over within the hour.

Filled with hope, I dialed the Levys' home number. I got the answering machine again. "This is Devon MacDonald," I began after the beep. "The Hoffman boy says he's—"

"Hello, Miss MacDonald. This is Ben's sister, Francine. Gloria asked me to intercept if you called again."

"Is she in? I have some good news for her and Ben."

"She's gone down to Rochester. Davy took a turn for the worse and the doctors wanted him down at Mayo right away."

My heart sank. Damn. David couldn't die now. Not yet. Not when I'd finally lined up two possible donors for him. "What happened?"

Francine sighed. "Leukemia's unpredictable," she said. "Sometimes I think Davy's been living on some sort of sheer will to survive for the past couple of weeks. Now—" She choked back tears. "Now, with Ben's not being home, the poor child seems to have lost his determination. Gloria hasn't told him his father's in jail; she thought that would be too upsetting. But we've been pretty hard-pressed to come up with a plausible reason why Ben's been gone since Friday. I suppose you know the judge set bail at a million dollars."

"How humanistic of him," I said. I quickly explained about Tyler Hoffman and asked how to have the boy tested as a potential donor.

"Thank God," Francine said. "Maybe there's hope left after all." She said she would arrange for Tyler to see Dr. Matsumi at the University of Minnesota Hospitals as soon as possible. I gave her my office and home phone numbers as well as Myra Hoffman's number.

It was with a renewed sense of urgency that I drove to the Hoffman house. Tyler had returned with several bags of groceries; he and his mother were in the kitchen putting them away when I arrived. Myra sent the two of us into the living room while she finished the task. I was grateful for a chance to talk to the boy alone.

"I remember you," Tyler said shyly. His blue eyes were sad. His narrow, olive-skinned face was the type that would carry a melancholy expression even at the best of times, and the past couple of weeks hardly qualified for that label. He wore jeans and a bright blue Oingo Boingo T-shirt that wasn't quite long enough for his lanky frame.

"Mr. Caldwell told me you overheard what your mother and I talked about the first day I came here, Tyler," I said. "I'm terribly sorry about that. I had no intention of your finding out that way."

He dropped to the old nylon sofa. "It wasn't your fault; I eavesdropped."

"Your mother says you're willing to do the bone marrow transplant for David Levy," I said. The boy nodded. "Do you understand what that will mean?"

"Yeah, I read up on it. The library had some medical journal articles on bone marrow transplantation, so I copied them." His face lighted up. "There's this Israeli biophysicist who developed a brand-new technique for transplants, using partially matched bone marrow. Did you know that?" I shook my head. "You see, an ideal donor would have exactly the same HLA-antigens as the recipient; an identical twin would be best. With regular brothers and sisters, you only get a twenty-five-percent chance their HLA-antigens will match, even with both parents in common." The kid certainly *had* read up on it. "David and I won't be a perfect match because we have different mothers, but with this new process, the transplant can still work if we have a partial match. They just have to add this stuff called soy bean agglutinin to the bone marrow I donate and—"

"I'm impressed. You really understand all this?"

"I think I've got it pretty straight," Tyler said. "Of course, there's some things I'll want to ask the doctors."

I could understand Roddy Caldwell's pleasure and pride in this boy. He soaked up difficult scientific data like my credit cards soak up my paychecks. I told Tyler the situation was becoming urgent, that David's condition had worsened, and the younger boy had been taken to the Mayo Clinic. "David's aunt is arranging for you to take some tests at the U as quickly as possible. If they turn out the way everybody hopes, then you'll go to Rochester for the actual transplant process."

"Okay by me."

"Did your mom tell you that I'm working for Dr. Levy, trying to find out who really murdered your father?"

"Dr. Levy is my father," he said stiffly. "Biologically speaking."

"Gilbert Hoffman was your legal father."

He frowned, as if to deny the truth of my remark. "I don't like to think of him that way. He was never a real father to me."

"Okay, I'll rephrase it. I've been hired to find out who really murdered Gilbert Hoffman."

"You don't think my real father did it?"

I shook my head. Tyler looked relieved. "I sure hope not," he said.

"You didn't like your dad—uh, I mean Gilbert— much, did you, Tyler?"

The boy's eyes darted toward the kitchen door. "Do we have to talk about this?"

"It would help me understand your family, and what kind of man Gilbert really was. Maybe that would help me find his killer."

He sighed. "I just don't want my mom to hear what I say. She kind of freaks out sometimes."

"How about your showing me around the neighborhood?" I suggested, gesturing toward the front door.

"I'll just tell Mom we're going out for a walk," he said, sprinting toward the kitchen.

Outside, the humidity was heavy. Someone in the neighborhood was mowing grass. I breathed in the pungent, grassy air and sneezed.

"Hay fever?" asked Tyler.

"In spades." I pulled a tissue from my purse. "About Gilbert," I said. "From what I've been told, there were some pretty heavy problems in your family."

Tyler stepped around a crack in the old concrete sidewalk. "Gilbert Hoffman was mentally ill," he said bluntly. "Sure, he was on medication, but all it did was keep him from getting real depressed. It didn't change his crazy ideas."

"Mr. Caldwell says you and Gilbert disagreed about your going to college."

He shrugged his thin shoulders. "We disagreed about everything. What happened is he'd yell and give me orders and I'd try to figure out a way to get out of doing what he said."

"Didn't you ever just tell him you disagreed, that you had your own ideas?"

"Sure, a few times."

"And?"

"You've got to understand the kind of man Gilbert was, Miss MacDonald."

"Call me Devon, please."

"Okay, Devon. If somebody challenged something he said, anything at all, he got real threatened. He liked to settle things with his fists, and he had pretty big fists." Unconsciously, he glanced at his own long, slender hands. "I know my mom told you how he used to beat her up," he said. "Well, he did the same thing to me if I ever crossed him and he found out about it."

A black Labrador chained to a front-yard stake lunged and barked energetically at us as we walked by, pulling against his restraints. I quickened my pace. "So if you disobeyed Gilbert, you figured out ways he wouldn't find out about it."

"Pretty much," he said, a bit sheepishly.

"Like what? Give me an example."

"Could be anything, any little thing. He wanted to run my whole life. Like . . . well, who I had for friends. He didn't like Marietta, that's my girlfriend. So I just didn't bring her around to the house. When I wanted to see her, I'd tell him I was going to the library to study or something. I just didn't tell him Marietta would be there, too."

"Sounds like fairly normal teenage behavior to me."

"Yeah, well, that's just the beginning. He had to control everything in my life. The clothes I wore . . ." He glanced down at his T-shirt. "Marietta bought me this shirt for my birthday, but if I ever wore it in front of Gilbert, he'd've ripped it off me. So I had to change clothes at school. And the college thing. Mr. Caldwell says I could get a scholarship. I wasn't even asking Gilbert to pay for anything. But did he say, 'Fine, son. Go ahead, better yourself'? Hell, no. He said, 'Get your ass down to the meat market and be a fucking butcher like your old man.' "

The boy's voice had taken on a desperate, pleading quality, as though it were important that I understand. "Sounds pretty bad," I said sympathetically as we turned and walked eastward on Randolph Avenue, past Holy Spirit Catholic Church. "You must have had some plan to escape. Soon you'll be a legal adult."

"I—I don't know. Sometimes I thought about just packing my clothes and disappearing, but I was afraid he'd find me," he said, tugging on the bottom of his T-shirt. "I was afraid he'd take it out on my mom, too. She's—she's not very strong. Don't tell her I said so, but sometimes I think he drove her a little crazy, too."

I couldn't argue with that. "So you didn't want to leave her behind, alone with Gilbert?"

"I couldn't. But now that I don't have to worry about that anymore, I feel kind of guilty."

"About what?"

"When I was a little kid, I used to lie in bed at night and wish he'd die, that he'd crash the car on the way home from work, or have a heart attack. He used to make me feel so damn powerless." Tyler made a fist and struck the palm of his other hand. "I was scared all the time, and I hated him for that."

"This was when you were a little kid."

"Yeah, and I guess later, too. I wished he was dead right up until the day he died." He kicked at a gum wrapper lying on the sidewalk, moving it an inch. "Then

I felt bad, like my wishing had caused his death. I was almost relieved when they said somebody poisoned him."

"Relieved? Why?"

"'Cause it meant it was somebody else's fault he was dead, not mine." He slowed and plunged his hands into his jeans pockets. "I know that's all bullshit. You can't just *wish* somebody dead."

"It takes a little more than that. How much did you know about the medication your father was on?"

"He was taking phenelzine sulfate, brand name Nardil. It's supposed to help relieve neurotic depression. I guess it did."

So Tyler knew the chemical name of Gilbert's medication. "That's a pretty potent drug, isn't it?"

"Yeah. It's got to be monitored pretty closely, and it can have severe side effects, if that's what you mean. But I think my fa— I think Gilbert was a paranoid schizophrenic; Nardil doesn't do a thing for that."

"Sounds like you've read up on that subject, too."

"Over the past few years, I've studied a lot about what makes people crazy."

"Such as?"

His voice was barely audible. "Like it can run in families."

"So you're relieved to find out Gil Hoffman wasn't your biological father?"

He stopped walking and faced me. "I suppose you think I'm ungrateful. The man fed and housed and clothed me. I know that." His face crumpled. "I tried to love him, honest I did. But he made it so goddamned hard!"

I put my hand on the boy's shoulder. He was trembling. "It's okay, Tyler. There's nothing wrong with you. What you feel . . . what you felt about the man you thought was your father is normal enough. You know, some kinds of mental illness can be caused by a person's childhood environment, too, and it sounds like Gil provided a pretty bad one for you. If I were you, I'd be grateful I managed to grow up with my own head straight."

He took a deep breath, struggling to get his emotions under control. "I couldn't win," he said, scuffing the sidewalk with the toe of his dirty white sneaker. "To be a good son to him, the kind he wanted me to be, I'd've had to be just as weird as he was. You know, be into guns and fighting and hating people different than me. I—I just couldn't."

Thank God, I thought. There seemed to be some inner strength in this boy that had insulated him against Hoffman's sick efforts to indoctrinate and contaminate him. Unless the father's torment had ironically turned the son into a murderer, his own father's murderer. That would be a different, maybe deadlier, kind of contamination.

"You want to know what the worst thing was?" Tyler asked. I nodded. "The time he got arrested. Christ, I wanted to die. Half my class is Jewish and my father's name gets in the paper 'cause he's with this hate group, picketing against the Holocaust. For practically a month, I got beat up every day—on the way to school and again on the way home." He stepped off the curb into the street, then up again onto the grassy boulevard. "Sometimes I'd wait at school till the principal was ready to lock up because I was so scared . . . but those boys always waited for me, no matter how late it got. 'Nazi, Nazi,' they yelled while they were hitting me. 'Fucking little Nazi!'"

I shuddered as a vision of a skinny, dark-haired kid living with fear all around him invaded my mind. "What did Gilbert say . . . about your being beaten up like that? Didn't he feel responsible?"

"Hah! That's a good one. Responsible! Gilbert Hoffman never felt *responsible* for anything in his whole life. Nothing was ever *his* fault. Know what he used to do if he found out I'd been beaten up? He'd tell me it was *my* fault. If I wasn't such a pansy, he'd tell me, I'd be able to 'beat the shit outa them kikes.' Then he'd whack me one."

"So first you got beat up and then you had to keep your old man from finding out."

Tyler nodded, his face grim like an old man's.

"An experience like that could be enough to make you agree with Gilbert's views on Jews."

He shook his head firmly. "Uh-uh. It made me mad, sure. But even back then I knew . . . I realized these kids were being just as bigoted as my father. Just 'cause my old man was an ass didn't make me one and they had—" His face spasmed. "They had no *right* to make me pay for what he did. They had no right to think I was as sick as he was."

"I'm glad Gilbert's views didn't rub off on you," I said.

Tyler stuck his hands in his pockets and chewed his lower lip.

"Did Gilbert ever talk to you about the Aryan Supremacy Party?" I asked.

"Sure. Or at least he talked about ASP all the time, not so much direct to me. It was supposed to be some sort of secret society—the membership list was secret, anyway. But he was always going on about this land they were buying out in Oregon and how they were going to set up this . . . what he called a 'pure state' where there wouldn't be any 'niggers or kikes or slant-eyes' or any of his other cute terms for people."

"Did any of the other ASP members hang around your house?"

"They'd show up off and on, I guess. Herb Keller was over practically every day. He lives next door."

"I've met him," I said.

"My dad and Herb'd talk about these guns they were stashing . . . to fend off some stupid attack they thought was coming. All sorts of paranoid survivalist bullshit. They'd spend hours on it, revving each other up." He pulled at his T-shirt. "They expected me to join, too, soon as I turn eighteen. But I would've figured some way to get out of it."

Tyler told me that Gilbert wanted to have the ASP emblem, the turquoise snake, tattooed on Tyler's arm as an eighteenth birthday gift. "And I was supposed to be grateful!" The boy's voice rose fiercely. "What kind of father would make his kid get a tattoo he doesn't even want and then call it a birthday gift?"

"A cruel, crazy one," I said.

"No shit." We turned a corner and headed back toward the Hoffman house.

"Was your father ever on any kind of stimulant medication as far as you can remember?" I asked.

"You mean like the stuff that killed him? Methylphenidate hydrochloride?" I nodded. "You think he might've committed suicide?"

"That's one possibility," I said, thinking that a couple of others were more probable.

Tyler shook his head. "I don't think he'd kill himself. Or, if he did, he'd go out in a blaze of glory, probably shoot himself, or set himself on fire in a public place. He'd probably take my mom and me out with him, too." Tyler really did seem to understand Hoffman's mentality. "I'm pretty sure he never took uppers," he said. "The problem was never pepping him up; it was calming him down, keeping him from flying into a rage."

"How did you know the name of the drug Gilbert was given, the fatal one?" I asked.

"I asked the county attorney's office," he said innocently, as though any seventeen-year-old would have done the same. "Then I looked everything up in the *Physician's Desk Reference.* Looks like the methylphenidate hydrochloride might not have killed him if he hadn't been on Nardil when he took it."

"I'm surprised the county attorney's people gave you that kind of information."

Tyler turned his palms skyward. "They didn't want to,

but I threatened to sue for it under the Freedom of Information Act—I learned about that in U.S. Government last year—so they told me."

I chuckled. This was one formidable young man. "Let's sit a minute," I said, perching on a low concrete retaining wall edging a raised front lawn. Tyler plopped his lanky frame next to me. "So what else did your library research tell you?" I asked him.

"Well . . . if you're taking Nardil, there's a whole list of things you're not supposed to mix with it. The doctor'd already told Gilbert about most of them."

"Like what?"

"Everything from foods that are aged, like cheese, to alcohol to caffeine to tranquilizers. Funny thing is, if you'd set out to kill Gilbert, you could probably be more certain it would work if you gave him a narcotic or a second kind of MAO inhibitor—that's the kind of drug Nardil is. Or . . . the *Physician's Desk Reference* also said people on that kind of drug have been known to die after taking a single dose of something called meperidine. It's some sort of depressant."

"So the murderer could've given him rat poison, too," I said. "Or he could've used a gun. That'd probably be more efficient, certainly more predictable. What's your point?"

"Sure, but don't you see? If you shot him or used an obvious poison, everybody'd know right off he'd been murdered." The boy shook his head. "I think whoever drugged Gilbert's drink hoped his death would be chalked up to natural causes."

"But you're saying that using methylphenidate hydrochloride might not have killed him."

"All I'm saying—if I understand it right—is that you'd have to give him quite a lot of methylphenidate hydrochloride to make sure he . . . well, to kill him. You could give him a smaller quantity of some of these other drugs and be more sure of the same result."

"And," I said, seeing the light, "if you were a doctor, you'd know that sort of detail."

Tyler nodded and pulled at a piece of grass. "If you were a doctor, you'd also have access to whatever drug would be most efficient, no questions asked." He thrust the piece of grass between his teeth and chewed on the tender base. "I think whoever killed Gilbert used what they used because they had it handy . . . and because they figured it would throw suspicion on Dr. Levy if it was discovered."

"That makes sense," I said. Yet I felt uneasy. Tyler Hoffman knew almost too much about which drugs might be fatal to Gilbert. He must realize his knowledge threw suspicion on himself, especially when he admitted despising his old man. So why was he telling me all this? Either he was completely guileless, I thought, or he was playing a sophisticated game with me. It was possible Tyler knew I'd probably find out all of this anyway. By being so frank about his feelings and his research, he might be trying to convince me that he—and his mother —had nothing to hide.

"Sounds like you've been giving this a lot of thought," I said. "Where do you think the murderer got the fatal pills?"

"Could be anywhere. Legal source. Illegal source. If you've got the money and you know where to look. . . . All you've got to do is go down to Selby-Dale or lower Hennepin Avenue, someplace like that, put in your order. You can get anything you want." He squinted up at the sun.

I knew that, of course. But I found it somehow disconcerting to hear Tyler Hoffman admit so casually that he knew it, too. I would have to learn more about this young man who'd been raised by two neurotic, possibly even psychotic, parents. I hoped I'd be happy with what I turned up . . . for Tyler Hoffman's sake, as well as for David Levy's.

— 29 —

I left the Hoffman house feeling uneasy. I wanted to believe that young Tyler's detailed knowledge about Gilbert's medication and his cause of death was innocent. Still . . . Tyler was different from any teenagers I knew. None of them would have attempted this kind of research. Or, if they had, they probably wouldn't have understood it. I decided Roddy Caldwell might be able to help me put my interview with Tyler into the proper perspective.

Highland Park High was only about a mile away and, on this visit, I got lucky. I found Caldwell in his chemistry classroom, calculating his final semester's grades.

I peered through the window in the closed door at the classroom with its two rows of tables holding Bunsen burners and various size beakers, flasks, and test tubes. A row of locked glass-front cabinets along one wall held bottles and jars of chemicals. Roddy sat on a tall stool at the head table, his head bent over a grade book, punching numbers into a pocket-size calculator. I knocked lightly on the door, then opened it. A pungent chemical smell assaulted me.

Caldwell looked up with a smile. "Devon, hi! Must be ESP. I was just sitting here, praying a beautiful damsel in distress would appear to brighten my day . . . and here you are."

"Anyone ever tell you you're full of shit, Roddy?" I asked, smiling back.

"All the time. But I've been told it makes me that

much more appealing to the opposite sex." His face had a boyish, eager-to-please quality.

I laughed. "You may have a point there. The girls in the school office find you pretty irresistible," I told him.

"I'm flattered, but the truth is I prefer older women. Let me guess—you've come to tell me you've changed your mind about going out with me."

I shook my head. "Maybe later, but right now, this damsel is too busy getting herself out of all this distress to think about a social life."

"So what can I do to hurry things along?" He clicked off the calculator and gestured toward a second stool. "Sit down and tell me about it."

I described my conversation with Tyler Hoffman and my concerns about the boy.

Caldwell shook his head. "That's just Tyler. I'm not a bit surprised he's learned everything there is to know about what killed his old man. Frankly, I'd be shocked if he hadn't."

"But don't you see, Roddy, how it looks to people who don't know the kid . . . and I don't mean just me. Here we've got a boy whose father abused both him and his mother. He's some sort of genius in chemistry. He learns what drug combinations will cause his old man's death. Then, lo and behold, the old man dies from just such a drug mixture."

"Isn't your timetable a little cockeyed there, Devon? You make it sound as though Ty learned all this *before* his father died, not afterward."

"So who knows? If it comes to that, can Tyler prove he didn't know all this weeks ago, long before his father swallowed those fatal pills, long enough before so Tyler could've scored the drugs, put them in Gilbert's Thermos, and tried to pin the whole thing on Ben Levy?"

"Hey, I thought you were innocent until proven guilty in this country."

"Sure," I said sourly. "Just like Ben Levy."

"So what do you want from me?"

"I don't know," I said. "Reassurance, I guess. To be honest, Roddy, I've never met a kid quite like Tyler before. And I've got a suspicious nature. I guess I want you to convince me he's not guilty."

Caldwell leaned against the table. "Ty had the motivation, sure. Old man Hoffman was a certifiable bastard. But, if you knew this kid, you'd know he hasn't got a violent bone in his body. Between you and me, there were times I tried to get Ty to be more aggressive, more physical. Maybe his father had a point about that. Ty doesn't impress people as . . . well, as terribly masculine, I guess, despite his size."

"What do you mean?"

Caldwell bit his lip and thought. "I'm not sure just how to put this . . . he's got sort of a bookish demeanor and it's hard to picture him defending himself with anything but his mind. It—it's like the minute Ty feels threatened, his hands go into his pockets. He cowers, he hides, he tries to run away, even if it's only mentally. He uses his superior intelligence to distance himself from people like his father. You just can't picture this kid ever punching somebody out, fighting back, no matter how much he might want to."

Maybe, I thought, Tyler just doesn't fight back openly.

"Listen," Caldwell said. "Why don't you talk to Marietta Tilsen? She knows Ty as well as anybody."

"Marietta's Tyler's girlfriend?"

"Right. She works here at school part-time." He glanced at the wall clock above the supply cabinets. "Comes in about four every day to tend to the animals in the biology room. She should be here in fifteen minutes or so."

Roddy unlocked the biology classroom and kept me company while I waited for Marietta Tilsen. The place had a faint smell of small animals in cages, reminiscent of zoos. I counted four white mice, a pair of gerbils, and three rabbits in cages, as well as half a dozen hen's eggs incubating under a warm light. The Tilsen girl was right on time. Caldwell introduced us and returned to his chemistry lab across the hall, leaving us alone with the animals.

Marietta was a tall, reed-thin girl with a curtain of blond hair that fell to her waist. Her features were a bit too severe for classic prettiness, but she was undeniably striking. She unlocked a wall cabinet and removed a large paper sack filled with food pellets. "I suppose you want to ask me about Tyler's father," she said, scooping out some of the pellets and transferring them to a clear plastic feeder on the side of the gerbils' cage.

"Yes," I said, "and about Tyler too. I'm investigating the murder of Gilbert Hoffman."

"Ty told me." Her blue eyes were clear and frank. "He tells me everything."

I smiled. "Did you know Mr. Hoffman well?"

She shook her head; her fair hair rippled over her shoulders. "I met him once or twice, but he made it quite clear he didn't like me. After that, I stayed away from the house if he was home."

"Does that mean you went there when Gilbert was away?"

"Sometimes after school. And once in a while I would stop by in the morning if Ty needed a ride to school. But not very often."

"Tyler didn't want his father to know he was seeing you."

She nodded, then opened the cage door, lifted out a small furry animal, and held it up at eye level. "I bet you're starving, aren't you, Laurel?" She stroked its tiny back with an index finger. "Her mate here is Hardy," Marietta told me. "You want to hold one?"

I declined, pleading my allergy to fur. As she reached for the male gerbil, the girl placed the female on her shoulder, where it balanced precariously, gripping her loose hair with its claws. I wondered whether gerbils carry fleas.

"What about Mrs. Hoffman?" I asked. "How did she feel about you and Tyler?"

Marietta shrugged and Laurel scampered to regain her balance. "I don't think she minded, as long as Ty's dad didn't find out. But with that sort of woman, it's hard to tell what they're really thinking."

"What sort is that?"

"Oh, you know . . . neurotic, I guess. Mrs. Hoffman seems scared of her own shadow. You saw her at the funeral . . . I remember you sat in the back row next to Mr. Caldwell." I nodded. "Well, she was shaking something terrible. Ty practically had to hold her up during the ceremony."

"Mrs. Hoffman did seem nervous," I said.

"And another thing. You'd think she'd be relieved to be rid of that man, but, no, all she does is moan and groan about how hard it's going to be for her and Ty to get along without him. You ask me, Mr. Hoffman's death is the best thing ever happened to her." She voiced her opinion firmly.

"Does Tyler share your view?"

"Well, *sure*. Why wouldn't he?" Her tone told me Tyler agreed with all her opinions.

"The man was his father."

She efficiently finished cleaning the gerbils' cage and affectionately replaced its occupants. They scurried greedily toward their feeder. "Mr. Hoffman was more like a warden than a father, Ms. MacDonald. Now Ty's got opportunities in front of him, and nobody holding him back. If he gets going on it right away, I think he can get a scholarship to Harvard next year."

"Why Harvard?"

The look she flashed me said only an idiot would ask such a question. "It's the best college in the country. If you go to Harvard, you're way ahead. That's where I'm going . . . for my undergraduate work, anyway. I haven't decided about grad school yet."

"Do you have a scholarship?"

"Not yet. I'll apply, of course, but even if I can't get a scholarship, that won't stop me. It's incredibly expensive, but my grandfather left me a trust fund for college, and I can always take out loans and work if I run short. I'm not afraid of work." Marietta Tilsen didn't look as though she'd be afraid of anything. She opened the rabbit cage, the most odoriferous of the lot.

"What did Tyler tell you about his father's death, Marietta?"

"Like how he died, that sort of thing?"

"Let's start with how he felt about it."

Her nose crinkled. "Well, he was shocked at first, of course. Who wouldn't be? But, frankly, after a while it started to seem like kind of a lucky break . . . at least until the police began saying Ty's dad had been murdered."

"And then what happened?"

The girl pulled a loose-limbed black rabbit from the cage and cradled it in her arms. "I—I think Ty got scared. You know how the police always think it's the family who did it. I guess he was afraid he'd be accused, or his mom would. I know that's crazy. I mean, anyone who knows Ty knows he wouldn't hurt a fly and Mrs. Hoffman is such a wimp. If she did want to kill her husband, I doubt she'd even know what to do, and where would she get the pills? Then, when the police arrested somebody else—"

"Tyler was relieved?"

"That he and his mom were off the hook, sure, but he didn't want it to be this Dr. Levy who did it. I guess you know about Dr. Levy's being Ty's real dad. Boy, was that a surprise!" She stroked the rabbit. "This whole thing has been really rough on Ty. I just hope he can get over it quick and get on with his life. I mean, if he screws up his senior year, he'll never get into a decent college, and then what? His whole future's at stake."

"A few grades can't be that serious, Marietta. Certainly any school would consider a boy with Tyler's brains an asset, even if he didn't get an A in every subject he ever studied."

She shook her head adamantly. "That's not the way the really top colleges look at it. You just don't know the kind of competition kids have today. Some of the best universities have two hundred applicants for every opening, and if you don't go to the right college, you'll never get into the right graduate school. If you don't go to the right grad school, you can't get the best jobs. Believe me, nowadays you can screw up your whole life just by slacking off in high school. Nobody cares why you did it, either." Her young face was a study in anguish. "Things were a lot different when you were young," she told me.

I tried not to dwell on my rapidly advancing age. Yet, although I hardly felt old, the girl was right. Things were different when I was her age. I couldn't identify with today's youth and their sense of urgency about acquiring that new BMW or designer wardrobe or house in the upscale neighborhood. I couldn't relate to their panicky efforts to achieve success—defined solely in financial terms—before they were thirty. Thinking about it depressed me. I forced my mind back to the case. "Marietta," I said, "Tyler seems to know quite a lot about what killed his father."

She put the rabbit back into its cage and added a dish filled with clean water, then latched the door. "Ty is going to be a research biologist," she said. "He'd be interested in that sort of thing even if it weren't his own father who died."

"What about you? What are you going to be?" Somehow I knew she'd have it all planned.

"A veterinarian."

If ambition were even half the battle, Marietta Tilsen

already had it won. "When Mr. Hoffman first started taking his medication—the Nardil," I asked her, "did Ty discuss it with you?"

She gave me a sideways glance. "Anything wrong with that?"

"No, Marietta, nothing's wrong with it. I'm just trying to get everything in perspective."

"Tyler didn't kill his father, Ms. MacDonald, so don't go trying to pin it on him." Mother cats protect their kittens with less ferocity.

"That's the last thing I want to do, believe me. Listen, Marietta, I'm sure Tyler told you about Dr. Levy's son, David, and the bone marrow transplant. Well, what I really want to do is clear both Ben Levy and Tyler. That's the only way little David is ever going to have a decent chance at life. I'm not trying to pin anything on Tyler; I'm just trying to get at the truth. If Tyler's innocent, the truth can only help him."

She was silent for a moment. I waited her out. "I guess you're right," she decided. "Sure, Ty told me about the medication. The truth is he was worried. He was afraid whatever mental illness his father had was hereditary. So we researched it. We learned as much as we could about mental conditions that run in families."

"And about the effects of Nardil."

"Uh-huh."

"This was when Tyler first learned about his father's medication?"

"Well, yeah, but actually we started reading about abnormal psychology way before that."

"I understand. Ty was worried he might end up . . . well, I guess you could call it crazy . . . like his father. So he read up on mental illness and tried to diagnose exactly what his father's psychological problem was. Then, when Mr. Hoffman's doctor put him on Nardil, Ty learned what he could about that medication."

"Ty was worried that he might be a carrier, too, that even if he was all right, he might pass it on to his . . . to our children. Ty and I plan to get married. Not until we've both finished school and we've gotten started in our careers, of course, but . . . well, Ty said it wouldn't be fair for me to marry him if our kids had any chance of being like his dad." Her eyes filled but no tears spilled over. "Ty's always been scared of insanity."

"He won't have to worry about passing on Gilbert Hoffman's genes anymore," I said quietly.

"That's something to be thankful for." She turned back and began to tend to one of the cages of white mice.

"Yes," I said, "it is." I wished I could reassure Marietta that the young man she'd so carefully planned her future with wasn't a murderer. But, unfortunately, what she had told me merely reinforced the idea that Tyler Hoffman had known exactly how to kill Gilbert well in advance of that fatal day. And so, I realized, did Marietta Tilsen.

— **30** —

It was almost closing time when I returned to Sherman and MacDonald, Private Investigators. I climbed the stairs to the second floor and, as I approached the office door, found a pale, balding man in a gray suit and maroon tie standing in the hallway. He looked uncomfortably warm in the late afternoon heat. "May I help you?" I asked him.

"No, thanks," he said, avoiding my eyes. He seemed embarrassed that I'd noticed him.

"If you're here to see somebody at Sherman and MacDonald, we're just about to close."

"I'll just wait out here," he said obscurely.

"It's a free country," I said, reaching for the doorknob.

It wouldn't turn. Damn Paula, I thought; she must have sneaked out early again. That habit certainly didn't help business.

I fished in my purse for my key and let myself in. Paula was sitting at her desk, staring into space. "What the— Paula, why is this door locked? It's not five o'clock."

She turned her bloodshot brown eyes in my direction. Her mascara was streaked and she had chewed the lipstick off her bottom lip. "Don't let him in, Devon," she begged. "I'm not going to talk to him."

"What are you talking about? Who is that guy?"

"Stuart," she said. "Stuart Lindblom."

"You mean *the* Stuart Lindblom, the dentist?"

Paula bit her lip and nodded gravely. I began to laugh. I don't know exactly how I'd imagined Paula's two-timing lover boy would look, but the meek little man cowering in our hallway wasn't it.

"It's not funny," Paula said, taking quick offense. "He kept calling and calling and now he's come over here, trying to get me to talk to him. I saw him coming and locked the door, but I know he's out there waiting for me."

"So why don't you just tell him to go home to his wife?"

"I can't do that, Devon. You know I haven't got any willpower. If I so much as see him, talk to him, I know he'll look at me with those sexy eyes of his and I'll just melt. Next thing you know, I'll forget all about his wife and end up stuck in another dead-end romance." She thumped her fist on the desk, careful not to chip her nails. "Why is it that nice men, the kind who want to get married and settle down and have kids, never fall in love with *me?*"

I thought it might have something to do with Paula's sexpot image, but I didn't say so. She was one of those women who'd never recognized that Marilyn Monroe has been dead for a quarter century. "So what are you going to do about it?" I asked. "You can't hide in here all night."

"I—I don't know." She looked forlorn. "Devon, do you suppose you could tell him . . . you know, just tell him I'm not going to see him? Ask him to leave? You're so aggress— I mean assertive. Maybe he'll listen to you."

I groaned, but agreed to do the dirty work. Tossing my purse on my desk, I returned to the hallway. Paula's suitor was still lurking. "Dr. Lindblom," I said in my most aggress— er, assertive manner. "Ms. Carboni asked me to tell you that she does not wish to see you again and that she wants you to stop bothering her."

For an uncomfortable moment, I feared the man actually was going to cry. Then he whined, "But why? All I ask is that she tell me why. I think I'm entitled to know that much."

Sometimes men really amaze me. "It's quite simple," I told him crisply. "You make her feel superfluous, unnecessary, redundant."

"I don't understand."

I sighed. "I'll spell it out for you, Doctor. You've got a wife, and Paula doesn't like auditioning for a part that's already been filled. Get the picture?"

"Wife? What wife? I'm not married."

I shook my head. "Dr. Lindblom, maybe you can bullshit my secretary, but it doesn't work on me. Paula told me she called your office last week and your wife answered the phone."

A look of astonishment crossed his face. "But that's impossible. I'm not married, I swear it."

"Try swearing to some more gullible female. The fact is Mrs. Lindblom answers your phone."

He broke into a fit of high-pitched giggles. "Mother!" he screeched. "Mrs. Lindblom is my *mother!*"

Ten minutes later I had determined that Stuart Lindblom's receptionist had called in sick two days last week. His mother, with whom he lived, had taken over until the woman returned to work. Feeling guilty for what I'd said to him, I promised I would relay his story to Paula and, a short time later, the two lovebirds had made up and asked my permission to flee to a more private perch. I agreed to close up for the day.

As I watched them leave, Paula's face alight with hope, I suspected she might find Mrs. Lindblom the mother to be a bigger obstacle to matrimony with Stuart than the dreaded, if fictitious, Mrs. Lindblom the wife.

Sam's office was empty, but he'd left a note on my desk. *Barry dropped this off. Sends his best. I'm off to courthouse on Levy case, then home. See you tomorrow a.m. with research. Sam.* Attached was a copy of Leon Jackson's rap sheet.

It had been a long day and I was tired. I sank into my chair and began reading the document. The story it told wasn't unusual for a troubled young man from a bad neighborhood. Jackson's arrest record dated back to shortly after his eighteenth birthday. He probably had a juvenile record, too, but that would have been sealed when he reached adulthood. This one began with two arrests for burglary, one resulting in a conviction and suspended sentence. A later conviction for assault had brought him ten months in Stillwater State Prison. Then he had apparently stayed clean for nearly two years. His most recent conviction was four years before and it had sent him back to Stillwater to serve two and a half. It was for possession and sale of a controlled substance.

I found this entry particularly depressing, although it really did no more than confirm what I already knew must be true—that Leon Jackson knew how and where to get any kind of drug he wanted. You could say the same about any streetwise twelve-year-old in the Twin Cities.

Jackson had a motive to kill Hoffman, that was certain. The man had ridden him mercilessly, yet Jackson had made it clear to me that he couldn't afford to quit his job. It was even possible that Hoffman had threatened to fire the black man for some real or imagined transgression. Had Jackson carefully planned to get rid of Hoffman permanently, then waited for a moment when his boss's death, if it were ever classified as murder, could be blamed on somebody else?

If so, Ben and Gloria Levy's visit to Hoffman would have provided Jackson with that perfect opportunity. He'd overheard what went on when the Levys came to see Hoffman at the meat market that first night. He'd even helped stop Hoffman's assault on Levy. Fact was, Jackson's intervention might have prompted Hoffman to give him his notice. Certainly the older man would have resented the interference.

Jackson easily could have put a handful of pills in Hoffman's Thermos the next morning and then, when Levy arrived, sneaked out to plant a few leftovers in the unsuspecting doctor's car. Then all Jackson would have to do was sit back and wait for Hoffman to drink his daily ration of juice. And make sure that Hoffman was close to death before he summoned the paramedics.

If I could prove that, or even present a strong enough case that Jackson *could* have killed Hoffman, it might be enough to cast reasonable doubt on Ben Levy's arrest. Yet that prospect didn't raise my spirits much. I certainly didn't want Ben Levy convicted, but neither did I want to pin the crime on a possibly innocent Leon Jackson. With his background, he'd be even less able to defend himself than my client.

With a sigh, I put Leon Jackson's rap sheet in my file on the case. Jackson's name would stay high on my list of suspects.

— 31 —

An hour later, I was at home trying to cool off my tiny attic oven of an apartment and preparing a cold tuna salad for my dinner. The five thousand BTUs of window air conditioner groaned and drooled down the side of the sweating old house. In half an hour, the indoor temperature had dropped a mere three degrees, to eighty-nine.

I'd poured myself a glass of iced tea and was adding low-fat mayo to a can of tuna when the phone rang. It was Francine Levy. "I have good news," she said. "The judge lowered Ben's bail and he'll be out in a couple of hours."

"That's great!"

"I'll drive him down to Rochester to see Davy as soon as he's packed."

"Have him call me before he leaves town," I said, wishing I'd taken time to talk to Ben Levy earlier.

Francine also announced she'd made an appointment for Tyler Hoffman to undergo blood tests at nine the next morning at the University Hospitals. The lab had agreed to rush the test results to the Mayo Clinic; by Monday, we would know whether Tyler was an acceptable bone marrow donor for his half-brother.

I called Myra Hoffman and volunteered to drive her and Tyler to the U in the morning. I wasn't looking forward to the unpleasant memories being back in a hospital would evoke, but Myra didn't drive. Only by providing transportation did I feel confident that the Hoffmans would show up for the tests. Although Myra agreed to the appointment, I could hear resistance in her voice. I hung up before she could change her mind and called Sam to postpone our information-pooling session. He had a lunch meeting scheduled with a new attorney client, so we agreed to meet at the office at three.

While I waited to hear from Benjamin Levy, I put some Mendelssohn on the stereo and picked at my tuna salad. The heat made me groggy; I had almost dozed off when the phone rang.

Ben Levy spoke rapidly. "I just can't take the time to talk now. Davy's waiting for me."

"It won't take long, Dr. Levy—Ben. I really need to ask you some questions about that morning when Hoffman—"

"Sorry. Not now. I'm just going to jump in the shower—God, I don't know if I'll *ever* get the stink of that place off me—and then I'm heading straight to Rochester. I'm sure you can understand."

I did. "Go ahead. Take your shower and pack a bag. I'll be there in twenty minutes to drive you to Rochester."

Benjamin Levy tossed a khaki canvas duffel bag into the hatchback of the Honda and, bending his tall frame to keep from hitting his head, climbed into the passenger's seat beside me. The past few days hadn't been kind to him. His narrow face was lined and gray, and he had the wild-eyed look of a man long deprived of sleep. His hands trembled as he fastened his seat belt.

Levy seemed to brighten when I reassured him that Tyler would undergo the awaited medical tests the next morning. "My sister told me you'd arranged it, but I was afraid the boy might back out."

It wasn't Tyler's backing out I feared; it was his unstable mother's, but I saw no point in burdening Levy with my own worries in addition to his own. As darkness fell, I drove south, then turned east on Highway 494 across the Minnesota River, then south again on Highway 55 to the junction with Highway 52. As I piloted the Honda through the sparsely populated farmlands south of the Twin Cities, I steered the conversation toward

Levy's confrontations with the man who had raised Tyler Hoffman. "I need to hear everything you can remember about that morning when you came back to see Gilbert Hoffman at the butcher shop," I told him.

Levy exhaled loudly and stared out the window at the passing scenery. "God, that was a stupid move." He made a fist and struck his right knee a sharp blow. "All I can think is that somebody wanted Hoffman dead. A man like him, they must've been standing in line for the chance to get rid of him, 'specially if they could pin it on somebody else. And there I was—'sucker' written all over me. What a jerk!"

"Just tell me what happened." I rolled up my window as we passed the stench belching from the Pine Bend refinery.

Levy's story was much the same that Leon Jackson had told me. "Hoffman assaulted me the night before when I tried to tell him about Davy. I suppose I deserved it. It was stupid of me to present that kind of information to him cold. Chalk it up to desperation." Levy took a monogrammed handkerchief from his pocket and wiped his damp face. "Then, the next morning . . . well, I—I just couldn't give up that easily. I guess I had this fantasy that he'd go home and sleep on it, talk it over with his wife. Once he'd cooled off, I hoped he'd do the right thing."

"Instead he went home and beat the hell out of his wife."

Levy shot me a pained expression. "I never meant—"

"I know that, and I hope Mrs. Hoffman knows that. But still—"

"I really screwed up, didn't I?"

"Sorry, I didn't mean to make it any harder," I said. "This case is getting to me and the heat never improves my disposition, either. Let's get back to the morning in question. You went back to see Hoffman for a second time about when?"

"Ten, maybe ten-thirty, I think."

"And you parked behind the shop?"

"I was hoping to catch Hoffman alone. I thought maybe part of the reason he got so riled up the night before was because there were other people around and he felt he had to defend his . . ."

"Manhood?"

"I suppose. Something like that. Anyway, I figured he might react differently if I saw him alone."

"So you went in the back door. Was it locked?"

"No . . ." He thought a moment. "I knocked and the other butcher—the young black guy who'd been there the night before—"

"Leon Jackson."

"Right, Leon; I remember his name tag said Leon. Anyway, this Leon fellow was sitting in the back room there, smoking. He opened the door and let me in, but I'm pretty sure it wasn't locked. It was only a flimsy screen door anyway, but— No, I definitely can't recall him unlatching it."

"Jackson seem surprised to see you?"

"I suppose he was. Made some smart remark—can't remember just what he said. What it amounted to was I must be crazy. Then he sort of smiled and told me to wait there in the back and he'd get his boss."

"How long before Hoffman showed up?"

Levy rolled down his window and sucked in air. With the refinery behind us, we were once again assaulted by the nighttime smells of pollen and freshly tilled earth. "I don't know. Ten minutes at the most."

"What were you doing while you waited?"

"Just waiting. . . . I don't know. Looking around, getting nervous."

"Anybody come in while you were waiting?"

"No. Well, Gloria came to the door. She was getting worried waiting out there by herself. But I sent her back to the car."

"Gloria?"

"My wife. You know Gloria."

177

"Sure, I know her. I just didn't realize she was with you that morning."

"Well, I wouldn't say she was exactly *with* me. Except for that minute or two, she was waiting out in the car. I didn't want her to come with me at all, but she insisted. So we compromised. I said she could come along, but she'd have to wait outside."

I digested that bit of information. "Tell me how Hoffman acted when he saw you'd come back."

Levy bit his lip. "He—he hadn't mellowed overnight."

"And?"

"He swore at me and I left."

"I got a somewhat more graphic description of your confrontation from Leon Jackson."

"So, what can I tell you? Jackson hung around in the doorway, watching. I don't know—maybe he was just nosy, or maybe he wanted to make sure Hoffman didn't become violent. Anyway, the man became verbally abusive, so I left."

"Did you come back again?"

"No way. I got back in my car and drove home."

"You're sure the only other person you saw in that shop was your wife?"

"Gloria only came as far as the back door. She didn't come inside."

"No meat deliveries, no customers, no maintenance people, no mailman?"

"Uh uh."

"Notice anybody parked out back?"

Levy fixed his vision on the divided road ahead. "I—I can't really say. I'm trying to picture it."

"Take your time. It could be very important."

"I think that alley handles parking for a couple of other businesses. So I couldn't say that anybody out back was there for the butcher shop."

"Just try to remember everything you can."

"There was a UPS truck, I think, but I can't remember

whether it was still there by the time we left. And a couple of other cars—"

"Anyone inside them?"

Levy shook his head. "I just can't remember. Might've been. Might not've been. The best I can recall is that the parking spots in the alley were pretty well taken up, but I really wasn't paying attention."

We drove in silence for a time, then, as we approached Rochester, Levy spoke of his hopes for his son. The man's anguish pierced my heart. I took the Southwest Second Street exit off Highway 52 and made my way around the one-way roads to Center Street. The Mayo Clinic dominates Rochester, but it isn't actually a hospital. Mayo's patients are hospitalized at either St. Mary's or Methodist Hospitals. David Levy was a patient at Methodist, a block north of the Mayo Building. "Ask your wife to try to remember any vehicles or people she may have seen behind the butcher shop that morning," I told Levy as I pulled the car into the curb in front of the hospital. "I'll need her observations."

Levy opened his door. "Come up with me and you can ask her right now."

I looked up at Methodist Hospital, a modern-looking tan building with glass picture windows across the front, and my spine tightened. "No . . . I'm parked on a red curb."

"Don't worry about it. If you get a ticket, bill me for it. Come on."

"But—"

"Come on, Devon. Just leave the car here. Nobody's going to bother it this time of night."

I sighed and turned off the engine. Grimly, I followed the lanky doctor through the sterile marble lobby and into the elevator. When we reached David's floor, I hung back. My legs were having trouble supporting me as we made our way past the empty family lounge. "It's got to be way past visiting hours," I said.

"On David's ward, nobody pays attention to those rules."

Because the cases there are so hopeless time doesn't matter, I thought. I was having trouble getting enough air into my lungs.

"We have to wash our hands here before we go onto the BMT ward," Levy told me, rolling up his sleeves and gesturing toward a stainless steel sink at the edge of the ward. I ran cool water over my wrists in an effort to calm myself; it didn't help much.

The Bone Marrow Transplant unit was built in a circular fashion, with the patients' brightly colored rooms around the circumference and the round nurses' station in the middle. Levy approached room number seven. "Wait here and I'll send Gloria out to talk to you."

I waited by the nurses' station. Through the glass door of the room, I could see Levy's long arms envelop his son. The tableau began to blur. I surreptitiously wiped my eyes. A young nurse, her tent-shaped white uniform covering a close-to-term pregnancy, emerged from the room. "He sure is happy to see his daddy," she said, smiling at me.

"Uh-huh." I tried to smile back, but my mouth was too crooked. I wanted to ask her how she could continue to work there—a baby growing in her belly—tending other people's dying children.

I'd regained some of my composure by the time Gloria Levy emerged from David's room. Tonight she was dressed in a peach-colored cotton knit shift and matching high-heeled sandals. Her hair was pulled back into the ballerina's bun she'd worn the night I met her and large gold hoops hung from her dainty ears. Tiny lines around her mouth were the only visible sign of the tension she must have been under. "Hello, Devon. I appreciate your driving Benjamin down. He says you want to speak with me."

I thrust my hands in the pockets of my skirt and

glanced at David's room, then back at Gloria. "It won't take long."

"It's all right. David needs a few minutes alone with his father. Shall we go down to the lounge?"

We sat on one of the pale tweed sofas. Our images were reflected in windows that were glossy black against the night—a cool brunette and a rattled strawberry blonde. A passerby might have mistaken me for the distraught mother and Gloria Levy for the well-controlled detective. Yet when it came to powers of observation, Gloria left something to be desired. I led her over and over the events of Gilbert Hoffman's last morning, with little to show for my efforts. "I'm sorry," she said. "I know the alley was crowded—we had trouble parking—but I can't remember anything specific. There was one truck, a big blue one, I think, with some sort of meat company name on it. It drove through the alley and the driver gave me a dirty look. Maybe I was in his parking place."

"Anyone else you can remember driving past? Anybody at all?"

"Not specifically. It seems as though there were two or three cars, American ones, I think. Nothing unusual about them. But I just can't be more specific than that." She glanced at the dainty gold watch adorning her left wrist. "It's getting late, Devon. I'd like to get back to say goodnight to David before he goes to sleep."

"Of course. If you remember anything, no matter how trivial it may seem, please give me a call."

I stood in the hospital hallway and watched Gloria Levy walk back to her dying son, her spine correctly straight and her heels clicking softly on the immaculate marble floor. Then I let out my breath and hurried toward the elevator.

Next morning, I stepped into a cool salmon-colored cotton dress and was at the Hoffman house by eight-thirty, exhausted from my night's drive but running on adrenaline. Myra opened the front door as soon as I rang the bell, but she was still dressed in a pink summer bathrobe, her hair disheveled and her face unwashed. She stepped back to let me enter the house. The living room was still a shambles, obviously untouched since the day before.

"Myra," I said, "you'll have to hurry or we'll be late getting to the hospital."

"What about the money?" Myra's pale hand made a grasping motion. "What did they say about the money?"

"The Levys will give you money, Myra, but I can't get it today. Ben just got out of jail last night. David's condition took a turn for the worse and they had to make an emergency trip to Mayo."

She shook her head stubbornly. "We need the money. Once Tyler donates this bone marrow they want, they won't need us anymore. They'll never pay then. Gilbert always said, give people credit, they'll cheat you every time."

Shit. I didn't need this. "Myra, listen to me. The Levys are honorable people. They won't cheat you, honest. They said they'd give you some money, and that's what they'll do, but there's just no way I can get it today. You'll just have to trust—"

"Don't pay any attention to her." Tyler was dressed neatly in casual gray slacks and a gray-and-blue-striped sport shirt. His wet hair had been meticulously combed into place. "She's just scared to go out to the hospital, so she's making excuses." He placed a hand on his mother's shoulder. "You don't have to go, Ma, but you can't stop me. I don't care about getting paid. David's my brother, and if I can keep him alive, I'm gonna do it."

Myra jerked away from Tyler's touch. "But your college, Tyler. They owe you that mu—"

"They don't owe me shit, Ma!" The boy's voice demonstrated a strength of purpose I hadn't seen in him before. "Anybody owes me, it's you. It's time you did something for *me,* instead of just protecting yourself all the time. Now keep quiet and sign whatever it takes for me to do this thing. It's me, Tyler, asking you, not the Levys . . . and you owe me this much. If they want to give us something afterward, okay, but I'm gonna do this for only one reason—because it's *right.*"

Myra seemed to shrink into herself as her son gained strength. She nodded meekly.

"You're not coming with us?" I asked her.

"I—I can't," she whispered. She bit her lip and hugged herself as though to keep warm; the morning heat was already above eighty degrees. The woman obviously needed psychiatric help, but David Levy couldn't wait until she got it.

I sighed. "Tyler, please get us a piece of paper and a pen." When he'd returned with the materials, I instructed Myra to write out her permission for her son to undergo today's medical tests, then to sign and date it. I put my signature under her name, as witness. I told her I would bring the proper hospital documents for her to sign later, but this written permission should allow Tyler's tests to begin.

As we left the Pascal Street house, I saw Myra Hoffman standing framed in the doorway. Her face was forlorn as she watched her son, her sole link to the outside world, leave her behind. Alone. I wondered how safe she felt now.

* * *

Tyler breezed through his tests, good-humoredly badgering the nurses and lab technicians with technical questions about what they were doing to him and how they would learn from it. I understood little about either his questions or the amused and patient staff's answers, but listening helped distract me from my discomfort over being in a hospital for the second time in about twelve hours. It was easier this morning, but this was just lab work; I didn't have to see any sick kids. What I was able to comprehend from Tyler's Q and A was that this preliminary blood workup would be the easy part. If the results turned out favorably, the next step would involve an extraction of his bone marrow, a much more painful procedure that would be done in Rochester.

"If I go down to the Mayo Clinic, will I be able to meet David?" Tyler asked eagerly as I drove him back to St. Paul.

"I suppose so," I said.

"They'll have him in a clean room, you know," he said, his face grave. "What they'll be doing is giving him chemotherapy to destroy his defective bone marrow. That's why he has to be kept away from germs; when his bone marrow is all gone, he won't be able to fight off infection. Then they'll inject him with some of my good bone marrow and, if things work out right, it'll start to grow in David's body . . ."

Suddenly I was hit with an image of a weak, bald little boy imprisoned inside a sterile bubble to keep him away from the disease-ridden outer world. In a way, it was not unlike Myra Hoffman's self-imposed exile, except this one might be fatal. Tears welled up in my eyes, but I refused to blink and send them careening down my cheeks.

". . . so what do you think? Will I get to see him?" Tyler continued.

I took a deep breath. "I—I don't know, Tyler. Maybe if you wear sterile clothing and a mask the doctors will let you into his room, but I can't promise. Say," I said, wanting to change the subject, "I met your girlfriend yesterday."

"Yeah, she told me."

"She says you two want to go to Harvard. Sounds like she's got your lives all planned."

A broad grin stole over his face. "Marietta's all right. She's just paranoid about missing out on something important in life." He laughed. "Harvard! Can you imagine *me* at Harvard? Geez, I never even thought I'd make it to the U."

I had no trouble whatsoever picturing Tyler Hoffman at Harvard. Any college should consider itself damned lucky to get him.

Myra was dressed in an old-fashioned middy blouse and black slacks when we returned to the house. Her hands fidgeted constantly with the blouse's black ties, rolling the ends between her fingers until they were limp.

I laid out the hospital papers on the dining table for her. She grabbed at them. "Just tell me where I sign." Her eyes darted nervously between the documents and the hallway. She was obviously eager to have the task of signing finished and me gone. It didn't take long for me to realize why.

A man's foot kicked open the hall door to the basement and Herb Keller emerged, carrying a large cardboard box. "I thought I heard voices up here, Myra." His cold eyes fixed on me. "What are *you* doing here?"

"I brought some papers for Mrs. Hoffman to sign."

"What kind of papers? What're you doing with this bitch, Myra?"

"It's just somethin' to do with Tyler, Herb," Myra said in a small voice. "It's nothin', really." She extended her arms across the table in a futile attempt to hide the printed forms. But Keller didn't approach us.

"Better be nothin'." Keller shifted the box to his left hip. "Gil wouldn't like you gettin' tight with this god-damn Jew-lover and you know it. Hell, woman, don't you know she's workin' for the kike that killed your husband? You know what's good for you, you'll get her outa here." He turned and stomped out the back door.

I took a deep breath and waited until I was sure most of the fury was gone from my voice. "What was Keller carrying out of here?"

"Just some of Gilbert's records," she said quickly. "Nothin' but old boxes he kept in the basement."

"ASP records?"

"I—I guess so. That's what Herb said, that he was takin' over for Gil and he had to get some club property Gil'd been keepin' here. I don't know anything about that stuff. I never go down in the cellar." I had a sinking feeling that enough information about the Aryan Supremacy Party to break the organization's back had been languishing in the Hoffmans' basement all along. Damn the woman's insufferable timidity. "Here," Myra said, shoving the signed papers toward me with shaky hands. "You better go before he comes back. Please."

I looked at Tyler. His face was a study in humiliation, his newfound maturity in tatters. My heart went out to him. "You did a good thing today, Tyler," I said, scooping up the signed documents. "I'll be in touch as soon as we know the results."

I sat for a while out front in my steaming car, its windows rolled down for ventilation, and watched as Herb Keller carried cartons from the Hoffman house to his own next door. He made five more trips before he had finished. I would have given a great deal for a chance to examine the contents of those half-dozen cartons. As I sat in the stifling midday heat, I thought about where Keller would be likely to put them and about my chances of ever having that look.

— 33 —

I returned the signed papers to the hospital and stopped in Dinkytown, on the university's northern edge, to buy a dish of frozen yogurt that would have to pass for lunch. Wielding my spoon with one hand and driving with the other, I snaked onto I-94 and drove westward through downtown Minneapolis, then south on I-35W.

The house into which Susannah Keller and her son had moved after her divorce was a boxy two-family dwelling of dark red brick on Colfax Avenue South. It was probably about a hundred years old, but it had been lovingly maintained; the bright white trim around the windows had a fresh coat of paint and the row of low bushes at the base of the building was carefully trimmed.

The woman who answered the door of the upstairs apartment was as solid-looking as her house. Susannah Keller was about forty and wore her long brown hair pulled back in a braid secured with a covered rubber band. Her broad hips were encased in rolled-up jeans, over which she wore a man's roomy white shirt. Her feet were bare.

I explained my business quickly. "I guess I can spare a few minutes," she said in a voice that could only be described as ear-splitting. "Come on in." She led me through the foyer into a spacious living room outlined by natural oak baseboards and archways. Midday light filtering through the leaves of the ash tree outside the living room windows gave the room a cool greenish tint reflected by dozens of green plants perched on every available surface. The gleaming floor was dotted with handmade braided and woven rag rugs in shades of blue and violet. Only the furniture, inexpensive Early American replicas obviously purchased some years ago, showed any signs of shabbiness.

Seating myself on the blue-flowered sofa, I complimented Mrs. Keller on her lovely home and meant what I said. Part of me longed to have a place like this, one with a sense of solidness, tradition, warmth. I could picture winter evenings here, with the tree branches outside heavy with snow and the fireplace blazing. Yet another part of me wanted to escape to someplace new, free of painful Minnesota memories.

"I'm glad you like it." Her steel gray eyes warmed. "I refinished the woodwork myself and, of course, the rugs are my work." I was sure her voice could be heard in the downstairs apartment; I wondered if she were hard of hearing.

"You actually made these?" I took a closer look at the intricate handiwork. "I thought this sort of thing was pretty much a lost art."

"Not quite. It's what I do for a living. I work at home as much as I can to be with Stevie—that's my son." She gestured toward a den at her left where I could see a large loom that took up most of the room. On the floor beside it sat a light-haired boy about six years old who was engrossed in building something complicated with a Tinkertoy set. Despite the volume of his mother's voice, he showed no sign of interest at her mention of his name. "I'm an artist, and I've been concentrating on weaving lately," Susannah Keller continued. "Not just rugs. Wall hangings, table coverings, even some clothing. Capes, tunics, that sort of thing." She opened a drawer in the end table next to the sofa, pulled out a card and handed it to me. It read, *Crafts by Susannah*. "If you know anybody who's in the market . . ."

"Sure. Be happy to." I slipped the card into my purse. Mrs. Keller insisted she could be of little help in my investigation. "It's been ages since I had anything to do with the Hoffmans. I never did like that Gilbert."

"But I understand he was friendly with your husband."

"*Ex*-husband. Those two rats deserved each other."

"How's that?"

"They were both fascists, that's why. If you've been investigating Gilbert Hoffman, you must know that much."

"The Aryan Supremacy Party."

"Yeah, and his general approach to life. Well, that good-for-nothing ex of mine's the same way. Tried to run Stevie and me the way Gil ran his poor family, but I wouldn't buy it."

"You mean your husband was physically abusive?"

"Not to me. I wouldn't put up with it. But we had plenty of trouble over Stevie. We still do."

I glanced at the child. His eyes remained fixed on his construction project, but now he thrust the sticks into the connecting pieces with added energy and he began to hum tunelessly to himself. "What kind of trouble?"

She lowered her voice a few decibels. "My son has a health problem, nothing particularly difficult or rare, but he needs medical attention. When I tried to get him treatment, that bastard I was married to sabotaged it. The way Herbert sees it, the only thing wrong with Stevie is that I spoil him rotten. He figures a good swat or two will take care of what ails the kid; all he needs is to learn who's boss." She made a spitting sound. "That's like saying you can cure cancer with a horsewhipping. And he wonders why our son ended up with emotional problems? Did you ever hear such a load of crap in your life?"

I had, more times than I could count. "So you divorced him?"

"You bet I divorced him. I'm no doormat like Myra Hoffman. If a man doesn't know how to treat his wife and child, he can damn well live without 'em, the way I see it. Got myself the best divorce lawyer in town and unloaded the bastard."

"Sounds expensive."

Susannah Keller smiled mirthlessly. "Fifteen thousand dollars. But I didn't have to pay the bill."

"You did have a good lawyer," I said.

"He got me a good settlement," she said smugly. "Not that it wasn't fair to Herbert. He got to keep the house in St. Paul *and* his precious printing business."

"And you?"

"I got a cash settlement, and this duplex. We bought it seven years ago as an investment. There's alimony and child support, too, of course—when it actually arrives."

"Isn't that always the story," I murmured sympathetically.

"Yeah, well, Herbert's not getting away with that crap, either. My lawyer's working on getting him cited for contempt of court . . . for being chronically late in paying his support obligations. If he doesn't shape up quick, he'll go to jail."

"How would that help support you and Stevie?"

She shot me a look that questioned whose side I was on. I kept my face noncommittal. "If I have to get the money from selling his house and his business while he rots in jail, that's where I'll get it," she said. "It's his choice, not mine."

Susannah Keller was a formidable opponent. If Herb Keller had been a decent human being, I might have been able to dredge up some pity for him.

A series of crashes began to emanate from the workroom. I turned to see Stevie Keller methodically smashing his Tinkertoy construction to pieces with his small fists.

"Gently, Steven, gently," his mother said, not moving. "Take the pieces apart carefully and put them all away in the box." At the sound of his mother's loud voice, the child paused only briefly, then began yanking the sticks from their connectors and throwing them forcefully into the colorful round tub that housed them. Susannah Keller rose to her feet. "You're getting tired, Stevie. It's time to calm down now and have some juice. Excuse me a minute," she said to me.

She walked purposefully into the den and firmly lifted her son to his feet. "No juice! No juice!" he screamed.

"So you'll have milk," she said calmly, expertly avoiding his flailing arms and feet. "Relax, Stevie." She tightened her grip on the child. "You know it doesn't do any good to fight Mama."

I had the distinct feeling it wouldn't do anyone much good to fight Susannah Keller.

"Now," she said when she had returned from the kitchen. "I think we got off the track here. What is it you wanted to know about the Hoffmans?"

Susannah and Herb Keller had lived next door to the Hoffman family for several years, but the Kellers had split up before Gilbert Hoffman bought into the meat market. "Like I said, Herb and Gil were friendly because of that silly club of theirs. But I didn't have much in common with the Hoffmans. With Herb, either, for that matter."

As we talked, Stevie came into the room dragging a tattered blanket behind him. He crawled onto the sofa next to his mother and nestled in close to her. His thumb went into his mouth as Susannah cuddled him close to her ample body and stroked his hair gently. The boy was subdued now, but I sensed terrible anxiety beneath his quiet surface, like an active volcano at rest, waiting to erupt.

Mrs. Keller told me about the times she'd witnessed Gilbert Hoffman's abuse of his wife and child. "I lost sympathy for Myra after a while," she said flatly. "You can only try to help someone who doesn't want to be helped so long before you get fed up."

"What makes you believe Myra Hoffman didn't want help?"

Mrs. Keller rolled her eyes skyward. "Look, I could see what was happening. Anyone could. Myra'd be covered with bruises and scrapes. She didn't get them cleaning that house like some sort of Donna Reed clone." She shifted her weight as Stevie pushed against her. "I offered to take her to a shelter. I offered to let her come to our house. I even offered to call the police myself if she was afraid to. But she wasn't buying any of it. Told me to butt out. So . . . eventually, that's exactly what I did." She shook her head. "I don't know what happens to some women once they get married. They turn into melting marshmallows—anything the old man says is just fine with them, any kind of abuse is better than fighting for their rights. Pretty soon they can't even think for themselves. Hell, you'd never know from looking at her today that Myra Hoffman was once a straight-A nursing student, would you?"

"Myra Hoffman studied nursing?"

"Sure. It was years ago, but she says she was good at it. Wanted to be a psychiatric nurse but she quit to marry her knight in shining armor. Too bad for her he turned out to be such a sicko. On the other hand, maybe that's what attracted her to him in the first place." Her voice was heavy with sarcasm. "Maybe Myra figured she could be a psychiatric nurse without ever leaving home. She just didn't count on ending up a nut case herself."

This was information I'd need time to process. It could mean nothing, or it could mean a great deal. It meant Myra Hoffman could have known precisely what combination of drugs would kill her abusive husband, or at least how to get that information. She'd certainly had the opportunity to poison him. But what about access to the drug? "Is Myra really agoraphobic?" I asked.

"I don't know," Mrs. Keller said. "Myra became more and more reclusive during the time I knew her. Whether she's certifiably phobic about leaving her house . . . you'd have to ask an expert about that." Her gray eyes became sober. "Did Myra kill him?"

"I don't know," I said. "It's certainly possible. What do you think?"

She raised her palms. "She never had much backbone. But if she'd finally had enough of old Gilbert, I think that's the way she'd do it, slip something into his food. She'd be sneaky about it, not straightforward."

"Have you seen the Hoffmans since you and Steven moved out of the neighborhood?"

She shook her head. "I haven't. But Stevie has. That's another thing Herb and I had words over."

"Oh?"

"Yeah. Herb was fighting me for custody. But every time he'd have Stevie stay with him, he'd palm him off on Myra Hoffman to babysit."

"Why?"

"Because he never really wanted our son. He just didn't want me to have him." Steven began to hum tunelessly once more, as though he were using a mantra to transport himself away from a painful reality.

"No, I mean where would your husband go that he needed a babysitter for Stevie?"

"Somewhere with Gil. Those ASP meetings, probably."

Susannah pleaded ignorance of ASP's details— "Women weren't allowed to join, not that I'd have wanted to. I think the whole thing is a load of crap."

"Why?"

"Because it took up a lot of my husband's time and money that should have belonged to me and my son." Nothing about the group's history of bigotry or violence.

"What about your brother-in-law? Did he ever belong?"

"Roger? Belong to ASP? Good lord, no. Roger votes a straight DFL ticket. Always has."

"What do you know about his taking on Gilbert Hoffman as a partner in the meat market?"

"Not much. Like I told you, Herb and I split up before that happened. My guess is that Roger must've needed the money pretty bad to paint himself into that kind of corner. Those two wouldn't get along for ten minutes."

"Because of ASP?"

"Because of everything. Look, Roger Pearson is a fairly decent guy, but he wants things run his way. He wouldn't be happy with *any* kind of business partner. Fact is, he quit the supermarket and opened his own shop because he wanted to be his own boss. Put him in partnership with a dictator like Gil Hoffman and you've got a recipe for disaster."

"I understand the partnership was your ex-husband's idea."

"Yeah, well, that sure wasn't the first bum idea he's had."

"Could Roger Pearson have been unhappy enough with his partnership to use murder as a way out?"

Susannah Keller thought for a moment. "I'm trying to picture Roger doing something like that but I just can't. Wouldn't it be a lot easier just to buy Hoffman out?"

"If Pearson had the money. And if Hoffman wanted to be bought out. Remember this was a man who couldn't hold a job anywhere else."

"Still, I can't see Roger deliberately poisoning anybody." She gave me an ironic smile. "Violence is against all his liberal principles."

"And your ex-husband," I said. "Do you know of any problems between him and Gilbert Hoffman?"

She looked at me with surprise, then stiffened. "You said it yourself. They were best friends. No, I can't think of any reason why Herb would want Gil out of the way." She glanced down at her son. "Even if I could, this wouldn't be the place to discuss it." She was right, but it was the first time she'd used Steven's presence as an excuse not to trash her ex. The boy certainly had had an earful of that subject. "Now, if you don't mind, Ms. Mac—"

"MacDonald."

"Ms. MacDonald. I've really got to get back to work.

When you're self-employed, it's no work, no money."
She tried to rise, but Stevie clung to her so tightly that he
kept her off balance. "Let go, sweetheart," she said.
"Mama's going to walk the lady to the door now." I
wondered if she always referred to herself in the third
person when she spoke to her son. He reluctantly loosened his grasp on his mother, trailing behind us as she led
me to the foyer.

I thanked Mrs. Keller for her help and then said,
"Good-bye, Stevie. I enjoyed meeting you, too."

The boy stared at me with troubled eyes, then suddenly pivoted and darted into the living room, sideswiping a
plant in his path. Ignoring him, his mother showed me
out.

There was something familiar about young Steven's
behavior, something that brought back memories of my
classroom days at Linwood Elementary. It could be
nothing more than a typical child's reaction to his
parents' messy divorce, or it could be something much
more serious. As I climbed into the Honda and headed
back to the office, I thought about why no one connected
with this case seemed to have a son living a normal,
healthy, happy life.

— 34 —

I found Sam sitting at Paula's desk talking into the
phone, a well-chewed cigar dangling from the left side of
his mouth. The reception area was stifling and it smelled
of sweat and wet tobacco. Sherman and MacDonald is
certainly a high-class joint.

I threw my bag on one of the Naugahyde sofas next to
an untidy stack of manila folders waiting to be filed.

"What the hell happened to the air conditioning?" I asked when Sam had hung up. I was hot and irritable after a stop-and-go, rush-hour drive back from Minneapolis.

Sam removed the mangled stogie from his mouth and balanced it precariously on the edge of Paula's desk. "It's certainly a pleasure to see you, too, Devon," he said.

"Hello, Sam. Now—what the hell happened to the air conditioning?"

"Groaned and died about noon. Repairman says he'll try to come by tomorrow, no promises, of course, given the heat wave and all."

"If it weren't hot out, we wouldn't need the damn thing."

"You're preachin' to the choir, kiddo. Why don't you take a load off and see if you can't jack your disposition up a notch or two. Some of us around here are tryin' to make the best of it and remain our usual charming selves."

I really hate it when Sam reprimands me. I hate it even more when he's right. I took a bottle of mineral water from his office refrigerator and drank half of it in one gulp. The phone rang and Sam answered it. He spent a good five minutes arguing a bill with a woman who'd wanted her missing sister located. Now that we'd found the sister, the woman had suddenly remembered that the two had never gotten along together. Predictably, she didn't want to pay our bill. I thought Sam showed remarkable restraint in simply threatening her with small-claims court. The look on his face made it clear that he'd sell his mother for a chance to meet this particular client in a dark alley. He hung up and the phone rang again. He switched on the answering machine and his recorded voice took over. "You have reached the offices of Sherman and MacDonald, Private Investigators. If you will leave your name and number . . ."

"Where's Paula?" I asked.

"Had a dentist's appointment."

"A what?"

"A dentist's appointment."

It was either scream or laugh. I chose the latter.

Sam gave me a disapproving look. "What's so funny?"

I began to shake and I felt tears rolling down my cheeks.

"Chrissakes, Devon. Get ahold of yourself. What's so goddamned amusing?"

I took a deep breath and gasped, "I nominate Paula for today's chutzpah award." Then I wiped my eyes and explained about Paula and her amorous Dr. Lindblom.

Sam uttered a graphic suggestion about what should be done to our errant receptionist. "I suspect the good dentist may be performing a variation on that theme right now," I said. "For their sake, I hope they've found an air-conditioned place for it."

"Sure. You can laugh. Go right ahead. *I'm* the one who's been stuck here all afternoon, sweatin' myself into another heart attack. Charlie Nice Guy . . ." He continued in the same vein for another minute or two.

"So you survived, Sam," I reminded him. "We'll talk to Paula about it tomorrow. In the meantime, I suggest you lighten up. Some of us around here are trying very hard to remain our usual charming selves despite—" He grabbed his soggy cigar and threw it at me. He missed. "Truce," I said, holding my hand up. "I suggest we get some work done so we can get the hell out of this steam bath." I picked the smelly cigar off the floor with two fingers and deposited it in the circular file.

Sam stalked into his office and re-emerged carrying a cold beer and three file folders he'd made up on the ASP members who had been arrested with Hoffman and Keller. "These beauties are all yours," he said, tossing the folders on the reception desk.

"Let's hear what you've got."

He opened the first folder. "Eldon Bergmann. He's a mechanic at Kelly Chevrolet in Mendota. Lives on Finn Street, near St. Thomas College. DMV says he's thirty-nine, five ten, one sixty-five. Brown hair, green eyes."

He handed me the file and opened the second one. "This one was a little harder to track down. Name's Orville C. Voss. Furniture salesman. Worked at Furnitureville in Bloomington when he was arrested. Left shortly afterward and nobody there seemed to know where he'd gone. Finally found a janitor at Furnitureville who heard Voss'd got himself hired on as a manager at Superior Bedding on Nicollet in Richfield. Home address's in here, too. Lives near Lake Nokomis. Driver's license is under O. Christopher Voss. He's thirty, five nine, one sixty, has brown hair, blue eyes." He drained the beer and tossed the bottle in the wastebasket.

"You earned your pay tracking down O.C., Sam. What about the third guy?"

He tossed the Voss folder across the desk to me and opened the third one. "Paul E. Mueller. This guy's a little different from the other two."

"How so?"

"Seems to be educated, wealthy, not your typical blue-collar redneck type like these other jerks. Herr Mueller's a forty-one-year-old stockbroker, got his own company, Mueller and Smith, offices downtown in the Hamm Building. Lives on Glen Wilding Lane in Bloomington, no less."

"On Nine Mile Creek?"

"Uh-huh. The guy's got bucks. Hard to see what he'd have in common with these other idiots."

"Hatred, bigotry, paranoia, for a start," I suggested. "You have a description for Mueller?"

"Yeah." Sam pulled out a sheet of paper. "Pudgy bastard. Stands five eleven and weighs two forty-five. Next to him I'm practically svelte." He patted his bulging midsection.

"So have another beer."

He shot me a dirty look.

"Then give me the rest of the particulars on this hunk Mueller," I said.

"Blond hair, hazel eyes. That's all I've got for now. I'll get Barry to pull the rap sheets on these cuties tomorrow and I'll check the civil files on 'em. The rest's up to you, sweetheart."

I already knew that.

35

The humidity was so thick as I drove home that the ominously still air seemed green. I wasn't the only one adversely affected by the heat and low atmospheric pressure. Plenty of other drivers were equally short-tempered. Screeching tires, blowing horns, and epithets yelled out open car windows were the order of the day. I was glad to get home.

My window air conditioner—for once I'd had the sense to leave it on when I left that morning—was still humming away. By the time I'd indulged myself in a cool shower and a glass of iced tea, I felt almost human again.

I examined my options for the evening. I could watch television, but *L.A. Law* was in summer reruns. I could go out for a bite to eat, but I was too broke. I could call Roddy Caldwell and suggest an air-conditioned movie, but that was still too intimidating. I could go back to work. . . . Somehow it always seemed to come down to that lately. Work through boredom, work through loneliness, work through life.

I threw together a salad for dinner and ate while I

leafed through the files Sam had made up on the ASP members. Was I wasting my time with them? After all, what did ASP really have to do with Gilbert Hoffman's murder? Was I using Hoffman's membership in the organization as an excuse to play my version of Simon Wiesenthal? Still, I rationalized, Hoffman's belonging to that ugly hate group may have had something to do with his untimely demise. And his fellow party members might know more about his enemies, both inside and outside the group, than anyone else.

The idea of confronting my trio of neo-Nazis in their homes didn't thrill me. I'm not into asking for trouble. Cornering them on the job, with other people around, made much more sense. That left out Bergmann and Mueller for tonight. Kelly Chevrolet's repair department and Mueller's brokerage office would be closed. Superior Bedding offered a possibility, though. I dialed the store's Richfield number and asked to speak to Mr. Voss. The woman who answered asked me to hold on. I hung up.

Forty minutes later I was winding my way through a sea of beds—brass ones and wood ones, platform beds and water beds, from crib-size to king-size. There were three salespeople on duty, the woman who had taken my call, a bald man well over six feet tall, and a shorter guy in a yellow-and-orange plaid shirt and black bow tie I figured must be Voss. He was giving the hard sell on a youth bed to a couple trying to control a squirming toddler. The child had remnants of a grape Popsicle smeared all over her hands and face. Just what every furniture store needs.

The bald salesman approached me. "Thanks, but I'm waiting for Mr. Voss," I said, shaking my head. I spent another ten minutes inspecting every conceivable variety of mattress ticking while Voss wrote up his sale. There followed a brief, whispered conference between the two salesmen; then Voss walked in my direction. He wore his medium brown hair in a crew cut that did nothing to hide his sunburned and peeling cauliflower ears.

I smiled and said, "I'd like to take a look at this round bed over here." When I'd led him into the corner, I took my ID from my bag and flashed it. "I'm Devon MacDonald, Mr. Voss. I'm investigating the murder of Gilbert Hoffman and I'd like to ask you a few questions."

"I don't know any Gilbert Hoffman."

"He was president of your group—the Aryan Supremacy Party."

His Adam's apple bobbed, wiggling the bow tie. "Never heard of it."

"You *are* Orville Voss, aren't you?"

"Yes . . ."

"Orville Christopher Voss, formerly employed at Furnitureville."

"Yes, but I don't know anything about any of this. Now if you'll excuse me—" He turned away.

"Orville Christopher Voss who was arrested at a violent demonstration against Jews along with—"

He turned back. His face had gone white below the angry patch of sunburn topping his nose and cheekbones. "Stop it."

"—Gilbert Hoffman, Herbert Keller, Paul Mueller—"

"Stop! All right, all right." He glanced surreptitiously over his shoulder at his co-workers, who were chatting at the other side of the sales floor. There were no customers in the store. "Look," he said, lowering his voice, "I did belong to ASP once, a long time ago. I'll admit that much. But I don't anymore. I quit the day we all got arrested."

My look was skeptical.

"It's true. Look, I only joined because my uncle was fanatic about it. It was never my thing. Look what it did to me—got me a criminal record, got me fired from my job. That was enough. I never went to another meeting."

"What's your uncle's name?"

"Arnie. Arnold Voss."

"Where can I reach him?"

He shook his head. "He's dead. Shot himself three years ago." Cheerful little group, the Aryan Supremacy Party.

"Tell me what you know about Gil Hoffman."

"Not a damn thing. I didn't even know the guy." He ran a finger under his shirt collar, which was beginning to look damp. "Look, lady—"

"You knew him well enough to demonstrate with him against some people who were simply trying to honor their dead. You knew him well enough to go to jail with him."

"Look, lady, I can't afford to lose this job, too. Why come here harassing me?"

"Just tell me what I want to know and I'll leave you in peace." I almost felt sorry for the guy. "Come on," I said. "I'm not trying to get you fired. Let's walk around the store and you can make like you're showing me the merchandise. Just keep enough distance so your cronies can't hear what we're talking about." We moved to the water bed section. "Now, tell me what you know about Gil Hoffman."

Voss sighed and tugged at the bow tie. "All I remember about him is he was a huge son of a bitch. Foul temper. Big mouth. Really took ASP seriously."

"Don't most members?"

"Not me. I guess most of them are into it pretty deep. You're screened pretty well before you can join. You have to have a sponsor, that sort of thing. In my case, my uncle muscled me in, so they didn't give me all that much inspection."

"What's the club's purpose, besides harassing innocent people?" I tried to keep the sarcasm out of my voice, but I didn't do too well.

"The big project was always the land."

"Land?"

"They were trying to scrape together enough cash to buy a big tract of land somewhere out west. Planned to live on it when the cities blew up."

"What do you mean?"

The ASP theory is that America's cities are just waiting to explode—too many minorities, too much crime, that sort of thing. They figure it's all going to come to a head one of these days in total urban war. They want to be ready to move out for the duration. They've got canned goods stockpiled, farm equipment, stuff like that."

"Guns?"

"Yeah, I guess. They're avid NRA supporters."

"What do they plan to do with all this stuff?"

"When it hits the fan in the cities, they'll head for their land and wait out the war. Then, when it's all over, they figure they can come out of the hills and take over, put America back together their own way."

We moved on to a section filled with sofa beds. "Very pretty," I said.

"It's a Simmons."

"I meant ASP's scenario and I was being sarcastic."

"Oh."

"Did ASP actually buy this land or was this just a pie-in-the-sky notion?"

Despite the store's refrigerated air, dark circles of sweat stained Voss's plaid shirt and his faint scent of Old Spice—deodorant or after-shave?—intensified. "Don't ask me. I'd guess they probably got some of it. They're pretty determined guys. But like I told you, I got out after that night in jail. I couldn't tell you what they've been up to since then."

Maybe not, but Voss had given me food for thought. "Did Hoffman have any enemies?"

"Nobody specific that I knew of." He bent over and straightened a cushion on one of the sofa beds, using the opportunity to steal a look at his co-workers. "But it's hard to believe a guy with his personality could live long without making enemies."

"That's the point," I said. "Gilbert Hoffman didn't live very long." When we had worked our way around to the front of the store, within earshot of the other employees, I handed Voss one of my cards and said loudly enough for the other salespeople to hear, "You've been very helpful, Mr. Voss. If that style I want comes in, do give me a call."

As I reached the door, I turned and saw him wiping his brow with a rumpled handkerchief. Somehow I doubted it was just sunburn that was making Orville Voss sweat.

— 36 —

A violent rainstorm turned the sky into a light show until the early hours of the morning. Cracks of thunder shook my tiny attic apartment and a gale-force wind rattled the windows. I awoke to find tree branches littering the streets and lawns. Driving to Mendota, south across the Minnesota River, was slow because of debris in the roads, but at least the air had cooled to a level at which humans could survive with some semblance of comfort.

The service department at Kelly Chevrolet was pungent with paint fumes and the stench of gasoline. The whine of an electric buffer competed with the *rat-tat-tat* of a power wrench removing a wheel on a jacked-up Corvette. I approached the teenage receptionist, a skinny girl in tight jeans and a pink T-shirt cut low to show her minuscule breasts. "Yeah, Eldon's out back, bay number three," she told me.

I found Eldon Bergmann bending over the engine of an old Chevy Malibu, adjusting something with a wrench. A couple of inches taller than I am, he wore grease-stained coveralls the same shade of brown as his close-cropped hair. "Yeah, I recognize you from Gil's funeral," he said when I introduced myself. His tone was less than cordial. "I hear you been botherin' my buddies." He did not put down the wrench. On the back of the hand that held it was a small turquoise tattoo of a coiled snake.

"Not the way I see it. Just trying to find out who killed your pal."

"Yeah, well, way we see it, what you're doin' is tryin' to find some sucker besides that Hymie doctor to pin it on." He wiped his left hand on his pants leg. "You ain't gonna find him here, lady, so why don't you just move along."

"I'd think you guys would want conclusive proof of what really happened to Gil Hoffman," I said. "Truth is, I find it a little suspicious that none of you want to talk to me. It's almost enough to make me think you took Gil out yourselves—"

"Fuck that. And fuck you." He tightened his grip on the wrench and raised it menacingly. I didn't move. There were enough other men in the repair shop—several of them staring openly in our direction—that I doubted Bergmann would risk assaulting me. But I was very glad I had decided not to confront him in his home.

"You're playing a real stupid game here, Bergmann," I said. "You and your cronies are getting my curiosity aroused. And I can be a real pain in the ass when I get curious. You know, about things like that stockpile of guns you guys have, and your land in—where is it?—Idaho? Montana?"

The mechanic's green eyes narrowed. "I ain't gonna give you the sweat off my balls, lady. And if you don't back off, you won't be the first cat curiosity wiped out." Eldon Bergmann certainly had a way with words. He gave me his best threatening look and waved the wrench in my direction one last time before his head disappeared back underneath the Malibu's hood.

"Just in case you change your mind, give me a call," I said, keeping my voice level. I placed one of my cards on the roof of the Chevy, turned, and walked slowly back to my car, my chin held high. Somebody wolf whistled; I feigned deafness. My body language said, "Nobody scares Devon MacDonald, crack private investigator." But my hands were shaking on the steering wheel as I drove the Honda out of the parking lot.

— 37 —

A call to Paul Mueller's office told me I couldn't see the stockbroker until mid-afternoon, so I spent some time at the St. Paul Library looking up drugs in the *Physician's Desk Reference*. What I found reinforced a suspicion that had begun to form yesterday. I still couldn't be sure who murdered Gilbert Hoffman, but I had a line on the source of the pills that did the job. Trouble was, that source was available to at least four people who'd had an opportunity to drug Hoffman's drink on the fatal day. And at least three of them had powerful reasons to want him out of the way. After I had made some notes, I left my car parked outside the library and walked across Rice Park and up Market Street to the Hamm Building.

The offices of Mueller and Smith, Stockbrokerage, were designed to project solidity and dependability. The walls of the reception area were walnut-paneled and the tables next to the modern brown plush sofas held copies of *The Wall Street Journal, Forbes,* and *Investor's Daily*. Mueller's office was paneled in matching walnut and featured a coordinating desk of suitable executive proportions. A table along one side of the room held a computer whose screen projected constantly changing stock quotations. On the opposite wall were charts detailing the performance of various stock indexes over a five-year period. I was impressed. Also snowed. My personal finances are so far from allowing any investment in the stock market that I've never bothered to learn much about it. When I can afford to pay off my MasterCard bill all at once, I'll feel successful.

Mueller was decidedly friendlier than Keller, Voss, and Bergmann had been. Or maybe it was just his professional polish. He held out a chair for me, moving with unusual grace for such a heavy man. His handmade charcoal gray suit flattered his bulky physique and contrasted starkly with his extremely fair hair and complexion. The light blue silk shirt he wore matched his eyes precisely.

"Now, Ms. MacDonald," he said, smiling congenially, "what can I do for you?"

My quest seemed not to surprise him. Undoubtedly he'd been warned by one or more of his cronies in ASP to expect a visit from me.

"I really think you have the wrong idea altogether about our little club," Mueller said. "Maybe some of our members have been a bit overzealous in the past, but we're not a violent group."

"Police records would argue that point, Mr. Mueller."

He dismissed this with a sweep of his manicured hand. "All a misunderstanding. The Aryan Supremacy Party is a positive force in society, not a negative one."

"What's positive about it?"

"We have a vision of a direction in which this country should go. It's nothing radical at all. That's what our detractors don't understand. We simply wish to return to the good, solid American values that made this country great. God, flag, family, strong moral fiber."

Bigotry, racism, triumph of the strong over the weak, I thought, but I hadn't come there to get into an argument. "Mr. Mueller," I said, "as you obviously already know, I'm trying to find out what happened to the president of your organization. You can help by telling me what you know about Gilbert Hoffman."

"That could take more time than either of us has available, my dear. I've known—I knew Gil for many, many years. Perhaps if you were more specific I could be more helpful."

"It seems to be a given that Hoffman had a temper, perhaps was mentally ill."

Mueller's brow furrowed. "Mentally ill is a gross exaggeration," he said carefully.

I shrugged. "Let's just say he was the kind of man who didn't make many friends."

"Gil had—uh, a strong personality. He stood up for what he thought was right. Sometimes he may have been a bit too forceful, but he acted from a strong internal sense of morality."

"And we all have our own definitions of morality, is that it?"

"I see you understand perfectly."

I sighed. In his own way, the slippery Mr. Mueller seemed more dangerous than ASP's less polished, more violent members. "Have you ever held an office in the Aryan Supremacy Party, Mr. Mueller?"

He smiled ingratiatingly. "That sort of information is supposed to be confidential . . . but I can't see what harm it would do to tell you, Ms. MacDonald. The answer is no. Some members are able to give their time by holding an office, others become involved in fund-raising, recruiting new members, the calling committee. . . . It all depends on what they're good at. My own contribution falls into a different arena."

"Which is?"

He gestured around him. "Investments."

"I don't understand. What does a stockbrokerage have to do with ASP?"

His voice took on the air of a teacher lecturing to a particularly slow child. "The party has certain financial goals. By investing what funds we have raised, we've been able to multiply our assets quite successfully."

"And you've handled these investments."

"The stock market has been good to us, allowing us to reach several of our goals well ahead of our target dates."

I took a wild shot. "You mean like the land you people plan to retreat to when the cities erupt into urban warfare."

The superior look melted from Mueller's face momentarily. "I don't know how you found out—"

"That doesn't matter." I decided to try a different approach. I flashed him my own version of an ingratiating smile. "I'm impressed. You must have a real talent for investment, Mr. Mueller. That land must have gone for—what?—a couple of million, maybe more."

"Not quite that much. Prices for Oregon land are depressed these days." His index finger stroked his burgundy silk tie. "But I'm not going to be modest. On my advice, we more than tripled our market funds over a five-year period. Then we chose to transfer our investment into real estate in an area of the country that offers both abundant physical resources and remoteness from the chaos of our modern civilization. We got lucky there, too. The land we bought will certainly be worth two, maybe three million in a few years. But we got it for a million five."

"And you chose the particular location?"

He gave me a self-deprecating wave lest I think he was taking more credit than was his due for ASP's financial astuteness. "I merely recommended an area of the country. Oregon looked good for the reasons I mentioned, Linn County in particular. The party's officers chose the actual parcel and brought back photos and price information. The entire membership voted to purchase, over-whelmingly."

"And you've been improving the land, have you? In preparation for this donnybrook you're forecasting?"

"We're adding buildings as we can afford them, yes. I think we've done quite well."

"You must have had mixed feelings about buying the land," I said.

"I don't understand. . . ."

"Well, it seems to me that switching a million and a half dollars from stocks to land must have cost you a hefty sum in brokerage commissions."

A new respect for the broad across the desk from him crept into Mueller's eyes. "You misjudge me, Ms. Mac-Donald. My only motivation in managing ASP's funds was to further the party's aims."

"Then you didn't charge brokerage commissions?"

"I'm not running a charity here, Ms. MacDonald, and I have my partner to think of. I did offer the party a reduced fee, however. We reached an agreement that satisfied all of us."

Even with a discount, I thought, Mueller must have made a pretty bundle managing an account of that size. Perhaps therein lay the real reason he had joined ASP.

I asked about Gil Hoffman's enemies, but Mueller insisted that the dead president had had none within ASP. "Look," he said, "the man lived and breathed ASP. Gave it twenty, thirty hours a week. When he went to those meetings, people respected him, they looked up to him." He leaned across the desk. "My dear, if that doctor they arrested didn't kill Gil, I'd look to Mrs. Hoffman." He gave me a saccharine smile. "I'd heard rumors for years that all was not happy in Gil's home. From what I understood, Mrs. Hoffman had refused to go anywhere with her husband for the past several years. Not even to the party's family events. Here the poor man's president and he has to go alone, or with that boy of his. Now you know that's got to be a disappointment, an embarrassment. Trust me, there was trouble in that home. Maybe fatal trouble."

I left Mueller and Smith, Brokerage, wondering whether I'd really learned anything I hadn't already known. I'd found out that the Aryan Supremacy Party was wealthier than I'd guessed . . . or feared. I'd learned that the land Orville Voss had told me about existed, and roughly where it was. Yet I had a feeling that I'd learned only what Mueller had intended for me to know. That he, not I, had controlled the interview. I drove back to the office wondering whether Mueller and Eldon Bergmann had just suckered me with a good cop–bad cop routine.

— 38 —

Sam and Rose were waiting for me at the office. "Come on, Devon. Even you gotta eat sometime," Sam said. "We'll even take you to a rabbit-food place, you insist."

"What about the records you were going to dig up on our suspects?" I asked. "I can't afford to quit working this early."

"Since when does Sam Sherman shirk when a job ain't finished? Who's quittin'? Rose and me, we just want a little nourishment first. We can come back to the office after and finish up."

"I've got a lot to go over with you, Sam. Rose doesn't want to sit here for a couple of hours while we finish up these files."

Diminutive Rose took my hand and patted it. "Devon, dear, don't you worry about me. You and Sam got work, I'll take myself home and keep outa your way. Just come and have a nice bite with us. You work too hard; you're looking pale."

"You got nothin' better to do anyway," Sam said. "Ain't like you got a big date waitin' in the wings."

"Thanks for the vote of confidence," I said.

"Devon's right, Sam," Rose pitched in. "You leave her alone. Time comes she decides she wants a man, the boys'll be standin' in line."

I let the two of them argue about my love life while I slipped into my own office. My desktop was clean, but my wastebasket was littered with candy and potato chip wrappers and two Coke Classic cans. Sam obviously had emptied his basket into mine before Rose arrived. He needed a bite to eat, all right. Question was how he planned to stuff it in. Still, I had to admit I was hungry; I'd forgotten to have lunch and my stomach was growling in protest. And they were right about one thing. I didn't have anything better to do with my evening.

Sam and Rose were still bickering good-naturedly when I returned to the outer office. "All right, all right," I said. "I'll have dinner with you on one condition: Sam and I come back to the office afterward and get this work cleaned up. Rose can take your car home and I'll drive Sam when we're finished here."

Sam chauffeured us to downtown Minneapolis in the dented and dirty old Chevrolet he calls his perfect surveillance car—there is absolutely nothing memorable about the sorry-looking vehicle—and we had a relaxing dinner at Ellington's. I was on my second glass of wine, enjoying the parkside view from the windows, when Sam announced, "I got good news and I got bad news."

I put down my glass. "Give me the good news first," I said, reluctant to lose the glow of the wine so quickly.

"Vince Vinelli's gonna pop for a little bonus for that libel work you did for him. Soon as you finish up this Levy case, figure on spendin' a couple o' days up at Gull Lake."

"Hey, that's great." I knew I could use a break, but what I found even more appealing was the implied praise of my work. Yet I've learned to be suspicious of Sam's apparently generous motives. "Let me guess the bad news—while I'm at the lake, you just happen to have a little job you want me to do up there."

Sam became indignant. "For God's sake, Devon. Here I am, tryin' to do somethin' nice for you, give you a gift free and clear, and you accuse me— Come on, now, would I pull a dirty trick like that on you?"

"You not only would, Sam, you have. Remember the time you told me I was going to spend Memorial Day weekend in the Wisconsin Dells?"

A smile stole over Rose's face.

"Well, that was different, an emergency sorta thing," Sam said defensively.

I held up my palms. "Okay. Okay. I'm sorry, Sam. I'll plan on spending a nice, quiet weekend out of town. A real vacation. And thank you." I suppressed a fleeting thought that it would be nice to have someone to share that kind of weekend. "Now you might as well get it over with. Hit me with the bad news."

Sam played with his napkin for a moment. "I knew you'd get upset," he said, "but you gotta find out sometime. The Meyers kid ain't gonna give little David Levy that bone marrow he needs."

My eyes flew to Sam's face; it was a study in concern. So this was why Sam and Rose had insisted upon taking me to dinner, to soften the blow. "What happened?" I demanded.

He shook his head. "Docs looked at those records they sent from Israel. The girl just hasn't got the right kinda blood."

"We always knew it was a long shot." I spoke more to myself than to Sam and Rose, but I couldn't keep my heart from sinking.

"Now don't you lose sleep, Devon," Rose said. "Sam

tells me the boy—what's his name, Tyler—is gonna help out. You only need one good match."

"And we've got one chance left to get it." The warm glow of the wine disappeared and I shivered.

An hour later, Rose had taken the Chevrolet home and Sam and I were entrenched in the office, the only people working in the old frame building at that hour. When I had told Sam about my interviews with the ASP members, he pulled out his stack of notes on his own substantial day's work.

"Let's start with your Aryan Supremacy buddies," he said, talking around his unlighted cigar. "You're right. This Eldon Bergmann fellow is a real asshole. Jerk's got two new arrests Barry O'Neil was able to dig up for me, both for carrying a concealed weapon. Charges were dropped, but Barry says the arresting officers say Bergmann gets real macho anytime he can pull out a gun."

"I'm not surprised. I bet he gets off on cockfights and Sylvester Stallone movies, too. What about the others? Find anything on Orville Voss?"

Sam flipped over a page of his notepad. "No real reason to believe Voss wasn't tellin' you the truth last night. No police record, 'cept that demonstration arrest we already knew about. Guy's divorced, three years ago, but the records show it was a pretty clean break. Doesn't look like there's anything there. No kids, no contested property."

"And Mueller?"

"Mueller's a high roller. His stockbroker's license is current and his business is one of the most profitable in the cities. Owns it fifty-fifty with a fellow name of Morton Smith. You could do worse than have a piece of that action. Both Mueller and Smith got megabucks, from the business and their personal deals."

"Such as?"

"Mueller's all over the real-estate transactions records in both Ramsey and Hennepin counties. Owns the house on Glen Wilding plus fourteen other buildings, mostly multiple units."

"Yet he says he didn't negotiate ASP's purchase of that Oregon property."

Sam shrugged. "From what you said, Mueller seems to think they did okay without him. Maybe he was too busy makin' deals here to split for the West Coast to help out them neo-Nazis."

That fit with my theory that Mueller was in ASP mainly for personal profit. There wouldn't be any profit in negotiating a real estate deal unless he owned the particular piece of property ASP wanted, or was licensed to sell real estate in Oregon, neither of which appeared to be the case. "Anything else on Paul Mueller?" I asked.

Sam grinned. "Guy's got a lead foot. Seven speeding tickets in the past five years. Drives a Porsche with a souped-up engine."

"And he's still got his license?"

"You can pay for heavy-duty legal talent to defend a speeding ticket, you stay behind the wheel."

I put on a pot of decaf and we settled in for another hour. Sam had researched Herbert Keller, whose divorce I already knew was far less amicable than Orville Voss's. "This one cost a bundle," Sam reported. "Keller paid the wife's attorney's fees, over fifteen grand. Plus his own lawyer's tab, whatever that was. Plus he's stuck for fifteen hundred a month in child and spousal support."

"Plus more attorney's fees every time they go back into court and bicker some more," I said. "I'm surprised the lawyers haven't ripped off everything the Kellers own."

"It's their own fault," Sam said, ever defensive of the profession that hires us most often. "You take people like these Kellers, they'll fight over the bathroom towels. Take it to court before they'll let the other one have 'em. This sort of thing's gonna cost money, but they'd rather both of 'em went broke than one of 'em wins. Here, take a look at this." He tossed a thick copy of the Kellers' divorce file across the desk. I groaned, knowing I would have to study it cover to cover. Reading marriage dissolution papers always depresses me.

"The Kellers were luckier than a lot of folks," Sam continued. "They started out with a nice portfolio and they still got plenty of it left. The printing business, H&S, belonged to both of them before they split up, but now Herb's listed as sole owner. He also got the St. Paul house. She got the Minneapolis duplex and a fifty-thousand-dollar cash settlement."

"Where, may I ask, did Herb Keller get fifty thousand in cash?"

"Refinanced his house and took out a loan against H&S."

"Were you able to get a peek at his credit rating?" I poured two mugs of decaf. Sam liberally added cream and sugar to his.

"It's in pretty good shape now. Wasn't so hot a year or so ago, but looks like the business is making more money these days. My gut says Keller's also running a little scam to make sure it does."

Brooding, I sipped my coffee and burned myself. "Ouch. Damn." I sucked my tongue for a minute, then said, "Let's hear it."

"Keller's got a habit of filing small-claims court cases against folks who don't like their printing bills jacked up over the original estimate. Four in the past year. I'll wager that for every customer who refuses to pay and spends half a day in court there's a dozen who just write the check."

"So Keller lowballs his bids, then tacks on extra charges to raise the price he finally bills the customer. Sort of like your average defense contractor."

Sam smiled.

"Anything else on Keller?" I asked.

"Not much. Drives a new Dodge; he's got it registered to the business. Clean driving record. And no arrests since that little bash at the Jewish community center."

Sam hadn't missed checking a name on the list I'd given him. He's nothing if not thorough. "Tyler Hoffman's name isn't anywhere in the public records after his birth certificate," he reported. "Hasn't even got a driver's license." I sighed with relief. "Course, I can't say he hasn't got a juvie record." Juvenile Court records are sealed.

It was possibly wishful thinking, but I didn't want David Levy's only remaining hope for a transplant—his half-brother Tyler—to have a dark side. And it would be hard to conceive of anything much darker than Tyler's having poisoned the man who raised him.

"Ditto for the boy's girlfriend, Marietta Tilsen," Sam said. "'Cept she drives. Record with the DMV's clean as a whistle. There any more of this stuff?"

I refilled Sam's mug. "What about Myra Hoffman?"

Sam shook his head. "No arrest record in the seven-county area. Her driver's license expired on her last birthday and she hasn't renewed it." That would tend to support her claim that she was too frightened to venture outside her home. "Her name ain't even on the ownership of her house or Hoffman's business partnership with Roger Pearson. Far as the public files go, Myra Hoffman barely exists." There wasn't much evidence outside the public records that she did, either. But that didn't mean Myra hadn't quietly dumped a handful of pills into her dearly beloved's Thermos.

Sam had found nothing new on Roger Pearson, but his search had provided a couple of new wrinkles for Leon Jackson. "Parking tickets," Sam said.

"Parking tickets?" I laughed.

"He's got six of 'em outstanding. He don't pay 'em off pretty soon, they'll swear out a warrant and he's gonna find his ass back in the jug." Sam shot me a can-you-believe-some-people look. "Got lucky last year, too. Picked up for driving under the influence, but he walked."

"Why?"

"Arresting officer had a schedule conflict and didn't show up in court. Judge dismissed the charge."

Sam set out his notes for Paula to type up in the morning while I cleaned out the coffeepot and mugs. I stuffed the documents Sam had collected into my brief-case for bedtime reading. Sam grabbed a stack of books and papers he intended to deliver to one of our attorney clients the following morning, and we left the office. I locked the door behind us, straining to fit my key into the lock by the dim light available.

It was a beautifully clear evening. The North Star sparkled overhead as Sam and I reached the sidewalk and headed toward my Honda parked across the street.

Grand Avenue was quiet except for the typical sounds of the city at night—traffic cruising on Summit Avenue a block away, a radio softly playing Beethoven near an open window, a small dog yelping in a nearby yard. There was no passing traffic on Grand at the moment and only a handful of cars parked on the street. Sam lumbered along beside me, his arms heavily loaded. His breathing was becoming increasingly labored. "Here, let me carry some of that stuff," I said.

I reached toward the pile of documents Sam clutched tightly against his chest, but he jerked his burden away from my grasp. "I ain't no goddamn cripple," he snapped.

"Well, excuse me! Go ahead and give yourself a heart attack if you want to." I stepped off the curb. Sam followed, muttering words I couldn't quite make out under his breath.

We were approaching the center of the street when I heard it, a low rumbling sound that suddenly quickened into a whine. My head jerked around, toward the source of the noise. A large car, its headlights dark, began to pull away from the curb maybe three hundred feet behind us. Instantly, it accelerated and the night air was filled with the screech of rubber tires.

As the specter bore down on us, I was paralyzed, like a deer caught in the headlights of an oncoming car. Memory froze me to the pavement. In less than a split second, I relived my darkest moment. I saw myself standing helpless as another dark vehicle bore down on my son.

A faint smell of burning rubber shocked me awake like smelling salts. From the corner of my eye, I saw my partner trying futilely to force his sedentary body into motion, to escape the vehicle's deadly path. "Sam! Watch out!"

It couldn't happen again. My briefcase slipped from my grasp as I lunged, throwing my full weight against Sam's midsection. Pain shot through my shoulder and neck; I felt as though I'd just rushed one of the Minnesota Vikings. Papers flew everywhere. Sam jerked slightly upward, then toppled. I heard the whoosh of his breath as I hit him. As we fell in tandem to the pavement, I caught a glimpse of my partner's eyes, startled and uncomprehending. *Roll, Sam,* I commanded wordlessly. *Roll, damn it!* We skidded to the ground, the rough asphalt excruciatingly scraping the skin from my bare arm. Then a black blur sped inches from my head and I heard a terrible, familiar thud.

Seconds later, the screech of the tires had faded and I lay prone on the street. Where was Sam? *Oh, God,* I prayed, *don't let him be hurt; not like Danny. Don't let Sam die.* Frantically, I rolled over and pushed myself unsteadily to my feet. I saw Sam, maybe six feet away, lying facedown on the pavement. My breath caught as I bent over him. It took all my strength to get a grip on his arm and roll him over onto his back; he was heavy, dead weight.

"Sam! Sam, damn it, wake up! Sam, *please* don't do

this." Tears blurred my vision and streamed down my face. The fabric of his shirt began to rip as my fingers grasped it, but still I pulled at it.

A groan emerged from the body lying beneath my hands. "Sam? Sam, are you all right?" I held his pale face between my hands. "Sam, talk to me."

Sam's mouth moved. He groaned again. "What is it, Sam? Tell me." I placed my ear close to his mouth.

His words were faint and slurred, but distinguishable.

They were the sweetest words I'd heard in years. "Jesus Christ, girl. Lemme the hell alone."

I sat down hard on the pavement and bawled like a baby while distant sirens grew louder.

— 39 —

Two hours later, my scrapes and bruises had been treated and bandaged at St. Paul–Ramsey Medical Center. My right arm looked like it had been massaged with a cheese grater and felt worse; I sported a similar abrasion on my right cheek. Otherwise, however, I'd escaped with only bruises. If you don't count the psychic damage inherent in nearly being run down by what still seemed a phantom from my painful past. A good-looking young intern announced solemnly that I would live.

The doctor discharged me, but I had no intention of going home. I spent much of the night sitting in a chair in Sam's hospital room, listening to the erratic beeping of his heart monitor and his irregular snores. My eyes kept straying to the plastic bags of medication hanging above the bed and the IV tubes leading to Sam's left hand. Danny had been connected to tubes like those. . . .

On the other side of Sam's bed, Rose sat sniffling, nervously wringing a handkerchief she kept forgetting to use. "If only his heart can stand the shock, he'll be all right," she kept repeating, more to herself than to me. "If only his heart is strong enough." She looked ten years older than she had a few hours earlier, when she'd left us alone in the office. I felt fifty years older.

The car that had tried to run us down had managed to deal Sam no more than a glancing blow. As a result, he now had a deep bruise covering most of one side of his body, some abrasions, and a cracked arm bone. Yet the doctor's main concern was not the wounds inflicted by either the dark car or Sam's fall to the pavement. It was his unreliable heart. Because of the stress of the ordeal, it had developed an irregular rhythm that could indicate a pending attack. Now the doctors had him hitched up to the heart monitor and an IV, trying to forestall a third heart attack.

I knew that my amateur tackle probably had prevented Sam from being more seriously—maybe even fatally—injured. But that did little to assuage my guilt. I was sure they—whoever had been waiting in that car down the block—had been after me, not Sam. If I hadn't offered to drive him home, Sam never would have been anywhere near Grand Avenue or my parked Honda at that hour.

It broke my heart to see the big man I loved like a father lying so helpless in that bed. And as I watched over him, I couldn't help envisioning a much smaller body lying in a similar hospital bed, a child who had never wakened. I chewed my lip until it was raw and bloody, and tears I didn't know I could still shed rolled down my cheeks, soaking my blouse.

Lieutenant O'Neil lumbered into the room carrying a boxful of papers and my briefcase. He dumped them on the floor, kissed Rose on the cheek, and clumsily attempted to hug me. I had all I could do to keep from screaming in pain. "You're turnin' into a regular punchin' bag these days, kid," he said. "Tryin' to get yourself killed?"

I wiped at my eyes with the back of my hand. "Yeah, Barry. It's my life's ambition." If you can't overcome fear, I always say, hide behind false bravado.

"How 'bout you do it on some other guy's beat?" Barry had spent the last couple of hours measuring skid marks on Grand Avenue and interviewing residents of the street's few apartment buildings in search of witnesses. There was little he wouldn't do to find anybody who dared threaten his old friend.

I wasn't much help. All I could recall clearly was that the car that took aim at Sam and me was large and dark, most likely American. It could have been black, brown, blue, green; it could have been a Chevrolet, a Dodge, a Buick, a Ford. There might have been a passenger sitting beside the driver. Or maybe not. I just didn't know. Half the time, when I tried to remember, all I could remember was the gray Chrysler that ran Danny down, and the drunk who'd been driving.

I would have to make a formal statement about the hit-and-run, but Barry agreed to postpone it for a day or so. I pleaded exhaustion, but the truth was that I had better things to do with the next few days.

"How 'bout a ride home?" Barry offered.

"Thanks, but I'm not going home yet. I'll stay with Sam a while longer." That resolution spurred an argument with Rose, who launched into her mothering routine. I didn't budge. I wasn't leaving until I knew Sam was all right. Besides, I was afraid of who or what might be waiting for me back in Ramsey Hill. If the people who wanted me dead knew the hit-and-run hadn't done the job, they might well figure on finishing it another way. No sense in making it easy for them to find me. Tonight I was in no mood, or shape, to fight fascists if, as I suspected, the Aryan Supremacy Party was behind this. Truth was, I was in no shape to fight anybody. I would hide out in the hospital until I could figure out a safer way to settle things.

I struggled to organize my thoughts, but I must have dozed off in the chair, for I awoke stiff and in pain. I looked around me. Sam's monitor was still beeping away next to his motionless figure. To my untrained ear, the rhythm of the beeps seemed less irregular, but that could have been wishful thinking. Rose, exhausted by her vigil, was snoring softly in her chair, her husband's hand held in her own.

I took a bottle of aspirin from my purse, swallowed two tablets with some water from Sam's pitcher, and began to look through the box of papers Barry had brought. Some of the documents inside clearly had been scattered on the street; they were soiled and wrinkled and two or three had tire marks across them. I wondered which of Barry's men had taken the time to gather them up. Over the next few hours, by the faint greenish light above Sam's bed, I skimmed hundreds of pages of legal documents.

By the time dawn was lighting the sky outside the hospital window, I'd found what I was looking for. I now felt certain I knew where the pills that killed Hoffman had come from, but I still wasn't sure why they'd been used.

I had half a grapefruit and three cups of bitter black coffee in the hospital cafeteria, then paced the corridors until my sore muscles began to loosen up. The intern was right; I would live.

When I returned to Sam's room, he was awake and grumbling in a slurred voice for breakfast and painkiller, in that order. Rose's face glowed. Both seemed very good signs. My spirits began to lift.

"I'm going to Oregon, Sam," I told him. "I have to check on that land the Aryan Supremacists bought out there. I'll be back as soon as I can."

Sam didn't argue with me. Maybe he was too tired or

too groggy from his medication. Or maybe he figured I'd be safer in Oregon than here in Minnesota. I kissed them both good-bye and took a cab downtown.

Dayton's department store had everything I needed for a quick trip out of town. I used my charge card to buy a change of clothes, some toiletries, and a carry-on bag, then cashed a check at the service counter. A second cab brought me to MSP International in time to catch Northwest's noon flight to Portland.

Walking stiffly and pumped up with caffeine, I was at the Portland Airport Avis counter renting a car before two o'clock.

By three-thirty, I'd driven to Salem, the state capital, and was busy studying records of real estate transfers for Linn County. Luckily, it wasn't hard to find a record of the parcel purchased by the Aryan Supremacy Party; it was one of the county's largest transactions in recent years.

My notes detailing the property's location in my bag, I headed south from Salem on Highway 5, then cut east on Route 20 toward the foothills of the Cascades. By the time I pulled into an inexpensive motel in Sweet Home, I was weary to the core, no longer able to keep going on adrenaline and caffeine. Tomorrow, I told myself, would be soon enough to check out the local real estate agencies. For tonight, I wanted nothing more than to ease myself into a hot bath, then pass out in my room's sway-backed bed for a solid ten hours.

— 40 —

It took only two phone calls to real estate companies to learn which salespeople had handled the property ASP bought. In an economically depressed area, people don't easily forget which of their peers split a sales commission in the neighborhood of ninety thousand dollars. Portland broker Bud Erwin represented ASP, I was told, while local agent Gladys Thompson had listed the property, known locally as the Mahoney Ranch, and represented the sellers. I decided to begin with Thompson.

The morning was brilliantly sunny as I drove east. This country was dryer than Minnesota—there were fewer lakes and streams and, as a result, also fewer insects and weeds—but the tall pines were reminiscent of my own state's northern regions. The area was sparsely populated, and the handful of people I saw from the road were all Caucasian. If the Aryan Supremacy Party ever actually moved in here, its members would see to it that would never change. The thought depressed me.

Thompson Realty consisted of Gladys Thompson and her sister, Mavis Prior, and was run out of a converted garage attached to the Thompson house in the small village of Cascadia, population under two hundred. The two widowed sisters lived in modest frame houses on adjacent lots and had made their living from their joint venture for the past ten years. Both were gray-haired women with friendly, open faces. Gladys wore her hair permed into corkscrew curls while Mavis, who was about three inches taller than her sister, opted for a more traditional bun. The two would look at home in a typical country kitchen, wearing gingham aprons, but today

Mavis was dressed in paint-spattered jeans and a man's lumberjack shirt. "Excuse my appearance," she said, wiping her hands on her shirt. "When I'm not showin' property these days, I spend my time buildin' a new bedroom and bathroom onto my place next door. Room for the grandkids to visit. Today I'm tapin' sheetrock."

The women seemed thrilled that "a real private investigator"—and "a girl" at that—had come to Cascadia especially to see them. Excitement was apparently hard to come by around here.

Gladys and Mavis insisted that I have a cup of coffee and a homemade brownie before we got down to business. I acquiesced, wondering how long it would take me to kick the caffeine habit I was quickly acquiring. I complimented them on the brownie, which did taste awfully good, particularly since I'd hardly eaten anything for the past thirty-six hours.

Undisturbed by any current customers, we talked for nearly an hour about Gladys's sale of the Mahoney Ranch, which was located a few miles farther along Route 20, higher into the foothills and closer to the town of Upper Soda. "We dickered on that deal for better'n a month, as I recall," Gladys told me. "Showed 'em the place on, I think it was a Fourth of July weekend."

"Showed who?" I asked.

She nibbled her lip and thought. "It's hard to remember names this long after. . . . There was the other broker, o' course, Bud Erwin. He's from up to Portland. And, I think, three men came out from Minnesota that first time. The one who made the final deal and two other fellas."

"Do you remember what they looked like?"

"I remember one of 'em real well," Mavis contributed. "Big man, big as Emil; Emil's my late husband. 'Cept Emil was blond and this gentleman was dark-haired."

"Was his name Gilbert Hoffman?" I asked.

A smile lighted Gladys's face. "Sounds right. Yes . . . I

remember now. Mavis is right about his size. Mighta been even bigger'n Emil, and this guy had blue eyes." She shook her head, making her gray corkscrew curls bounce. "Made me nervous. Talked in a bossy sorta way all the time, like he was accusing us o' trying to cheat 'em."

Sounded like Gil Hoffman, all right. "And the other two men?"

"The one was the fella signed the papers. Hank? Harry? Somethin' like that. His name'll be on the purchase agreement." She began to dig through a messy file cabinet in search of the paperwork. "Here it is." She flipped through some pink-and-white sheets of paper and read from the bottom of one, "Herb, that's it. Herbert Keller, Treasurer, ASP, Incorporated. Funny name for a company, ASP."

So both Hoffman and Keller had come to Oregon to inspect the property. "You said that Keller is the man who did the negotiating," I said. Gladys nodded. "Did he make a second trip to Oregon or was that all done through Mr. Erwin?"

"Part was on the phone, dickerin' back 'n' forth. Fella drove a hard bargain, but between you 'n' me, them Mahoney kids were so anxious to unload that place, they mighta taken even less." Gladys drained her coffee cup and accepted a refill from her sister. "As I recall," Gladys said, "that Keller fella come back out to set the deal. Musta done—he signed the purchase agreement. Then he come again for the closing. Brought the cashier's checks from Minnesota."

"Why was the Mahoney family so anxious to get rid of the property?"

"Nothin' sinister about it," Gladys assured me firmly. "Just that all three o' old man Mahoney's kids moved to the city. When he died, they didn't want the property, they wanted the money. Had the place on the market for better'n six, seven years, wasn't it, Mavis?" Mavis nodded. "Not a single offer till them fellas from Minnesota come along. But don't get me wrong, it's good land. Got its own water, some forest that can be harvested for lumber, plenty o' pastureland. More'n twenty thousand acres."

"Any buildings?"

"There's the farmhouse, but to tell the truth, it's seen better days. Real value's in the land."

I asked to see the purchase agreement that Gladys held in her hand. She hesitated, then handed it over. "Can't see what harm it'd do now the deal's set," she told her sister, whose head bobbed in agreement.

I skimmed over what appeared to be a standard property-purchase agreement. "Why is this section about mortgage financing crossed out?"

"It was to be a cash sale from the start," Gladys explained, "so that standard stuff about cancelin' if the buyer couldn't get his mortgage wasn't necessary."

"And this was the total purchase price?" I pointed to the figure typed in on the agreement.

She nodded.

"Do you remember the original asking price?"

Gladys looked to Mavis for assistance. "I think it was originally listed at, what . . . two million?"

"One million, nine-fifty," Mavis said.

"That's right. Then they dropped it to a million seven fifty 'bout a year later. Come down to a million six hundred and willin' to listen to offers by the time them Minnesota fellas showed up. They got themselves a darned good deal."

I asked about construction done on the Mahoney Ranch since its sale to ASP.

Gladys and Mavis looked at each other, then shook their heads. "Hasn't been any permits pulled, that much I know," Mavis said slowly. "All building permits are listed in our local weekly and I'd've noticed. Now that you think of it, seems strange. Here they bought all this land 'n' it's done nothin' but sit idle ever since."

"What do you know about the men who bought it?" I asked.

"Nothin', 'cept they had the money and they offered the Mahoneys a clean deal," Gladys said. "Have to admit I wondered at the time. Worried a little, even. Up to Washington State, folks've had some of them religious cults move in. People wanderin' around in long robes, chantin' and sellin' flowers on the street. I was hopin' this wasn't one of them groups—our neighbors'd never forgive us—but so far it seems okay."

"It is, isn't it?" Mavis leaned forward anxiously. "It's okay?"

I hesitated, not sure I wanted to disillusion the sisters. Still, they were bound to find out sometime.

I explained about the Aryan Supremacy Party and its plans for the property. "Good lord! We had no idea." Gladys chewed on her thumbnail nervously. "I read about one of them groups moved into a town up to Idaho. Next thing you know, these fellas are runnin' 'round totin' guns, scarin' women and kids half to death. Oh, dear, oh, dear . . ."

I thanked the sisters for their help and tried to reassure them that ASP's moving into their backyard was not exactly imminent. There was nothing they could do about it anyway. And, if the plan that had begun to form in my mind worked the way I hoped, the Hoffman murder case might well blow up the Aryan Supremacy Party long before it ever came near the West Coast.

I could see no reason to explore the Mahoney Ranch. I'd found what I'd come to Oregon for in that purchase agreement and the Linn County building permits. Unless Paul Mueller had been wrong. Or had lied to me.

Gladys used the office Xerox machine to make me a copy of the agreement Herb Keller had signed on behalf of ASP. I exchanged it for a promise to keep the sisters posted on anything I learned about ASP's plans for the property Thompson Realty had sold.

The sun was high in the clear sky when I left the little converted garage. If I could leadfoot it back to Portland in time, I thought, I might still make the afternoon flight back to the Twin Cities.

— 41 —

I used the three hours' flying time to plan what I hoped would be a trap for Gilbert Hoffman's murderer. The idea I conceived was not perfect, but I couldn't afford to let that stop me from trying it. Eventually there might be another way to prove who had killed Hoffman. But eventually would not be soon enough. A dying child was depending on me to clear his dad of a murder charge. Self-preservation was involved, too. Since that car had tried to run me down, I'd realized I would have to get Hoffman's killer before he got me.

I used a pay phone at MSP International to call Paul Mueller's Bloomington home. When he answered, I launched into the first part of my plan, appealing to the stockbroker's inflated ego; he took the bait.

"You'd better be telling me the truth, Miss MacDonald," he said.

"You'll have plenty of proof tomorrow."

"All right. You're sure you got the address right?"

I suppressed an urge to respond sharply to his patronizing tone and repeated the address he'd given me. "It's just south of the State Fairgrounds," I said.

"Right. You'll have to be there early, no later than seven. I'll meet you at the south edge of the parking lot." Mueller rang off. I replaced the receiver, my heart thudding. Now there would be no turning back. It had to work right. If it didn't, my life wouldn't be worth a dime.

My second call was to Barry O'Neil at the St. Paul PD. I was told he'd already signed out for the day, but when I identified myself, his partner said Barry had planned to see Sam on his way home.

I took a cab directly from the airport to St. Paul–Ramsey Medical Center. Sam was sitting up in bed. He was still connected to his heart monitor, but his IV had been disconnected. He looked like hell—a mass of bruises and his arm in a sling—but I could sense the old Sam was back. Rose was still sitting beside the bed, patiently knitting something with blue angora yarn.

"Jesus, you look as bad as I feel," Sam growled as I entered.

"You're not winning any beauty contests yourself, handsome," I said. "So what's the verdict? You going to make it?"

"He's so good he's already complaining about the food," Rose scolded, her voice filled with happiness.

"So I get knocked around a little, I can't talk for myself anymore?" Sam said, glaring at his wife. "Look at me. Does it look like the doctors got my mouth taped shut?" Rose laughed girlishly and shot me a you-know-how-Sam-gets-when-he's-convalescing look. "The sooner they let me outa this prison," he grumbled, "the sooner I get back to work. And the sooner I'll be back to normal."

"Maybe normal is just what the doctors are afraid of," I said.

"This I really need. You girls ever hear of respect? You oughta try givin' a man a little once in a while."

My eyes met Rose's. Sam would recover. I vowed silently not to cause him any more stress until that day came. From here on out, wrapping up the Hoffman case was all my job.

I cornered Barry O'Neil in the hallway outside Sam's room. He was carrying a white bag that smelled suspiciously like hamburgers and fried onions. "Rose will kill you," I said, eyeing the bag. "For heaven's sake, she's trying to nurse the man back to health."

"So Sam calls me this afternoon and he says to me, 'Barry, they're tryin' to starve me to death in this place. Makin' me eat boiled cardboard without so much as one grain o' salt.' Says he's dreamin' o' sinkin' his teeth into one o' Mickey's specials." He shrugged his big shoulders. "Can't convince me one hamburger's gonna kill my best friend, Devon. Way I figure, a good meal will give old Sam somethin' to live for."

I silently admitted defeat and changed the subject. "I need your help, Barry." Keeping my voice low so it wouldn't carry into Sam's room, I told Barry about my plan for tomorrow evening.

"You're the craziest damn broad I ever knew," he said when I'd finished.

"But do you think it'll work?"

"I think you're playin' with fire, girl. These're probably the same assholes that tried to flatten you not two days ago. Now you figure you're gonna walk into the midst of 'em and play cop. You were my daughter, I'd seriously consider havin' you committed."

"I've got to do *something,* Barry," I insisted. "I have to prove Ben Levy isn't a murderer. And I'm not going to sit around waiting for a bunch of right-wing zealots to come and get me, either."

"What you can do is turn over whatever evidence you think you got and let us handle it."

"When? By Christmas? Let me remind you, Barry O'Neil, your people think they've *already* arrested Hoffman's murderer. Besides, I've been trying to explain to you that I don't have the kind of evidence you're going to need in a court of law. Not yet. I can show the weapon, the opportunity, and now I've got a probable motive, but I haven't got an eyewitness and I haven't got a confession. A clever lawyer could take everything I've got and turn it around to show somebody else could've done it."

"Why're you botherin' to tell me this, Devon? I say you're makin' a stupid move and you don't wanna hear it."

"You guys can't trick him into confessing," I said. "It'd never hold up in court. But I think I can."

"So what do you want from me? Approval? You ain't gonna get it." Liquid soaked through the white bag and began to drip onto Barry's rumpled pants.

"I need a couple of things, Barry. One is a witness to back up whatever I can get on tape." He stared at me silently. I took a deep breath. "Another thing is that I'm worried about walking into the middle of these guys with no backup," I said. "If something goes wrong . . ."

"First sensible words I heard outa your mouth today."

I looked him in the eye. "I'll go alone if I have to, Barry. You can't stop me. But I'd feel a lot better if you were in that parking lot just in case. Nothing official, just hanging around in the background . . . to radio for help if I need it." He lowered his eyes and busied himself with the dripping bag. "Barry," I said, "if Sam were able to help me out of this, I wouldn't even come to you. But he mustn't even suspect what's going on here. It could kill him."

Barry sighed. "Where'd you say this shindig was gonna be?"

— **42** —

I drove the Honda into the parking lot at a quarter to seven on Sunday night, choosing a parking spot on the southern edge. The Aryan Supremacy Party meeting wasn't scheduled to start for forty-five minutes, but there was already a handful of cars parked in the lot outside the low brown building. It was a prefab warehouse in a now-deserted industrial neighborhood. I guessed that the warehouse belonged to a loyal ASP member who allowed the group to use it for Sunday night meetings. The privacy it offered at that time of the week would have strong appeal for a secret society.

Although the sun wouldn't set for more than an hour, the sky was becoming ominously dark as storm clouds moved in from the west. Pollen hung heavy in the humid air and my nose itched. I hadn't dared take an antihistamine; it might make me drowsy.

Floodlights flashed on, illuminating the lot and making me feel uncomfortably exposed. Mosquitoes swarmed around the lights. Nervously, I fingered the remote microphone hidden in my bra; it was still in place under the loose, lightweight blouse I'd borrowed from Rose this afternoon.

Everything was quickly coming to a head. Tomorrow we would have the hospital's verdict on whether Tyler Hoffman's bone marrow had a chance of saving David Levy's life. And tomorrow, if tonight went as planned, the charges against Ben Levy would be dropped. Someone else would stand accused of Gilbert Hoffman's murder.

I remained in my car, waiting. One or two at a time, men arrived, parked their cars close to the building, and went inside. I looked at my watch. At exactly seven o'clock, a silver Porsche pulled into the lot from the west and parked next to my car. Paul Mueller carefully extricated his heavy body from the small car and approached me, a monogrammed leather briefcase clutched under his arm. I quickly activated the tape recorder under my seat, grabbed the stack of papers I'd brought with me, and climbed out of the Honda.

"Mr. Mueller, did you bring those financial records?" I asked him.

He nodded solemnly. "I want to see what you've got first. If everything's in order, then we'll discuss these records."

I set down my papers on the roof of his Porsche; it was considerably cleaner than my car's. "Here's a copy of the purchase agreement for the Oregon ranch," I said, taking the top sheet from the stack.

As Mueller scrutinized it, more ASP members drove in. We became the subject of several pairs of curious eyes. The stockbroker ignored them. "Let's see what else you've got," he demanded.

Out of the corner of my eye, I saw Barry O'Neil's unmarked Ford arrive. Barry parked and stayed in his car; I breathed a little easier. "Thompson Realty says there've been no building permits pulled for construction on that property," I told Mueller.

"I know." He grimaced. "I called Oregon yesterday, after I talked to you."

I nodded. "That's good. I wouldn't expect you to take my word for it." I dug deeper into the pile of papers. "Here," I said, pointing to some paragraphs circled in a legal document, "is where the pills that killed Gil Hoffman came from."

Mueller read silently for a moment. I rubbed my pollen-irritated eyes and glanced back at the warehouse. A small group of men emerged, stared in our direction, and began talking among themselves. I recognized two or three of them from Hoffman's funeral. Mueller opened his briefcase. "These are the numbers you wanted," he said, handing me copies of ASP's financial reports to members for the past two years.

I read them quickly and nervously. The group of men grew larger. Now I recognized Eldon Bergmann and Herb Keller. "There's even more money missing than I figured," I told Mueller, looking up. "Well over half a million dollars. There's your motive for murder."

"You're jumping to conclusions, Ms. MacDonald."

Mueller was using his condescending tone again. "What you've got here may point to embezzlement, but murder's something else entirely."

"You told me yourself that Gil Hoffman was fanatic about ASP. If he found out about the stolen funds, he'd never have agreed to keep quiet about it."

"You can't even prove he knew."

"But you believe what I'm saying. I can see it in your eyes." He glanced away.

The men began walking toward us, Keller and Bergmann in front. They brought to mind a lynch mob from an old Western movie. I wondered if any of them were carrying pieces of the secret arsenal Orville Voss had told me about. It looked like I wasn't going to need Mueller to get me into the ASP meeting after all; the meeting was coming to me.

"If your theory is right," Mueller said, "we'll take care of the situation ourselves."

I shook my head. "No way. This is a police matter."

The group reached us, then fanned out. My shoulders tensed. Eldon Bergmann approached Mueller and jerked a thumb in my direction. "What the hell's she doin' here?" Despite the mechanic's threatening demeanor, Mueller displayed no sign of anxiety.

"I'm perfectly capable of answering that for myself, Mr. Bergmann," I said. "I've come here to talk about some money that's been stolen from ASP by one of your members—several hundred thousand dollars. And about how the thief murdered your president to keep him quiet."

Bergmann spat. "This broad don't take a hint. She's so stupid she don't even know where she ain't wanted."

"Trying to run me down the other night was a bit more than a hint, but it didn't kill me. And it doesn't change the facts." I glared back at him, trying not to show my apprehension. "Did Keller get you to do that piece of dirty work for him, Bergmann, or did he do it himself? Or maybe you just supplied the car."

Herb Keller took a step forward. "We want you out of here," he said.

The other men stared, waiting to see what would happen. One of them, a musclebound young guy with a red beard, raked my body with his eyes. His inspection lingered on my breasts. He smirked and exchanged winks with a buddy. The classic male intimidation of the female. It made my skin itch.

"Mr. Mueller will tell you that what I'm saying is true. Herb Keller has stolen more than half a million dollars from the ASP treasury."

Keller's face went purple. "That's bullshit!"

"It's the truth," I said. "That property you men bought in Oregon—Keller drew checks from your stock accounts for a million and a half dollars. He told you that's what he paid for it. I have proof right here that the land really cost just under a million." I thrust the copy of the purchase agreement forward. "The difference went into his own pocket. And there's more. Keller cut new checks that were supposed to be for construction of buildings on that land. But not so much as a shed has ever been built. He's stolen every last—"

"This broad is dangerous," Keller yelled belligerently. He snatched the paper out of my hand and crushed it in his fist. I took an instinctive step backward. "She and her Jew buddies are out to destroy us, tryin' to get us to suspect each other, tryin' to start trouble."

Paul Mueller's face was grim. "What Miss MacDonald says about the money is true. I've seen the papers."

"So you're on this bitch's side," Bergmann said. "You take her part against Herb? You fuckin' traitor."

The big stockbroker stepped forward, grabbed the smaller man by the front of his shirt, and lifted him to his toes. "Don't you ever call me that again." A quiet menace lurked in his voice. "I worked my ass off for ASP. I'm the one who made that money. *Me!* My company. My expertise. I'm not going to sit by while one of our own people steals it. If you do, you're even more ignorant than you look." Abruptly, he released Bergmann, who stumbled silently back into the crowd, a whipped dog look on his face.

The onlookers began to whisper among themselves. I could feel their uncertainty, their growing hostility. Yet I still had nothing usable on my tape.

"Gil Hoffman found out what Keller was up to," I said, "and it cost him his life."

"She's fuckin' crazy." Keller's voice took on a hysterical edge. "You can't prove a damn thing you're sayin'."

"Oh, but I can, Mr. Keller." I took another bunch of papers from the roof of the Porsche. "Keller's son is hyperactive. His doctor put him on Ritalin—that's methylphenidate hydrochloride, the same drug that killed Gil Hoffman. I've got the proof right here, in Keller's divorce papers." Keller reached for the documents I held, but I pulled them away from his grasp. "Susannah Keller testified in court that Herb refused to give their son his medication," I said. "Now we know where all those pills ended up . . . in Gil Hoffman's Thermos jug. All except for one or two little leftovers. Keller planted them in a good man's car to pin the murder on him."

The eyes of the crowd snapped toward Keller. I could feel the level of suspicion rising and some of the hostility shifting from me to the party treasurer.

"I want a look at those papers." A tall man in jeans and a plaid sport shirt reached for them with a snake-tattooed hand.

"Me, too." Others in the group took up the cry. "Give us a look at what she's got."

Keller balked. "You can't believe her. It's all lies. I wouldn't—I didn't— Hell, Gil was my best friend."

"There isn't going to be any Oregon retreat because Herb Keller's greediness has ripped it all off," I told them. "This man only wants to be your president so he can keep right on stealing you blind. He'll kill any—"

"Shut up, shut up, you stinkin' bitch!" Keller pulled a

small-caliber handgun from under his jacket and pointed it at me. "I shoulda killed you the minute you stuck your nose in my business." He grasped my right arm, yanked me toward him, and pressed the gun against my cheek-bone.

"This is a stupid move, Herb." Not surprisingly, the voice of reason was Paul Mueller's.

"Shut up, you bastard," Keller said. "If it weren't for you, none o' this ever would've come out. Think you're so goddamn smart, so fuckin' better'n the rest of us. Playin' your money games with Jews." Fists clenched, the portly Mueller stepped toward us. But Keller yanked me closer. "Stay back, rich boy. Come any closer and I'll blow the broad's brains all over that expensive wop suit you're wearin'."

Keller had his left arm around my chest now, crushing my breasts painfully. The smell of him, a mixture of nervous sweat and Aqua Velva after-shave, was becoming overwhelming. The odor was familiar; I had smelled it before, in another time of danger. I no longer had any doubt that it was Herb Keller who'd attacked me that night in my apartment. This was the sweet smell I'd identified then. It was that night Keller had read my files and learned why I was investigating the Hoffman family. And he'd coolly used Myra Hoffman's secret to kill his friend and frame Ben Levy.

A low rumbling in the cloud-filled sky overhead was echoed by voices in the crowd. Snatches of the men's angry comments intruded into my thoughts.

"—never would've believed—"

"—fuckin' murderer—"

"—had us fooled—"

"Hell, I wasn't never no fan o'—"

"Sure, you had it figured. Sure! When'd you get so goddamn smart, hotshot?"

"—thief—"

"—traitor—"

Keller tightened his grip on me and I could feel his

body trembling. As he half dragged me away from the increasingly angry crowd, a few tentative drops began to fall from the sky. The crowd moved after us.

"Back off. I swear I'll blow her brains out." Keller's voice was close to hysteria, but the men weren't listening. They kept coming. Keller shifted the gun so it was aimed at the crowd, but he didn't loosen his grip on me. I realized with sudden terror that these men couldn't care less if I ended up dead on the pavement. They had their own business to settle with Keller.

Sirens wailed in the distance. Barry had managed to radio for help. If only it arrived in time. Suddenly I caught a direct whiff of Keller's odor. I could feel the beginnings of a spasm that I couldn't control. It started from my diaphragm and moved upward; I sneezed violently. Startled, Keller shifted his hold on me for a split second. I shoved myself away from him, elbowing him in the ribs, then fell forward. An instant before I hit the pavement, a shot rang out, quickly followed by a second. I landed on my left elbow. Pain ricocheted through my body.

I rolled onto my side and saw in a blur that Keller, too, had dropped to the parking lot. He grabbed his right shoulder with his left hand; his gun skidded inches away from his grip. I dove for it, wrapped my fingers around the trigger, and pointed it at him with shaking hands.

Dark blood spurted from between Keller's fingers and his face paled. He made a low, primitive sound and curled into the fetal position. I spun the gun around and pointed it at the crowd.

The red-bearded man who'd visually undressed me a few minutes earlier held out his hand to me.

"Keep away from me. I know how to use this."

"Shit, lady, I'm just tryin' to help."

"Stay back." I gripped the gun tighter. "I don't want your help."

"Fuck you." He stalked away.

As the sirens grew louder, the ASP members scattered,

rushing toward their cars. My view from the pavement became a sea of retreating backs. Except for one familiar form. "You okay, Devon?" I nodded at Barry, realizing that Keller's shot had missed me. He gripped my arm with one chunky hand and helped me to my feet. His other hand held his service revolver steady. The stench of gunpowder from both guns was strong. I sneezed again.

Barry gave me an exasperated look. "You really oughta do somethin' about that hay fever," he said.

As two squad cars pulled into the lot, the ASP members raced for the exit. Keller writhed on the pavement, clutching his bloodied shoulder and moaning. Lightning cracked overhead and a cloud burst, quickly drenching us.

"Thanks, Barry," I said, kissing him on the cheek.

He shrugged. "Figured them extra sessions on the target range hadda pay off someday."

My nose began to run and I sniffled. Barry handed me a handkerchief. "It's just this damn allergy," I mumbled as I blew. But I really think it had more to do with the tears streaming down my face. I was glad it was raining hard enough that nobody seemed to notice.

— 43 —

When I got back to the office on Tuesday afternoon, I felt like a million bucks. I looked like I'd barely survived a pit-bull attack, but that couldn't dampen my high spirits.

"So did you deliver the kid all right?" Sam asked. This was his first afternoon back on the job, too, and he looked tired.

"Right on schedule," I said with a smile. I'd driven

Tyler Hoffman to the Mayo Clinic in Rochester yesterday afternoon, a few hours after we'd learned his bone marrow would be a good match for David Levy. We'd spent the night at the Kahler Hotel, where Tyler had a chance to meet Ben and Gloria Levy, and this morning the medical procedure for the bone marrow donation had begun. "Tyler was an absolute prince," I said. "Not a word of complaint, but I think he's going to drive the hospital staff crazy with all his questions. Why are they doing this? What will they do with that? What's that stuff in the hypodermic? Have they seen something he read in some medical journal?" I laughed, recalling the tall, serious boy putting the medics through their paces.

"How long before they'll know if it worked, Devon?" Paula asked. A new set of braces glistened on her teeth. I suppressed an urge to ask about them.

"It'll take several weeks before the doctors will feel confident the transplant's a success, but they say David's chances look excellent. The boy really perked up when he saw his dad, and he couldn't wait to meet his new big brother."

"Sounds like everything's workin' out," Sam said. "The Levy boy's gettin' his transplant. His old man's outa jail and off the hook. And I hear the minute Barry 'n' his boys started haulin' them assholes on the ASP membership list in for questioning about the hit-and-run they tried on us, the whole party started fallin' apart. Rats desertin' the ship. The boxes o' ASP records Keller stashed in his house're makin' interesting readin', too." He grinned. "Couldn't happen to a nicer bunch o' guys."

"Tyler told me his mother has agreed to see a psychiatrist," I added. "And Ben Levy has promised to help Tyler go to any college he chooses. I have a good feeling about that young man, Sam; he's going to do great things."

"One more thing I wanna say." Sam wore a sheepish

look. He stared at the paper clip he was straightening. "About the other night. I—I guess I didn't really get a chance to— What I'm tryin' to say is this—" The paper clip snapped. "You deliver a helluva mean tackle, girl. And . . . well, thanks."

"You're welcome, Sam. That means a lot to me." I planted a kiss on his cheek, which promptly reddened. Truth was, the past few days had proven a kind of catharsis for me. Ever since the moment I realized Sam would survive the hit-and-run, I'd felt lighter, even happy at times. There still was no way I could bring Danny back, but now it seemed possible to stop blaming myself for failing to save him.

"Well, girls," Sam said, leaning back in his chair, the sling holding his injured arm resting on the mound of his belly, "much as I hate to admit it, looks like I may be gettin' too old for this game. Can't seem to get around the way I used to. Devon, I gotta admit you're the one gets the credit for solvin' a helluva difficult case here. As well as for savin' my ass." His expression was serious. "Just see you don't let it go to your head."

"You're full of crap, Sam Sherman, and you know it," I said, pulling a check from my bag. "I didn't pull this off by myself. You're the one who got me the clues. You found out who owned that sperm bank. You got backgrounds on every one of our suspects. Sure, I guessed the Keller kid was hyperactive, that he might be on Ritalin. He acted a lot like a couple of kids I used to teach. And the *Physician's Desk Reference* told me that methylphenidate hydrochloride is the chemical name for Ritalin. But where was the proof for my theory? In those divorce papers *you* dug up. Even Herb Keller's need for a lot of money he didn't have was in the legal and financial records you got. So I don't want to hear you putting yourself down."

I placed the check carefully on Sam's desk, next to his freshly opened Coke can. "As you'll notice, this nice fat bonus check from Ben and Gloria Levy is made out to both Sherman and MacDonald. That's who earned it, and that's who's going to spend it."

Sam's face brightened and he took a gulp of Coke. "How 'bout we celebrate," he said. "The three of us can go out to dinner tonight. Rose's with the grandkids and there's nothin' I'd like better than to sink my teeth into a nice, juicy, rare steak." His face took on a look of ecstasy.

"Gee, thanks, Sam," Paula said, smiling at the floor. "But I can't. I'm going to meet Stuart's mother tonight."

"Then I guess it's just the two of us, sweetpea," he said, turning to me.

"Uh, me, too." Suddenly I felt more self-conscious than Paula looked.

"Whaddya mean, 'Me, too'?" Sam asked.

"I mean I can't go. I've got a date tonight, too."

Sam and Paula looked at each other and then at me. You'd think I'd just announced I'd decided to seek the Republican nomination for President.

"Why is that so strange?" I demanded. "I'm entitled to have a date if I want one."

"It's that schoolteacher, ain't it?" Sam asked, a superior grin creeping across his face. "I could tell he had the hots for you."

"If you mean Roddy Caldwell, the answer is yes. And I'd hardly call it 'the hots,' Sam. Please try to treat my social life with a little dignity."

"Call it whatever you want, girl, you gotta admit this is something of an about-face for the ice maiden of the north."

"Maybe I just changed my mind," I said, stalking out of Sam's office. Somehow, once I'd begun to let go of that packload of guilt I'd been carrying, it seemed time to start living again. To start taking some risks that were more than just physical.

Sam pulled his feet off his desktop and shuffled after me. "Hey, Devon," he said, sounding genuinely contrite.

"I didn't really mean that the way it came out. How 'bout we make dinner tomorrow night?"

I thought for a moment and grinned. "I know why you *really* want me to go to dinner with you, Sam."

"Why?"

"Because," I said, my eyes resting on his sling, "you're going to need somebody to cut up that steak."

About the Author

NANCY BAKER JACOBS has worked as a private detective, a newspaper reporter, and a freelance journalist. She now teaches journalism at California State University, Nothridge. She is the author of six nonfiction books and one previous novel.

ELIZABETH PETERS

presents

MALICE DOMESTIC

An Anthology of
Original Traditional
Mystery Stories

Presented by the acclaimed Elizabeth Peters, here is an
outstanding collection of original mystery tales in the classic
Christie tradition, now practiced so successfully by authors on
both sides of the Atlantic.

Featuring Carolyn G. Hart, Charotte and Aaron Elkins, Sharyn
McCumb, Charlotte Macleod and many others!

Available from Pocket Books

POCKET
BOOKS   510